Copyright © Robert Richardsc ~~~~

Robert Richardson asserts the
identified as the author of thi:

CW01521903

This novel is entirely a work (
characters and incidents portr
of the author's imagination. Any resemblance to actual
persons, living or dead are entirely coincidental.

ISBN 978-1-291-56150-0

Neptune's Parlour

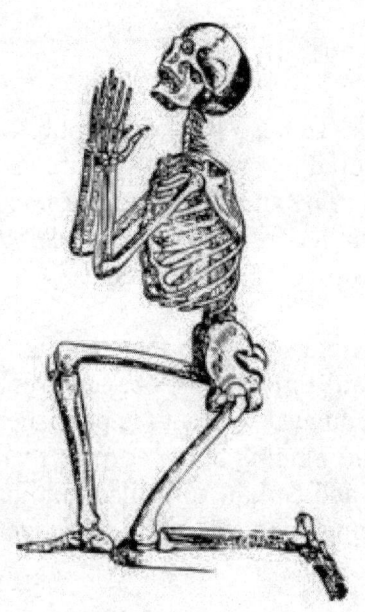

A gruesome tale of murder at sea

Neptune

I'm Neptune! Lord of the sea am I, am I!
My right of rule there is none to deny, to deny;
The great vessels o'er my kingdom come and go,
I hold in my sway, in my sway, all the winds that do blow, that
do blow!
With soft and gentle gale I fill the ready sail,
That bears the wealth of nations o'er my broad domain;
With voice of stormy might I fill with fear the night,
To show the world to show the world I reign!
I'm Neptune, I'm Neptune, Lord of the sea am I,
The stormy winds of every sky,
Come to me when they hear my cry,
And woe betide who dare my pow'r defy
The King of the Deep and all it's might,
The Lord of the sea am I! The Lord of the sea am I!
I'm Neptune! Lord of the sea am I, am I!
At my commanding the bravest must die, must die.
My breath can be soft and light as summer breeze,
Or shake with the might, with the might of my rage,
of my rage the seas,
No monarch on the land holds at his proud command
As free and open as my Kingdom wide:
And when my lightnings flash, My thunders roll and crash,
I laugh "ho ho" in pride!
I'm Neptune, I'm Neptune, Lord of the sea am I, am I!

Words by Clifton Bingham
Also set to music by Stanley Gordon.

The Caribbean and St Lucia

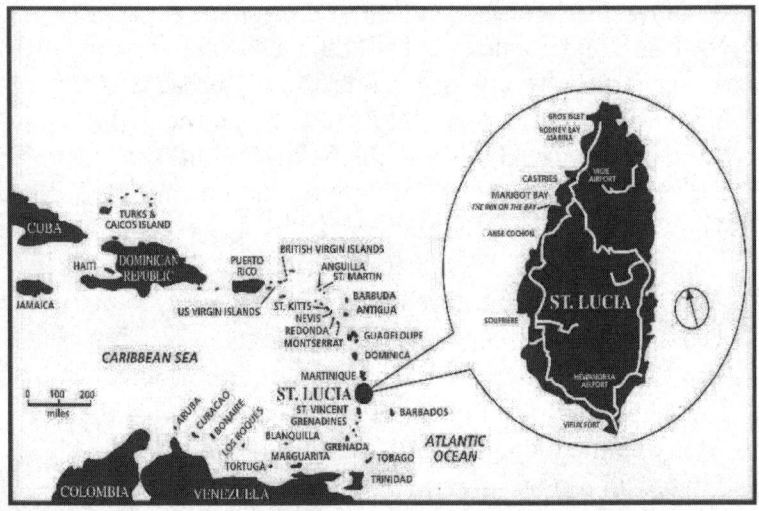

Dennery Prison is on the East side of the Island opposite the north facing arrow.

Dedication

To our much treasured Granddaughters and Grandson who have brought great joy into our lives.

Doctor Heather Richardson.

Kathryn Richardson.

Who became Mrs Page

When Kathryn married Luis on August 10th 2013

&

Callum Richardson

The happy memories over the years spent with our grandchildren, has resulted in a deep love and an unbreakable bond between us.

Grandparents Robert and Elsie

Acknowledgements.

It is a laborious task taking many weeks of concentrated effort to check each printed line in a manuscript of three hundred pages looking for errors made by the author.

My very good friend Mike Foster has done this on more than one occasion and I am indebted to him for giving up his precious time on my behalf.

Prologue

The yacht riding at anchor was rising slowly up and down in the slight swell with the two occupants lying in a double bed in the main cabin; the woman wide awake and the man snoring, not loudly, rather the result of adenoid problems.

Outside, the Caribbean evening had darkened a few hours earlier. The illuminated pointers on the clock fixed to the bulk head at the foot of the bed showed the time as 11.15pm.

They had both retired shortly after ten thirty after a tiring day ashore with too much walking, as they behaved like tourists enchanted by the Capital Castries they had visited as a stopover point in their four week holiday cruise of the Caribbean; timed to avoid the start of the hurricane season in June.

Now after a short cruise in untroubled waters, they were anchored in Rodney Bay, a few miles north of Castries with other yachts moored within hailing distance. They planned to go ashore the following morning to stock up with further provisions before their next port of call at Bridgetown in Barbados.

Although they had already been on the yacht for two weeks, Julia Warren was still wondering why her husband had suggested such an unexpected holiday. It was so unlike Walter Warren her husband of three years. She soon realised after a whirlwind courtship and a registry office marriage, that the man who had charmed her into his bed and slipped a large golden ring inset with diamonds on her finger, was a very different person from the one she had fallen so hopelessly in love with. Ruthless, self opinionated, opportunistic, and physically aggressive at times, were just a few of his many moods that she had found difficult to cope with once the original sexual extravagant dreams had quickly run their short explosive period.

Walter was pedantically aggressive in their home and would round on his wife in anger for failing to put the breakfast dishes in the dishwasher, or for leaving a wet towel on the bathroom floor.

When Julia responded innocently that the cleaning lady normally dealt with these mundane activities, Walter reacted by slapping her face and calling her a lazy idle slut who regarded bed as her work station and the rest of the house as some else's responsibility.

Julia, on the other hand, regarded herself as a responsible wife and loyal lover, who tried hard to fulfil all her wifely obligations. She was a good cook, paid constant attention to Walter's grumbles about her shortcomings, and made sure she was regularly dressed to please and encourage his manly demands, by wearing figure enticing short dresses over delicate underwear. She had learned early on in the marriage that bikinis did nothing for his libido, but lace knickers and bras and see-through nightdresses encouraged a quick short journey to the marital bedroom.

Julia had been awake for some time, mainly because the motion of the yacht when anchored instead of lulling her to sleep made her feel nauseous. She was never too happy when the boat was moving, but as she was mostly on deck during the day, the beauty of the surrounding Islands detracted from the motion of the hull as it sliced through the blue green waters of the Caribbean.

Below deck when she had to prepare meals was a constant torture where she regularly threw up but managed to conceal the fact from her husband, who would have enjoyed belittling her in front of others at this childish weakness, as he would have put it.

There was a sudden unmistakable thump as if something had fallen on deck, but Julia was well aware that Walter was a stickler for everything being shipshape on deck in case the weather turned nasty, which it often did in these tropical waters.

When the thump occurred again, Julia thought it advisable to nudge her husband awake, prepared to accept a volume of abuse when she disturbed his slumbers.

The forty feet yacht called Sunray had been hired by Walter from a Marina in Puerto Rico the day after they flew in on an Island Hopper aircraft after a short break in Jamaica, where her husband insisted he had some unexpected business opportunities to discuss with a local contact.

The yacht's owner, an American ex marine, had spent a few hours sailing with Walter until he was satisfied Walter had the appropriate skills necessary to take his precious boat out to sea. Walter had produced his Yacht Masters Certificate suitably endorsed with the qualification that he was able to use the navigational equipment and ship to shore radio. The owner provided him with the various wavelengths he needed to make contact with harbourmasters at each of his ports of call, also the important call sign necessary to keep the coastguard stations continuously aware of his position on these busy and often turbulent waters.

The owner stressed the need to be able to handle the distress rockets and send the appropriate distress signal to alert the coastguard if he needed urgent help. Walter, being full of his own importance, decided his wife should be excluded from the advisory information given by the owner of the vessel.

Julia would have preferred her husband to have paid the owner to accompany them as captain, because she was well aware that her husband had done very little sailing when they were in England, always ranting on that the North Sea, English Channel and Irish Seas were far too cold and the weather unpredictable for him to enjoy sailing in those waters. In other words his certificate may have been genuine, but his experience was extremely limited.

Walter woke up sending his wife a string of unprintable verbal abuse, mouthing at her that everything was shipshape on deck and if she was concerned, to get her own arse out of bed and go and see for herself that everything was secure and the anchors were not dragging in the gentle breeze.

A further thump and a slight movement in the stability of the yacht at last caught Walter's attention as he reluctantly slung his legs out of the cot and prepared to go on deck stark naked.

Grumbling continuously that he needed a good night's kip before they set sail the following morning, he staggered up the short companionway steps leading to the stern of the boat and disappeared through the open hatch to the deck above.

Julia now thoroughly frightened by the unexpected noises from above her head, slid down into the cot and pulled the one and only sheet covering her nakedness over her head to await the wrath of her husband when he returned from a wasted trip on deck.

Another loud thump was followed by a short period of silence, before she heard a scream of pain and assumed her husband had jabbed a toe on some piece of deck equipment, or accidently stood on a fastener holding the metal cover over the yacht's engine housing.

That a beating was inevitable from her angry husband was the accepted consequence she expected for her stupidity in waking him from a deep sexually related sleep.

As the cabin door opened, she awaited the wrath from her husband's tongue; instead a coloured man entered the cabin followed by another coloured man. They stepped quickly towards the bed and one of the men without uttering a word held an automatic pistol against the side of her head. The other man again without uttering a sound held a large knife across her throat.

'Stay quiet white bitch or your head will depart from your body.' Turning to the gun holder he said 'Pescie never mentioned this perq, so it's obviously a freebee.'

Leaning over, he yanked the sheet away from her naked body and his eyes gleamed and as he undid his fly. She screamed as he force her legs apart, mounted her, and proceeded to rape her. As soon as he had finished he stepped away and indicated to his silent partner that it was his turn. The invitation was initially declined, but a growl from the older man changed his mind, and Julia found herself raped again as the knife was pressed closer to her throat.

'Open the bloody safe' whispered the first man who had violated her body.

'I don't have the combination' she whispered, completely terrified and devastated by the combined attack on her vulnerability. 'Where is my husband?' she asked wondering why he had allowed these intruders to enter their cabin.

'Come and see' replied the older man as he dragged her from the bed and marched her up the companionway steps to the deck by the simple expedient of dragging her by her hair.

Walter was lying in the aft well deck, and like her, naked, but trussed up with rope round his ankles and his hands tied behind his back. His nose was bleeding heavily and looked like it was broken; two deep cuts across his breast were also bleeding heavily. The fact that he was still breathing and his eyes were open showed he had received a serious beating and some form of torture before he was tossed unceremoniously onto the aft deck.

Julia was dragged in front of her husband who gave the impression from his glazed semiconscious state that he hardly recognised her.

The coloured man with the knife leaned down and stuck the blade up Walter's right nostril. 'All we want white pig is the combination of your safe so we can get the list.'

When Walter shook his head, the knife was forced higher up his nostril until the nose split and more blood appeared. The scream of pain resulted in Julia fainting.

When she came round she found the coloured man with the knife tying another line round her husband's feet. Glancing to the end of the line she saw it was still attached to the aft anchor that was now lying on the deck, instead of in the sand below the boat keeping it secure.

'All we want is the combi to the safe you stupid bastard then you and your blond slut can sail into the wide blue yonder,' he growled.

When Walter again shook his head from left to right indicating that he was not prepared to surrender the combination, the elder looking black looked at the other and nodded. He grabbed Walter's feet and the younger of the two his head and lifted him on to the gunwale obviously intending to hurl him over the side into the sea.

Walter looked at his wife and gave out a despairing scream before he was dropped over the side with the anchor attached to his feet as he disappeared quickly below the surface.

Julia was struck dumb with shock as she watched her husband murdered before her eyes.

The intruder with the gun turned to his partner and whispered 'Pascie is going to be really pissed off when we tell him we haven't got the list.'

The man with the knife stared at her naked body that filled her with fear that she would soon suffer the same fate. He grinned and raised the knife above his head before whipping it down and using the blunt end of the handle to strike her forehead where she dropped mercifully onto the deck unaware of her fate.

It was daylight when she recovered consciousness. The first thing she did was vomit onto the deck. She lay still for a while until the deck stopped spinning and gradually clawed her way into a sitting position. The yacht appeared to be drifting further away from the shore as she noticed that the other anchored yachts were some distance away from the place where they had first anchored.

From the lowly position of the sun she guessed it was about seven am and no one from the other boats was visible on deck. The pain in her head was unbearable so she lay back on the deck and tried to collect her thoughts on how she could get out of this serious predicament.

Understanding the possible consequences after being raped, she staggered below deck and crawled into the shower cubicle where she turned on the hot shower and used a douche to hopefully cleanse her vagina of any of the unwelcome semen from the two scum. She quickly dried herself, got dressed, and went back up on deck scanning the other yachts to see if anyone was moving about.

Suddenly a man emerged from the nearest yacht and stretched his arms as if he had just woken from a deep sleep.

Julia screamed across the water and yelled 'help me, please help me'.

The man turned and appeared to say something to someone below deck. Another man appeared on deck and Julia could see they were starting their engine as one man pulled the anchor aboard. The yacht turned towards her boat and within a few minutes pulled alongside.

'What's the problem' a tall man with a ginger beard asked her.

'We were boarded during the night by two coloured men who raped me and then murdered my husband,' she cried, before dropping in a dead faint.

When she regained consciousness the man with the ginger beard was holding her head and attempting to get some water into her mouth. 'Lie quiet' he said. 'I have radioed the harbour master and asked him to call the police who should be here in about thirty minutes.

'My wife is coming aboard as soon as she is dressed and will take you down to your cabin until the police arrive. 'Can we get you anything to eat?' he asked, and when Julia shook her head, he briefly examined the large bump on her head and told her his wife would make her a cup of tea and give her a couple of aspirins to alleviate the pain.

Ch.1

Julia was lying on the bed being comforted by the wife of the man who had come to her aid, when the coastguard cutter drew alongside, with three police officers and a doctor waiting to board the yacht.

After the wife of her rescuer quietly and briefly explained to the police what had happened during the night, the doctor quickly examined her and declared her fit to be moved to the cutter and be taken ashore for hospitalisation and a more detailed examination.

Julia was shocked when the senior police officer with no hint of concern for the present state of her mind, informed her that the yacht would be impounded for detailed examination, and that she would be required to make a formal statement regarding the tragic happenings on the previous evening as soon as she was cleared for interview by the hospital doctors.

While the senior police officer looked on with an indifference that frightened her, Julia Warren had to accept that everyone else, including the other police officers, treated her kindly during her transition from the Sunray to the coastguard cutter and thence to Castries harbour where an ambulance waited to take her to the nearby Victoria hospital.

At the crystal white hospital a nurse was waiting with a wheel chair to take her to the first floor, where she was ushered into a small private room and assisted into a single bed. The nurse explained that she would be seen by a doctor as soon as her basic particulars had been recorded by another nurse who was sitting by her bed.

As Julia glanced round the room she noted that the view from the window was quite spectacular. She could see the harbour where the cutter was moored and the wide bay looking out over the Caribbean. She involuntarily shuddered as she recounted what had changed her life forever in the last twenty four hours.

The nurse asked her name, date of birth, nationality, whether she had had any other illnesses or surgery, and what medication she took, before taking her blood pressure and a sample of her blood.

As the nurse finished her ministrations, a coloured doctor walked into the room and introduced himself as Doctor Semple.

'I understand you have had a serious traumatic experience and witnessed the murder of your husband during last night whilst aboard your yacht moored off Rodney Bay'

When Julia nodded her head, he told her she was extremely lucky that the thugs who had boarded the yacht had not killed her after she witnessed the murder of her husband. He examined the lump on her head and asked her what she had done when she recovered consciousness. She told him that she was confused and naked when she eventually came round from the heavy blow to her head. Before attempting to look for help she told the doctor she had crawled back to the cabin taken a shower, used a douche to try and clear her vagina of any male sperm, and then got dressed.

'It's unusual for a young married female such as you to have a douche readily available,' the doctor suggested.

'My husband did not want any children and occasionally failed to use any contraception. Just after we were married and he had made his intentions clear, I had a coil fitted. After a few periods I found it painful in that area so I had the coil removed and told him to use contraception, or he had to accept that I could become pregnant. I bought the douche as further insurance that I would not become pregnant.'

Doctor Semple finished taking down some notes and looked her squarely in the eyes as if contemplating what he was about to say. 'You do realise Mrs Warren that by taking a shower and using a douche effectively destroyed any forensic tests we could have obtained which might have aided the police to apprehend the killers of your husband.'

Julia shook her head in exasperation. 'Doctor I had just been raped by two coloured men and the first thing on my mind at the time was not that I was lucky to be alive, but that I might become pregnant, and if that happened, suicide was the best option open to me. Hopefully cleansing my body gave me a small chance of helping the police to bring those killers to justice.'

Doctor Semple made a further note and told her he would provide a sedative so she should rest for the next few hours. 'You will be discharged from this hospital tomorrow morning and arrangements have already been made for you to be accommodated in a nearby hotel. Once you have given a statement to the police I assume you can make arrangements to return to the UK.

After a night's undisturbed rest Julia was visited by another doctor, who, after checking her records and examining her head informed her that she could get dressed and leave the hospital. 'The nurse will arrange a cab to take you to your temporary accommodation. If you do not possess any money the hotel owner has offered to pay the driver until you can sort out your finances. The police will be informed of your discharge and will, no doubt, arrange to take a statement from you a.s.a.p.

Ch.2

The small hotel on the promenade looked a bit run down from the outside and looked as if it needed a coat of fresh paint to brighten up the facade. Once inside the vestibule, it gave the impression of something resurrected from the Victorian age with heavily panelled woodwork, a mahogany staircase winding to the first floor, and a large chandelier above a mahogany reception desk. The first impression on entering the hotel was how clean and welcoming it was, with a colourful bowl of flowers adorning the reception desk.

The female owner and receptionist standing behind the counter was middle aged, dressed in a plain green two piece, and obviously expecting the arrival of a patient from the local hospital.

'Mrs Warren I presume' she announced, as Julia walked in the door. 'We have given you a quiet room at the rear of the hotel as the sea front can be quite noisy in the evening with all the bars open until after midnight. However, if you want to change just let me know and I will find you a room with a view at the front.'

At that moment all Julia wanted to do, was lie down in some quite place and die quietly; the shock of her changed position in life as a widow; and the fact that she was far from home without a friendly face to comfort her, was slowly beginning to register.

'I have no luggage of any kind' she explained to the receptionist. 'Everything I possessed on the yacht is currently in the hands of the police. I will need to call them and ask them to let me have my clothes, my handbag containing some of my makeup, and my important credit card, so that I can pay my hotel bill and buy a few essentials. Have you got the number of the police station please?'

The receptionist told Julia while she consulting a book open on her desk, that her name was Cara Phillipé. 'I'll call the station and you can speak to the officer in charge. Use the telephone on the desk when it rings.

Julia, feeling extremely tired, partly from the shock of her current situation and partly because of the oppressive heat of the morning, leaned on the desk and closed her eyes. When the phone rang she picked it up and heard a male voice say 'Sergeant Costelan here, how can I help?'

Introducing herself, Julia told him she was the lady rescued from the yacht two days ago; explained her current dire situation; and asked if she could have her personal belongings if she came to the station to collect them.

'One moment please,' the sergeant replied and Julia heard him whispering to someone in the background before he responded. 'I'm sorry Mrs Warren but all your possessions are impounded for the time being.'

'Could I have my credit card out of my wallet so that I can buy some necessities and pay the hotel bill for my temporary stay?'

More whispering took place before the sergeant replied. 'I'm sorry Mrs. Warren but nothing can be released until I have the authority of the Chief Inspector in charge of this station and that is not possible. I suggest you contact your card agent and arrange for a replacement.'

Julia replaced the telephone on its carriage and started to cry.

Cara stepped forward and placed her hand on Julia's shoulder. 'I couldn't hear what the sergeant said to you, but I have an idea it was not good news.'

Julia explained her predicament. Cara assured her that she would not be pressed for any payment until she was solvent. 'Who issued you with your credit card?' she asked.

'HSBC' replied Julia.

'Good, there is a branch in Castries,' replied Cara. 'Leave it to me to contact the Manager. I am an important customer and feel sure he will see you without having to make an appointment. I suggest you take a taxi to the bank and explain your predicament to the Manager. Don't worry about the taxi bill. The driver will charge it to the hotel and I will add it to your bill. Use the same taxi firm to get you back here after the manager has resolved your problem.'

Glad that at least she had one person on St Lucia who was prepared to help her, she thanked Cara profusely and made her way to the entrance to await the taxi.

— — —

The bank from the outside looked as ancient as the hotel, but the opulence inside reflected the profit levels of the world international banking giant HSBC with its headquarters in Hong Kong.

When Julia informed the Teller at the desk that she had an appointment with the manager, the Teller looked her up and down obviously wondering how a stranger in a rather tattered dress could obtain permission without first making an appointment to meet his God in the inner office.

'Name please?' When Julia replied 'Mrs Julia Warren' she noticed the alarmed expression on his face. Obviously he had seen the headlines in the local paper that morning and was forming his own uninformed opinion about what had occurred on the holiday tourist's yacht.

Picking up the telephone he announced in a low voice, (but sufficient for Julia to hear), the arrival of the 'news headline' before informing Mrs. Warren that she could go straight in.

On the manager's desk was an ebony plaque announcing to all visitors to this illustrious office that he was Simon J Bellos. Inviting Julia to sit down in the chair opposite his enormous teak desk inlaid with a dark green leather insert, he told her he had been informed by the owner of the Adelphi Hotel that Julia was seeking a replacement credit card

When Julia explained that the police were holding her personal belongings and had refused to release her handbag, including the wallet that held her credit and debit cards, the manager told her that there would be no problem replacing her card, but first he would need to check her credit rating with the branch she normally dealt with in the UK.

'Can you tell me in confidence of course, roughly what the balance is in your account?'

'There should be about ten thousand pounds in the current account, and about thirty thousand pounds in the deposit account.' Without thinking she added 'there is somewhere in the region of five hundred thousand in various shares in my husband's name deposited with HSBC, and I would assume his business must be valued in the region of ten million pounds if it was on offer on the open market.' (She failed to add 'late' in respect of her husband). 'Our HSBC Branch is in Liverpool and the manager is a Mr. Percy Lowe'

Simon J Bellas didn't bat an eyelid as Julia casually mentioned that her late husband was a multi millionaire. 'Obviously I will need to check the facts with Mr. Lowe, but in the meantime I will arrange for you to be allocated a credit card with a limit of ten thousand pounds credit. The card will be available for you to collect from this office within the next twenty four hours.....subject of course to your manager in the UK confirming your credit rating.'

Julia was completely shocked by the callous approach of the manager. 'Why are you placing a restriction on my purchasing ability? 'I need a complete new wardrobe as this is the only dress I possess. I also need underwear, shoes, coats, handbag, makeup, waterproofs in case the weather changes and enough money for me to be upgraded to a five star hotel where my husband and I usually stay when away from home.'

The Bank Manager stroked his chin as if considering how to deliver a piece of news she would not appreciate. 'I am sorry Mrs. Warren but the circumstances surrounding your husband's death are expected to result in a long drawn out investigation. Until the circumstances of his death and the beneficiaries of his Will, assuming he made one, are known, then I have no alternative but to place a restriction on your spending power while on St Lucia.'

Julia had to swallow hard before commenting. 'If my local branch manager confirms my credit worthiness, what happens then?'

Mr. Bellos remained unmoved, which was typical of Bank Managers throughout the world. 'Ten thousand will remain your limit until I am instructed otherwise,' he replied, rising from his chair to draw the meeting to a close.

Ch.3

The following morning not only did Julia receive her credit card from the bank, but when she returned to the hotel two plain clothes detectives were sitting in the foyer awaiting her return.

When they were pointed out to her by Cara, she told Julia that she could use the hotel's small conference room if she did not want the detectives in her room while she was alone. Julia agreed, so Cara showed the three of them into the small conference room that was equipped with a mahogany oval table surrounded by ten comfortable dining type chairs. A small sideboard had facilities for hot and cold drinks plus space for a small buffet if one was required.

'I'll get the chef to bring you coffee in about half an hour' she told Julia. 'However, if you require company I can arrange for one of the staff to take charge of the reception desk for a while.'

Thanking her for being so helpful, Julia told Cara that she doubted if she would require her services.

As soon as the three were seated, the obvious senior of the two detectives showed her his warrant card and introduced himself as Detective Inspector Harry Bishop and his companion as Sergeant Lane Totti.

'I am English Mrs Warren so there will be no mis-understandings in interpretation. Sergeant Totti is St Lucian, but everyone on the Island speaks and understands English. We are here so that you can make a statement that you will be asked to read and sign. In the meantime the Sergeant will make a verbatim report of this meeting that you can read and alter before a final document is typed. Even at that stage you may make alterations in ink before you sign. Is that understood?'

When Julia nodded her head and asked if she needed to have a lawyer present, Inspector Bishop told her that as she was not being formally charged with anything, the purpose of this meeting was to collect some facts that would aid the police investigations into her husband's alleged murder by persons unknown, so a lawyer was not required at this stage.

Julia was sharp enough to note the 'alleged' addition by the Inspector.

Detective Inspector Harry Bishop had cold fish like eyes that appeared to generate no warmth to those who came under his icy stare. His hair showed roughly his age as it was turning grey and receding at the temple. A rather red bulbous nose with large nostrils gave the impression that the inspector liked more than an occasional tipple. Julia suspected she was in for a hard time from this man, who conveyed the impression that everyone he interviewed was presumed to be guilty until proven innocent which appeared to be contrary to the laws of the Island.

His colleague on the other hand was rather slim for a police officer. As a local, his skin was coloured brown with black curly hair and a similar coloured moustache adorned his upper lip, giving the impression he was ten years older than his early thirties. His smile in her direction as he opened his pad to take her statement seemed to convey a degree of sympathy for her present situation. It went through Julia's mind that first impressions are not always correct. It appeared obvious to her that the sergeant had not worked with Inspector Bishop for very long as he appeared to her to be unimpressed with the way his superior grilled witnesses, ever hoping to find loopholes in their statement.

As soon as Sergeant Totti indicated he was ready to take down the statement, Inspector Bishop introduced his opening gambit.

'Mrs Warren I will be asking a lot of questions that you may find unusual and not necessarily specifically relevant to the tragic incident that occurred this week on your husband's yacht. Please answer each question to the best of your ability and don't answer my questions with a question as I will not be responding.'

'First tell me how, why, and when you and your husband arrived in the Caribbean?'

'My husband (still no mention of 'late') has an Import/Export business in the UK. He rents a large warehouse facility on a trading estate on the outskirts of Liverpool and travels a lot to all corners of the world in search of business opportunities. Just four weeks ago he told me he had some business to do in the Caribbean and suggested it was incorporated with a cruising holiday for both of us.'

'Although I have never been keen on sailing I naturally agreed, so we left our home, took a train to London, and flew from Heathrow to Kingston in Jamaica where he left me for two days while he conducted some business in the capital. While we were in Jamaica he flew to the Cayman Islands on another business trip and when he returned we flew to Puerto Rica where he hired the yacht Sunray. After a few hours of supervision by the yacht owner to check my husband's competence to handle the boat, he sailed to St Lucia where we moored for the night. It was his intention to sail to Port of Spain in Trinidad where I understand he had further business interests to pursue. Finally we intended to sail along the coast of Venezuela to the capital Caracas for a final business meeting before we flew directly back to the UK, a total of four weeks give or take few days.'

When Sergeant Totti indicated to his boss that he had got all the answer down on paper the inspector continued.

'What did your husband's Import and Export business deal with?'

Julia shrugged her shoulders. 'I have no idea because I was not involved. I presume it was British made goods in exchange for foreign imports. I heard him mention furniture, pottery, self assembly units for both business and homes, building products and even literature. My husband would trade in anything that realised a healthy profit margin.'

'Do you have any idea what the business meetings were about that he had in the Caribbean?'

'None; it was something he never discussed with me.'

'Didn't you ask?'

'Not after he told me it was none of my business and my role was to act as a good wife and to look after our home.'

'Have you any idea why he flew specifically to the Cayman Islands?'

'No.'

'You must be aware that the Cayman Islands are where smart business men hide their ill gotten gains?'

Julia bristled. 'I find your suggestion extremely insulting.'

'Am I right in presuming your husband was a very rich business man?'

'I accepted the fact that we were comfortably off, as we lived in a large detached house in a wealthy suburb of Southport, a town a few miles from Liverpool. We had two luxury cars in the garage, and cash was available for anything I wanted for personal needs, such as designer clothes, hair does, etc. Does that answer your question?'

Her question was ignored.

The Inspector suddenly changed tack. 'Did your husband have any enemies in the Caribbean or surrounding countries, like Mexico, the United States of America, or South America?'

'All successful business men have jealous competitors,' she replied. 'But I have never heard of anyone who would be prepared to commit murder to win over new customers.'

'Ah' replied the Inspector, 'now we get to the crux of this interview. You claim two coloured men boarded your yacht late at night, raped you, killed your husband by throwing him overboard while still alive, and finally knocking you unconscious with the handle of a knife.'

Julia nodded her head to acknowledge the facts.

'You also claim that when you came round, you went below to your cabin, had a shower, and used a douche before getting dressed?'

Julia also acknowledged that that was how it happened.

'Yet it was well past daylight before you sought help from the adjoining anchored yachts, why was that?'

'It was daylight before I recovered consciousness. There were no movements from any of the other yachts because I assumed the persons aboard would be asleep at that time in the morning. As I was naked I thought it advisable to get dressed before I sought help. When I went on deck after having a shower, one man appeared on deck. I called out for help and he brought his yacht alongside to ask what the trouble was. As soon as I told him what had happened, he called the coast guard and asked for assistance. The rest you know.'

Inspector Bishop paused for a while to allow his sergeant to finish writing.

'Mrs Warren you claim you had never seen either of those two men before they raped you, is that true?'

Julia nodded.

'Did they say anything while they were in your presence?'

She nodded. 'They asked for the combination of the yacht's safe. When I told them I did not know the combination, I heard one of them say something like 'Pasco or Pascie will not be pleased''.

'Is that all?'

Again she nodded.

'When you were taken up on deck was there another boat of any kind nearby?'

'I never saw one. Then I didn't look as I was too shocked when I saw how my husband had been badly beaten.'

'Those men could only have got aboard from another boat....it must have been nearby.'

'I told you I didn't see any other boat.'

Another long pause, that caused even Sergeant Totti to look up from his writing.

Inspector Bishop looked long and hard at Julia who wondered what sort of searching question would come next. This interview was taking much longer than she had anticipated and she was beginning to feel both tired and concerned at the way the interview was being dragged out.

'Mrs Warren, during the whole of this interview there is one particular aspect that is causing me some concern. Since we met you in the foyer and until this minute, you have not shed one tear for your dead husband, looked particularly distressed after your traumatic experience, or asked us if we have found your husband's body. Can you explain why?'

Julia looked long and hard at the table top before turning her head and looking directly at Sergeant Totti who gave the impression he too was wondering how she would answer those questions.

'Inspector, I married Walter Warren three years ago. Before that he was outgoing, humorous, extremely thoughtful, an excellent dancer. He lavished me with expensive gifts, sent flowers every week, and took me out to dine at some of the most expensive restaurants in Liverpool. He charmed me into his bed and was a great and experienced lover. After we were married he remained a great lover but there was a ruthless side to his character I had not seen before we were married. Ruthless, in that he got very angry when I asked about his business interests, or his friends. There were times when he became violent and left me frightened and physically abused. My early love of the man was beginning to wane and I have to admit that shortly after arriving in the Caribbean I was bored by his idea of a holiday. Most of the time I was on my own and days can become exceedingly long when you are marooned on a yacht at anchor in a cove or bay. I was shocked and overwhelmed by the ferocity of the attack on my husband, but in retrospect I have to admit I feel as if I have been released from a huge burden I expected to bear for the rest of my life. Only a short while ago I considered asking for a divorce but realised that such a question would bring physical retribution so I considered suicide as another option.'

'After a few weeks I may miss the leisurely life I led and the availability of an unlimited expense account. But at this moment I don't feel any sense of loss which I suppose is a rather heartless thing to say.'

Inspector Bishop stood up and stretched his arms, while Sergeant Totti collected his papers together, indicating to Julia that the interview was over.

'Inspector may I ask a question?'

'Depends on the question' was the considered reply.

'May I have my handbag back and my passport? My handbag contains my notebook listing a number of friends telephone numbers whom I would like to call and explain what happened, because I assume they will have already seen the newspaper accounts of my husband's death and are worried about me. I need the passport because I am short of funds with a huge restriction on my spending with the new credit card that has been issued by my bank. Overseas tourists making any purchases in Castries can get an exemption from paying customs duty and purchase tax if they produce a passport.'

Inspector Bishop frowned. 'Everything you possessed on that yacht is impounded, including your note book and passport. Saving a few pounds on purchases is in my view Mrs. Warren, the least of your worries. Before we leave, Sergeant Totti will read your statement to you. You may alter anything if you disagree with what he has written down. When he has finished I would like you to sign each page which will then be typed at the police station. You will then be asked to read the typed script again and sign each page that you agree to the contents.'

Julia read the notes before signing each page. The Inspector wished her good day before leaving.

As soon as they departed Julia broke down and cried. Which was how Cara found her when she came looking for her in the conference room.

Ch.4

Cara turned out to be real gem. She comforted Julia and when she discovered that Julia now possessed a valid credit card and desperately needed a change in clothing, she suggested they visit the main shopping street in Castries that very afternoon. 'The hotel is always quiet in the afternoon as most residents are either on the beach, around the swimming pool, or taking a siesta,' she said.

Julia was introduced to two ladies dress shops one of which was in the town's Departmental Store, smaller but not unlike a Marks and Spencer Store in the UK.

In two hours she was fitted out with three suits two of which were made up of lightweight cotton trousers with matching blouses. The third was a khaki skirt with matching top. Underwear, an urgent necessity, quickly joined the bags Cara was carrying and a nearby Chemist supplied her with makeup. The final purchase was a cheap handbag suggested by Julia as she realised her credit card was not made of elastic.

Much more relaxed now that she possessed a small wardrobe, Julia told Cara how the police had refused to surrender her passport that now restricted her to remain on the Island for the time being. 'I'll have to find somewhere cheaper to live. I cannot continue to live in your hotel, or my credit will soon run out. Is it possible to find a cheap furnished flat on the Island, where I could do my own cooking and save on hotel bills?'

Cara pooh poohed the idea of moving. 'We can change your status to that of a long term tenant that will half the cost of your hotel bill. You need someone to take care of you until the police have completed their enquiries and released your passport. Please stay in the hotel where I can be of some help.'

The two of them in a much lighter mood arrived back at the hotel to find the Detective Inspector, his Sergeant and a woman police officer waiting in the foyer.

When the two women burdened down with all their shopping marched into the foyer delighted with their afternoon's purchases, the Inspector rose from his seat and approached them looking very stern.

'Are you Julia Warren from the yacht Sunray and wife of the late Walter Warren?'

Julia looked at the Inspector as if he had had a touch of the sun. 'You know who I am we met earlier today.'

'Please answer the question with a 'yes' or 'no'.

'Yes but....'

'Mrs Julia Warren you are hereby charged with the premeditated murder of Walter Warren and will be remanded in custody until you appear before the Castries Magistrate next Monday morning at 10am. The Prosecuting Attorney will be demanding you are denied bail and ask that you remain in custody until your trial later this year. In the meantime Sergeant Totti will read you your rights and Woman Constable Filisa will secure your arms behind your back. A police car is waiting in the forecourt to take you to the Bordelaise Correctional Facility in Dennery, where you will be held until the court decides otherwise.'

Julia staggered with shock and felt the blood rushing from her head as the Sergeant grasped her arm to prevent her falling to the floor.

Her arms were dragged behind her back and she felt the handcuffs click as they locked around her wrists.

'I explained what happened to my husband on the boat, why don't you believe me?' she cried in dismay as Cara looked on with shock and horror registered on her face. The purchases they had so recently enjoyed buying lay scattered on the floor of the foyer.

Too stunned to react further, Julia was led out to the police car where she was placed on the back seat by the female officer. A uniformed male police officer drove the car away from the hotel on the cross country journey to Dennery on the Atlantic coast of the Island, a place Julia had never heard of before today.

The journey over the mountain chain running down the spine of St Lucia would have been spectacular under normal circumstances, only this journey was far from what anyone would consider normal. It was only seven plus miles across the Island from Castries to Dennery, but to Julia the journey seemed to take forever.

When they arrived outside the prison, its brilliant white stylish buildings disguised the fact that it was a penal establishment. The police car was stopped at a barrier where the officers' warrants and the remand order were carefully scrutinised before the car was allowed to proceed to the main entrance.

The same procedure was followed once again before the car was allowed through the a large barred gate into the inner courtyard where Julia was helped out of the car, her handcuffs removed and she was handed over to a warder before being escorted to the office of the Governor, a hard faced rather fat individual who looked her up and down, much to her embarrassment as if undressing her.

'You will be taken to our remand centre that is part of this prison complex' he said rather haughtily. 'You will have to share a cell with one of the very few women we have to detain in this prison. Only 1.5% of females in St Lucia are ever confined within these walls and only for minor offences,' as if Julia Warren was interested in the prison's statistics. 'You will become the most infamous female ever to enter this prison and will be treated accordingly. Punishments for any form of misbehaviour are harsh, so behave yourself, follow the rules strictly and you will find your stay less troublesome. As a prisoner on remand you may wear your own clothes, but you will be responsible for certain duties like cleaning your cell and the ablution facilities. You will stand to attention when being addressed by any officer and will answer 'sir' to all male warders and 'ma'am' to all female warders. Is all that clear?'

When Julia nodded her head he quickly rebuked her and told her he had to be addressed as 'Governor' at all times.

Dismissing her with a casual wave of his hand Julia was taken to the remand wing where she was instructed to take a shower after she was photographed and finger printed. The female wardress a local from Dennery who was grossly overweight, led her to a line of cells where she was introduced to her cell mate, a women about her own age, who smiled as she entered the cell muttering 'at last someone to talk to.'

When the cell door clanged shut behind her the woman introduced herself as Violeta, pointed to the top bunk locked against the cell wall and invited Julia to take the top bunk as she already occupied the lower one. Glancing round the sparse cell Julia saw there were a small table, one chair, a toilet, and a small hand basin in the corner, beneath a small barred window set so high that it only gave glimpses of the sky from the floor of the cell.

'There's no privacy in this bloody place,' explained Violeta. 'Just when you decide to have a crap, the wardress looks through the spy hole, so get used to it or you'll be bunged up within a week. What you in for?' she concluded without drawing breath.

'I'm completely innocent,' Julia replied, that brought a smirk from Violeta's mouth.

'Ain't we all' was the laughing reply. 'I'm in for prostitution, possession of drugs, and a knife. The Magistrate will tell me I've been a naughty girl, give me one month for possession of a knife and ask the court usher to get my telephone number and address before I am brought back here for a brief holiday. His Honour doesn't expect to pay for services rendered, by reminding me that he could have sent me down for three months for possession of drugs.' With that she laughed until the tears rolled down her face.

When she recovered her composure she again asked Julia why she was in the remand centre.

'I am accused wrongly of my husband's murder' she replied. 'How do I get in touch with people who can help me?' she asked plaintively.

Violeta stood up, placed one hand on her stomach and the other behind her back and bowed formally at the waist. 'Bloody hell, I'm sharing a cell with a celebrity. My boyfriend *will* be impressed,' she said as a great big smile spread broadly across her face.

Julia was not at all impressed with the accolade. 'I asked you how I can get in touch with friends who can help me get out of this awful predicament?' she repeated.

Violeta quickly apologised and told her that she was entitled to one free local call each week while on remand. 'Any other calls have to be paid for at exorbitant rates charged by the Governor, or you can make a call asking for the receiver to pay the phone charge. All you do is ask the operator to inform the receiver of your call that it is a reversed charge call.'

How do I get to make these calls?' asked Julia, quickly beginning to realise that prison regime included both major setbacks and cruel exploitation.

'When you hear the wardress clomping along the landing wait until she peers into cell then shout out that you want to make a telephone call. Sometimes they let you out straight away, other times you have to ask two or three times before they admit they are not deaf. And don't forget to say please ma'am, or you'll be totally ignored.'

The next time the spy hole was opened Julia asked if she could please make a local telephone call. The wardress opened the cell door and pointed to a wall mounted phone at the end of the landing. 'You got five minutes then you'll be cut off,' she said before continuing with her round of inspection.

Julia ran to the phone and quickly dialled the hotel. It was Cara who answered the phone, expressing surprise when she found Julia on the other end of the line. 'Cara, will you accept a reverse charge call from me if I call you again?' When Cara said ok Julia put the phone back on its hook and breathed a sigh of relief.

She made the same call again informing the operator it was a reverse charge call. Cara immediately answered the call, asked Julia if she was ok and how could she help?

Julia told her that the prison cell was clean and she had a companion to keep her from going absolutely mad. She explained that she urgently needed a change of clothes and clean underwear, asking Cara if she could despatch these to the prison a.s.a.p.

'Better than that' Cara replied. 'I'll bring them across and ask for permission to see you for a few minutes. Is there anything else I can do in the meantime?'

'Could you ring this number in the UK I'm going to give you, asking for the charge to be reversed and inform my friend in the UK that I would like her to call me at the prison a.s.a.p. She gave Cara the number, told her that her friends name was Marion Cosworth and asked if she could briefly outline to Marion what had happened to cause her to be in the remand centre. 'If you bring her up to date it will save me time and hassle from the wardress while I outline the help I need.' Realising the wardress was listening to every word, Julia decided to cut short the conversation. 'Cara, I appreciate having you as a friend and don't know how I can ever repay your friendship. However, put the reverse call charges on my hotel bill and I will give you my credit card number so that you can be paid what I owe you.'

Cara told her she would do no such thing. 'Friendships are made to help each other so anything you want, and I do mean anything, you can call on me day or night and I will be happy to help.'

A tear ran down Julia's cheek as she replaced the telephone. This friendship had just been cemented for life, she thought.

Ch.5

It was the following afternoon when Julia was released from her cell to take a long distance call on the telephone.

Marion was on the other end apologising for the delay by explaining that the time difference between the UK and St Lucia meant she would be calling in the middle of the night if she had returned Cara's call to her. 'I didn't think the warders would be too impressed if I asked to speak to you at midnight.' She added.

Julia thanked Marion for calling, asked her if her friend Cara had updated her with the present situation and asked if she had a pen handy. When Marion confirmed Cara had been extremely explicit she said she was ready to hear what Julia wanted.

Julia told her she was extremely concerned that the local police and their Public Prosecutor appeared to have made up their minds that they had the murderess under lock and key. 'You know me Marion and I'm sure you believe me when I say I am innocent. I can't really trust any lawyers in St Lucia to believe me and look after my interests, so I would like a reliable lawyer from England to come out to St Lucia and hear my side of this dreadful saga.'

'You work in a law firm's office. Could you ask your boss who would be the best criminal lawyer to represent me bearing in mind Walter's assets have been frozen so I have no idea whether I can meet his or her costs, so they might have to apply for legal aid before they can accept my case.'

'Will do' replied Marion. 'As one school days friend to another, is there anything I or my husband can do to help?'

'Find me a brilliant good lawyer,' replied Julia, 'or I'll be spending the rest of my days in this godforsaken prison,' she replied.

'Julia, don't ever give up hope, because I won't until you're safely back home with us. Love you,' she said, as she replaced the phone on its cradle.

Julia went back to her cell far from confident that even the best lawyer in the world would have great difficulty proving her innocence.

Later that morning the wardress opened the cell door and ordered Julia to follow her. She was led down a flight of stairs, through numerous doors to a block of offices where she was shown into a small interview room where a female was sitting at a table.

'I am a civilian administrator from the Central Police Station in Castries.' She said without mentioning her name. 'I have a typed copy of your statement for you to read and sign on each page please. If you feel any of your earlier statement has been misquoted you are entitled to amend and initial the amendment. If you have any doubts I also have your original statement with me if you wish to check what you originally signed.'

Julia sat down and re-read her statement signing each page at the bottom to confirm her acceptance. Having nothing further to add, the interview was terminated and Julia was returned to her cell to await the meeting with the magistrate on Monday morning.

– – –

It was Sunday when Cara arrived at the prison and Julia hugged her in the interview room. Cara had brought along a change of clothes and underwear, also makeup and reading material for which Julia was eternally grateful.

They chatted for a while during which time Julia explained how her friend in the UK was trying to get her an English lawyer to conduct her defence. Cara suggested that if her friend found a lawyer willing to come to St Lucia it might be advisable if that person stayed at her hotel as she could act as a guide if he or she required any services whilst on the Island.

Julia thought this an excellent suggestion and when Cara confirmed she still had her friend's home number, she suggested Cara ring Marion and put the suggestion to her.

When the time for the interview expired, Julia hugged Cara who brushed aside her thanks saying she should regard Cara as a personal friend who would always be on hand to offer help. 'All you have to do is ring me, tell me what you need, and I will come and see you a.s.a.p.

There were tears of gratitude in Julia's eyes as Cara departed from the prison.

— — —

On Monday, much to Julia's dismay she and Violeta were taken by prison van rather than an unmarked police car to the Magistrates Court in Castries.

Violeta, as predicted, was given a sentence of seven days that meant her immediate release as she had been on remand for that time. Julia was then taken into the court where she was met briefly by a solicitor who had been allocated her case by the Police Department. He explained that this was only a preliminary hearing to hear her plea and determine whether she could be granted bail.

The magistrate's clerk read out the charges of premeditated murder, or complicity to murder one Walter Warren and using unknown assailants to assist her carry out that murder. The clerk asked her how she pleaded. Her completely strange lawyer who she had met only a few moments ago, stood up and pleaded not guilty to the charges. He asked the Magistrate to grant bail which was immediately refused.

In five minutes flat, Julia was ushered out of the court and returned to the remand centre completely bemused by the way her future was so hastily conducted without her being able to say a word in her defence.

On arrival she found another occupant in her cell only this time it was a middle aged local who was laying on Julia's made up bed. Her rank body odour hit Julia's sensitive nose as she walked into the cell. It looked as if her new cell mate had slept for months in the clothes she was wearing, rather than days, and had never seen soap or water.

When Julia told the filthy woman she was occupying her bunk bed the women leaned over, glared at her and told her to f... off and take the empty bed below.

When the disinterested wardress locked the cell door Julia asked the women once again to move off her bed. When she again refused and reiterated her previous foul mouthed abuse Julia lost her cool.

She reached up, grabbed the woman by her forearm and literally yanked her off the upper bunk, bringing the bedclothes and mattress with her. As she fell to the floor Julia jumped on top of her grabbed her hair and banged her head on the floor.

'That is my bunk and you, you miserable stinking old bag can take the bottom bunk.' Julia grabbed the mattress off the bottom bunk and the newly laid out blanket and pillow and threw them onto the top bunk.

The woman got up from the floor, screamed in anger and flew at Julia hurling a string of curses she had never heard before.

Julia was having none of it. She gave the woman are hard slap across the face just as the cell door was opened by the wardress. The officer drew her baton, and hit Julia hard between the shoulders causing Julia to fall to the floor.

When Julia got back on her feet she told the wardress that the other woman had been occupying her bunk and refused to move. The wardress looked at Julia with cold eyes. 'You have no right to claim the bunk as yours. This woman was within her rights to accept which ever bunk she wanted when you were not here. Now give her back her bunk and get the other bed made up on the lower bunk, or you'll be before the governor for disciplining before your feet can touch the ground.'

The other woman smirked and climbed onto the top bunk throwing a kiss at the wardress.

When the cell door closed Julia decided to surrender and set about making up the bottom bunk. She realised immediately that the woman had contaminated the blanket and pillow with the stench of her body odour. Julia felt sick at the very thought of having to lie on the bedding for the next few days until it became time to change the bedding on laundry day.

That night she lay with her back to the wall of the cell and felt sick at the odour contaminating the air in the confined space. The following day she asked the wardress if she could be move to another cell and when that was refused she asked if the bedding could be replaced which was immediately refused, so Julia had to accept that life in the future was going to one hundred per cent worse than she had ever expected.

What bothered her further was why the wardress was so obstructive. She had done nothing to upset the woman and as she was only on remand, she failed to comprehend why the wardress was being so difficult. She would soon learn that everyone was on the take and had designed devious ways of achieving their objectives.

Ch.6

In England on her first day back at work in the solicitor's office, Marion went into her boss's office on the fourth floor of the building, with views of the Maritime Building and the River Mersey in the background. She caught a glimpse of the ferry leaving the landing stage on its regular daily journey to New Brighton on the coast.

She quietly explained the terrible incident and the charge of murder that had happened to her friend on the tropical island of St Lucia, and of her friend's urgent request for help.

Lawyer James Crosby, the senior partner of Crosby and Welland, asked Marion if she was convinced that her friend had not committed any murder.

Marion emphatically confirmed that she knew her long standing friend's temperament too well to know that she would never be involved in any form of violence, let alone murder.

James Crosby pondered over the problem for a few moments before responding. 'I appreciate that your friend is requesting you to find the best Barrister in Britain to conduct her defence, but no top of the range barrister would accept the case unless he had sufficient evidence to conduct a reasonable defence. He pointed out that a lawyer of that calibre would cost the earth if he was required to fly out to St Lucia and spend several weeks there during a trial.

'I am guessing something in the region of about five hundred thousand pounds, and no one in their right mind would wish to spend that sort of money, even if they had it available. The fact that most people with average means in this country could never afford such a person is at the moment irrelevant. What we need is some concrete evidence that can be use in your friends defence.'

He paused for a moment because Marion looked puzzled. 'What is needed is someone who will not be influenced by local officialdom and biased attorneys and who can think laterally before making hasty decisions. You may think this is nepotism but that man is my son Edwin and to prove how strong my opinion is of his legal capability, I am prepared to ask him to take on the case at no cost to your friend. We will of course sound out her finances and if applicable I will make an application for legal aid. Although I can ill afford to spare him due to the current work load in the office, I'm sure Edwin will enjoy a few weeks from the office particularly when he finds he is on his way to the Windward Islands.'

Marion was overwhelmed by her boss's generous response and said so.

Before she left the office, her boss told her that if she wanted to go to St Lucia and visit her dearest friend she could have a few days off gratis free and could fly over at the Company's expense accompanied by his son as soon as he was ready to leave.

A tear trickled down Marion's cheek. There were so few people in the world that could be so kind, she thought.

– – –

Edwin Crosby had been qualified for only three years and was in his opinion, still learning the trade as he put it. However his court record was proving otherwise. He had won some very difficult cases for the Chambers, proving to be a challenging adversary for the prosecution with numerous new clients specifically asking for his son's services.

He was tall, and superbly fit, following the fitness regime of a professional sportsman. With cropped blond hair and penetrating blue eyes it was not surprising that many young ladies in the clubs he visited tried to catch his attention. That they were unsuccessful was because Edwin was only interested in one girl who was currently playing the hard to catch bit, although even she recognised that with a bit of guile she would sooner or later become Mrs Crosby.

The first thing Edwin did when his father suggested he go to St Lucia for an unspecified period was ring his girlfriend to inform her he would be abroad for a few weeks but promised to ring her every day.

When she suggested she could get time off for two weeks to accompany him he told her he would be involved in a gruesome murder trial and needed to be free from any commitments to apply his mind to what he anticipated would be a very complex case.

Reluctantly she had to concede, but warned him that if he was away too long she might, just might, find someone else interested in entertaining her while he was away.

The threat came as a complete shock to Edwin who told her he missed her and promised to come back with a large diamond ring for her left hand providing she behaved herself. Having successfully put his girl friend in check, he replaced the phone and walked into Marion's office to discuss flight arrangements and explain the problems facing him once he arrived in St Lucia. 'I know you are going to the Island to visit your friend and if that is all you want to do during the visit it is ok by me. However, I will require someone to handle all the paper work and you understand how my father and I work. If you could spare some time to help it would be greatly appreciated.'

Marion smiled. 'Your father has already agreed to pay my air fare, and my salary, while I am away, the least I could do is offer my services to you. In any case I assume visits to persons on remand will be restricted, and I won't know what time I am allowed until we get there and I can check the visiting times. Keeping me busy will help to take my mind off the dreadful situation Julia now finds herself in.

Before she left for home Edwin told her that the only seats available were on the flight the following evening so they would be travelling overnight. 'We change planes in Jamaica and should arrive on St Lucia in the early hours the following day bearing in mind the time difference. I'll book us into a hotel in Castries so we can be reasonably near the scene of the crime and the police headquarters where I expect to spend a lot of my time.'

When Marion arrived home she found a message on her answer phone from Cara offering her hotel accommodation.

'My hotel is not up to the standards of the five star hotels in town, but I will be able to assist you in getting to the prison to visit Julia and I can be useful if you need to make any purchases for either yourself or Julia,' was the message on her answering machine.

Marion immediately rang back, forgetting the five hour time difference between the two zones and got Cara out of bed, before apologised for disturbing her. She explained she would be travelling with a Lawyer who would take charge of Julia's case and they would be delighted to stay in her hotel when they arrived in two days time. Marion then telephoned Edwin Crosby and suggested he cancel the hotel he had booked for them both, while suggesting that Cara would be extremely useful to recommend any other help they may need to expedite the investigation into the murder of Julia's late husband.

Edwin agreed with her observations. 'It will also provide you with company while I am involved with the hum drum legal argy bargee I am anticipating with the local police, who are bound to be suspicious of someone from England being involved with their case. 'Ring Cara what's her name, tomorrow morning, and ask her to organise a boat with a reliable captain as I will need to visit the scene of the crime. I will also need to hire a car with an experienced driver who can wiz me round the Island, and particularly to the prison, where I will have to spend some time with Mrs Warren while I use the services of a local lawyer in preparing her case for the trial. I may be back in England long before the trial is scheduled to take place, but I do intend to be at your friend's trial to make sure the very best case is presented to ensure her release.'

Again when Marion put down the phone she thought to herself how very lucky she was to have such wonderful employers.

Ch.7

Marion's husband listened to the sudden change about to take place in his regimented lifestyle.

'I'm sure you will manage while I am away,' she told him. 'Have an occasional meal at the golf club; go and visit your mum who will be more than happy to feed you; and when you run out of options do what you always do....cook yourself a chef's exclusive dish of baked beans on toast.'

Gerald shrugged his shoulders accepting that his wife's visit to St Lucia was a fait accompli and he had better grin and bear it. 'When you eventually get to see Julia assure her that we will assist with any unexpected costs she hadn't anticipated, including legal fees etc. 'Please tell her that she has our love and that we will fully support her even if she is eventually found guilty and is kept in prison.'

Marion rounded on her husband angrily. 'I've told you not once, but dozens of times over the last few days, that Julia is totally innocent, and I will not have you even thinking that she is guilty.'

Gerald raised his hands in the air in abject surrender. 'I am not inferring that she may be guilty, I'm only suggesting that if the court finds her guilty she can still expect our undivided support.'

Marion was not in the mood to be appeased. 'No court could find her guilty, Julia is too nice a person she wouldn't harm a fly. However, your proposal that we support her financially has my total support. I'll even mortgage the bloody house if she needs that much money.'

Gerald hoped to hell that her proposal would never get that far.

– – –

The following night Marion and Edwin Crosby flew out of Heathrow en route to the Caribbean, accepting that the odds that they had gleaned on reading the national press were heavily stacked against Julia Warren.

Marion was completely confused after an eight hour flight when they arrived at Kingston International Airport in Jamaica at one am the following morning, failing to take into account the five hour time difference. They had to hang about in the airport lounge until daylight before they flew on an internal flight to St Lucia where they landed at 11.0am local time. Having cleared the passport control without any problems they took a taxi to Cara's hotel where she welcomed them with open arms.

Turning to Marion she said 'Julia will be delighted to see you and when she hears you are staying for two weeks will be looking forward to every visiting time to have a chat with her dearest friend.'

'How many visiting times are there?' asked Marion.

'Not enough,' replied Cara, 'but we'll apply for extra visiting rights as you have travelled such a long way to see Julia.'

She eyed Edwin up and down and quickly came to the conclusion that this young man could be more than a match for that despicable Inspector Bishop, who, in Cara's opinion, had already decided that the case was already solved. Only time and wasted court appearances would have to be endured by the Inspector and his team before Mrs Warren could be locked up for life.

Cara, remembering that she had promised to fulfil a number of requests from Edwin Crosby, told him that she had arranged for a deep sea cabin cruiser with a reliable captain to be on standby in Castries harbour. 'When you wish to use the boat I'll be happy to show you where she is moored in the Marina. Her owner will remain on board as long as he is required.' Glancing at Edwin's face to see how he would react she added that hiring his boat was not cheap, but pointed out the captain was very reliable.

Edwin shrugged his shoulders and commented that if he achieved the right results the cost would be irrelevant. As far as he was concerned he could imagine the cost of this case escalating out of control.

Cara showed them their bedrooms with a view of the harbour area and the promenade. Once they had deposited their travel bags Edwin excused himself saying he had business with the police department that needed to be dealt with that very day.

After Cara pointed him in the right direction, Edwin walked out of the hotel onto the street and immediately realised how popular a holiday resort is St Lucia. Tourists from all over the world thronged the streets festooned with cameras, mobile phones, and street maps. There appeared to be a prominence of Americans among the tourists bringing much needed dollar currency to the small Island.

He hailed a passing taxi and asked the driver to take him to the Police HQ at Bridge St. The driver gave him a quizzical glance before shrugging his shoulders and pulling away from the curb. The journey took about three minutes making Edwin understand the reason for the gesture because he could have walked to the HQ and stretched his stiff legs.

Entering the station he asked to see Detective Inspector Bishop. When asked for what purpose by the desk sergeant he told him it was in connection with the Warren incident.

'You a reporter?' demanded the sergeant.

'No, I'm a lawyer by the name of Crosby and I need to speak to the Inspector as a matter of urgency.'

The sergeant picked up his desk phone, pressed two or three buttons before mumbling into the mouthpiece that a Lawyer called Crosby was at the custody desk.

Edwin was kept waiting on a hard seat for fifteen minutes before a plain clothes officer arrived and asked Edwin to follow him. He was shown into a small office at the rear of the building overlooking the parking bays for the police vehicles.

The man sitting at the desk introduced himself to Edwin as Detective Inspector Bishop and asked what he could do to help.

'I've just arrived from the United Kingdom and am registered and staying at the hotel Adelphi. I am here to represent a Mrs. Julia

Warren who I understand is currently detained in the remand wing of the Dennery Correctional Facility.'

Harry Bishop's eyebrows moved up towards his receding hair line as he tried to estimate the age of the young man who was standing before him purporting to represent the young woman in the remand centre. Guessing his visitor was less than 30 years of age, the Inspector wondered what experience Crosby could have to be heading the defence team. 'Hell of an expensive exercise to bring a lawyer out from Britain to represent someone who professes to be desperately short of money,' he exclaimed.

Edwin ignored the sarcastic comment. 'I expect you have already obtained a statement from Mrs Warren. I will show you my credentials as I wish to obtain a copy of her statement.'

Inspector Bishop openly breathed a sigh of relief. 'You can show me all the credentials in the world, but I will not release anything to you until I have a signed authorisation from Mrs Warren and you are granted visiting rights by Chief Inspector Bailey who is Senior Officer in charge of this HQ.'

Inspector Bishop underestimated the young man standing in front of him, who was getting quietly pissed off by this pompous old prick who had not had the decency to ask him to sit down. 'Inspector Bishop all that is required is a quick telephone call by you to the Governor of the prison asking him to confirm with Mrs Warren that I am her legal representative. Please tell the Governor who I am and that I have been accompanied by her friend Marion Cosworth who will be visiting her as soon as she is granted special visiting rights.'

Edwin found it necessary to take in a few deep breaths to control his rising temper. 'While you are arranging the call, I wish to make the point that from today; no one, and I repeat no one, will discuss any aspects of her case with Mrs Warren unless I am present. Anyone who attempts to bypass my instructions will be brought before the local Judge for breach of legal procedure, and any information they have obtained will not be allowed to be presented as evidence, or be communicated to any other person, and that includes you Inspector. I hope of have made myself perfectly clear?'

'I also propose to visit the crime scene that I understand took place in the sea off somewhere called Rodney Bay. I will require the map co-ordinates of the anchored yacht which I am sure will be on your police records. I do not require a police presence while I visit the scene, as the captain of the boat I have hired will be perfectly capable of reading his map.'

Inspector Bishop swallowed so hard his Adams apple took a swift upward trend. With the young man staring hard into his eyes awaiting his reaction, he leaned forward, picked up the telephone and asked the operator to put him through to the prison governor. Explaining the reason for his call he listened to the reply before replacing the phone and at long last invited the angry looking lawyer to take a seat.

Making small talk as if he had not literally been punched below the belt by this smarmy intruder to his island, he spoke about how many problems he currently faced, dealing with small time criminals who were using every device to remove the cash from the visiting tourists. When the phone eventually rang and Inspector Bishop said 'thank you sir', Edwin assumed it was the governor replying to his call.

'Mrs Warren has confirmed you are authorised to represent her so I will arrange for you to collect a copy of her statement tomorrow midday, when I will also hand over the co-ordinates you are requesting. As to your instruction that no one interviews Mrs Warren without you being present I will raise this point with the Public Prosecutor later today and will give you his answer when you call tomorrow.'

Edwin Crosby leaned across the Inspector's desk. 'I am sure your police department has moved out of the Victorian era into the twenty first century and possess a photo copying machine or computer printer. Excuse me for not trusting you, but I want that copy made while I am here, to ensure your staff have no time to doctor her original statement......do I make myself clear once again Inspector?'

Inspector Bishop rose from his chair angry at the insinuation. 'I resent your inference Mr Crosby. My police officer's would never do such an illegal act.'

Edwin Crosby smiled sweetly at the Inspector. 'I am well versed in what happens when nosey lawyers start to ask serious questions about a case. I apologise if I have offended you, but I still want a photo copy within the next fifteen minutes, or the statement will be declared null and void once I appear in court.'

Edwin left the station half an hour later with a copy of Julia's statement in his pocket.

As soon as he left the station Harry Bishop called his team together. 'The bloke who just left my office is a clever dick lawyer from England. If you come in contact with him with regard to the Warren case, don't be deceived by his youthful appearance. I have a strong feeling he is going to be thorn in our bloody side, so don't be obviously obstructive, but at the same time don't offer him any help or advice, and if he asks any awkward questions refer him to me.'

Edwin had taken only a few hours to make his first of many enemies in the Caribbean.

Harry Bishop had never cared very much for lawyers per se, but this upstart from England had already got seriously up his nose. He felt confident between the Public Prosecutor and himself, that they could soon show this over cocky guy that *they* decided between them what was in the best interests of the citizens of St Lucia; and that they were more than capable of dealing with a piddling little murder case without having the technicalities of the law quoted at them by some clever dick from the UK.

The proverbial 'fly on the wall' would have come to the conclusion that war had been declared without a shot being fired.

Ch.8

The following day he, Marion, and Cara in the hired car, made the journey across the mountains with Cara acting as guide. They arrived at the Prison one hour before the official visiting time so Edwin invited both ladies to join him in a local bar where they were served with delicious coffee. When Edwin indicated he was not having any alcohol as he wished to keep a clear head, Marion and Cara also declined.

Passing through the outer barrier of the prison they queued to await the opening of the small door leading to the inner court yard. They were eventually led with other visitors into the visitors meeting room, where a warder and wardress stood by the outer wall and watched to see that no narcotics, cigarettes, or small parcels, changed hands under the various tables.

When Julia arrived from her cell, the embrace between her and Marion and the show of tears showed how emotional this first meeting was going to be.

When Julia was asked if she had any problems tears welled up in her eyes. When Marion insisted that Julia should tell them what her problem was, she told them how she was now sharing a cell with a down and out, who not only suffered from serious body odour problems, was infested with lice, mean as hell, smoked pot, and used language the like of which Julia had never experienced.

While Julia, Marion and Cara where chatting, Edwin walked over to the two warders. He explained that he was one of Mrs Warren's approved visitors and was concerned when he discovered she had to share a cell with a local layabout who had a serious odour problem. He asked if there was anything that could be done to improve Mrs Warren's current situation.

The wardress stepped forward and told him that there was nothing that could be done to improve her lot but..... And there she hesitated.

'But what?' asked Edwin knowing quite well what was coming next.

'Some prisoners are willing to pay extra for special treatment, such as improved food and better sleeping conditions.'

'And what would that special treatment cost?' he asked.

'Are we talking in American dollars, or local Caribbean dollars?'

Edwin brought out his wallet. 'I would like Mrs Warren transferred to a cell on her own and be given five star treatment where food and health are concerned. What would that cost in English pounds?'

The warder standing beside her was quick off the mark. 'One hundred pounds per week might improve her lot,' he said with an annoying smirk on his face.

Edwin handed over five twenty pound notes and promised to pay weekly as and when he visited his client. Pretending to act like a novice tourist he asked if he could pay by bankers order to the prison service. The male warder in a lowered voice told Edwin that he, or the lady accompanying him, should be paid in cash each week on the prison visit. 'Either Wardress Javendes, or me, are normally on duty for these visits so hand over the money to us.'

What if you are not on duty?' asked Edwin quietly.

'Then pay us two weeks on the next visit.'

'And what is your name may I ask?' asked Edwin.

'I'm Warder Rodney Bona and can assure you that we will take great care of Mrs Warren from now on.'

I bet you will. Two blood thirsty sharks, thought Edwin.

He walked back to the table were Julia, Marion and Cara were in animated conversation with hands being waved in the air to describe something they were discussing.

When he sat down, he quietly informed Julia that he had spoken to the two prison officers who had promised to improve her conditions after the visit was over.

Julia's short stay in prison had taught her a lot about the character of both warders and inmates. 'How much did you have to pay to get me out of that abominable cell?' she asked.

'Not very much' laughed Edwin, 'but I hope it was enough to ensure you peace of mind for the next few weeks until you come to trial.'

'You do realise I can't afford it,' she said with a deep sigh.

Marion told her friend not to worry. Placing her hands over Julia's hands she told her that her husband had promised to meet any unforeseen costs until Julia could get her finances sorted out.

Edwin suddenly interrupted the ladies. 'We do not have much time left before the visiting time will expire and I have a couple of questions I need to ask Julia. He produced the copy of the statement he had acquired from the Inspector and asked Julia if she would glance down the pages and confirm that was what she had said. As she was doing so he asked her who had written down the original statement, and where and when after she was rescued from the yacht?

Julia told him that the Inspector and a sergeant had come to the hotel the day after she was rescued and had interviewed her in the hotel conference room by agreement with Cara; who nodded that that was so. 'The Inspector asked the questions and the sergeant wrote down her answers and asked her to read the notes and sign them that they were correct.'

Julia handed back the typed copy of her statement and confirmed it was correct just as the alarm bell sounded to warn the visitors it was time to leave.

Marion hugged Julia and whispered in her ear to put her trust in Edwin. 'He looks far too young to be an experienced lawyer, but I trust Edwin's father's judgement who told me his son was far advanced in legal matters for his age.'

When the visitors had departed the wardress told Julia to follow her and she was taken to a cell on the ground floor with a barred window looking over the prison courtyard where there was a finely mown lawn surrounded by beds of brilliantly coloured flowers. There was only one bed in the cell and the wardress pointed to a single sheet of paper lying on the bed. You order your evening meal from that list each day and give it to one of the trustee prisoners who arrive each morning to clean your cell. 'Welcome to the Ritz,' said the smirking wardress as she closed and locked the cell door.

Julia glanced around her temporary new home. The sheets, pillow case and blankets looked as if they had freshly laundered. On the solitary table was a blotting pad, writing material including a biro pen, and two paperback novels. The toilet was hidden behind a seclusion panel and possessed a plastic seat. The hand basin possessed a plug and a soap dish complete with a bar of scented toilet soap. A hand rail next to the basin included a clean roller towel. As the wardress had so sarcastically told her, this was indeed the Rolls Royce of all prison cells. Julia realised her newly appointed defence counsellor had spared no expense to ensure her personal comfort while she was on remand.

Ch.9

Edwin was in a black mood as they drove away from the prison.

When Marion asked what had annoyed him, he told her what had happened when he went to speak to the warders. They quickly assess the worth of the prisoner in their supposed care and if there is an opportunity to earn a quick buck they make sure the prisoner is housed with someone they will not like. Julia was first placed in a cell with a known prostitute and drug addict, but the girl was released the next day so they replaced her with a stinking, bug ridden, down and out, knowing that Julia would complain to her visitors. As soon as I asked for her to be moved to better accommodation the two sharks were quick to tell me what it would cost and for how long.

'As far as I am concerned the money is incidental if Julia is given a cell on her own. We'll find out on our next visit and if she has not been re-housed to better conditions, then those two cold blooded sharks will wish they had never been born.'

Marion had a feeling that a number of unsuspecting persons who were directly, or indirectly, involved in this murder inquiry on St Lucia, would find the devil incarnate had invaded their cosy territory.

– – –

The discussion over the evening meal with Edwin and Marion centred on the visit to the prison. Marion expressed her horror that appointed government officials like those two warders at the prison could be so devious in a cold and calculated effort to enhance their income. 'Surely if the Governor and his deputy can't see what is going on they shouldn't be holding such responsible positions,' she said with such feeling, that Edwin felt dreadfully sorry that Marion's first visit had presented her with such an awful dilemma.

Although Edwin's plan of action was firmly fixed in his mind, he thought it advisable to update Marion with his first intention. 'I am concerned that Julia was represented at the Magistrates first hearing with a lawyer appointed by the prosecution service that has a vested interest in keeping her in custody. The impression I glean from Cara is that the Magistrate, the police, and the prosecuting officers are a small cabal of local government servants, who tend to cosy up to each other to protect their positions in the hierarchy. I intend to rock that little boat a bit, to try and relieve the pressure on us about constantly having to worry about Julia's situation as it currently stands.'

Marion who was beginning to enjoy the quietude of the small hotel where the staff was so attentive to detail, and the food was of the highest quality, asked what Edwin had in mind.

'Now that I have been accepted as Julia's appointed lawyer, I am going to request that the court be reconvened a.s.a.p. to hear my plea for bail to be granted.'

'Do you think you have a chance with all the odds stacked against you?'

'They had it damned easy the first time round with no palpable opposition. This time I have a few cards up my sleeve they may not have encountered in the past.'

'When is this likely to happen?' asked Marion well aware of what was said at some of the regular weekly meetings in Crosby and Welland's Chambers when schemes were devised, first to allay the opposition, then hit them with a broadside when least expected.

'I will make the application tomorrow, pressing for an early hearing as I must return to England to deal with other urgent cases piling up on my desk.'

Marion put down her knife and fork and looked aghast at Edwin. 'You never said you were returning to England so soon?'

'I'm not, but the magistrate doesn't know that, so he might allow the hearing this week.'

'Devious bastard,' muttered Marion laughing, before apologising for the language.

When Edwin applied for a hearing to present an appeal on behalf of Mrs Julia Warren the Magistrates office informed him that because bail had been rejected by the magistrate he would have to apply to the Central Appeals Court for permission to present his case before the presiding judge a Mr Justice Bell.

Edwin ever persistent did just that and was informed that under normal circumstances he would have to wait at least three months for a slot in the court programme. However, luck was on his side when he was informed that a case scheduled for the following week had been cancelled because the applicant had died. That particular case had been set aside for three days so the clerk of the court asked if Edwin's case would last as long.

'In my opinion no,' asserted Edwin. 'I wish to question only two witnesses and subject to their responses and the reaction of the Public Prosecutor, I expect my application to last only two days at the most.'

The clerk asked for the names of the witnesses and was told that they were Detective Inspector Harry Bishop and Detective Sergeant Lane Totti.

'Have you asked them to attend voluntarily?' asked the clerk, having experienced some difficulty with the Inspector in the past.

'No' on both counts,' replied Edwin. 'I cannot see Inspector Bishop attending my hearing without having to be dragged here.'

'In that case I will issue an order for them to appear before the Judge.'

Expressing his profound gratitude for the assistance he received, Edwin decided another formal visit to Julia was necessary to clear up a few points he suspected were missing from her statement. When he contacted the prison administration office he was asked what date and time he had in mind. When he suggested two days hence at 2pm, Edwin was taken by surprise when it was agreed.

From the hotel he walked down to the harbour's Marina and found the boat he had hired tied up alongside one of the many piers. The boat's owner was on deck busy polishing the brasses trying to keep his cruiser looking spick and span.

'Captain Bellis?' Edwin asked the man with a large polishing cloth in his hand.

'At your service Mr Crosby, when do you require my services?'

'Right now, if you are ready to go to sea?'

'You are paying the bill Mr Crosby so you call the tune,' he replied with a hearty laugh. 'I have an idea why you require my services. I assume you want to visit the scene of the crime?'

Edwin acknowledged the warm welcome and the immediate response to his request, well pleased with Cara's selection. The cruiser was large and powerful looking and the boat looked as if it had an owner who cared about its appearance. 'You seem well informed and yes I want to visit the scene of the crime.'

'I read the local papers to keep myself informed. The murder has been headlines for weeks, with reporters forming opinions as to who is suspect and expressing some negative opinions that the main suspect is already in prison.'

Turning the ignition key as he chatted, the engine roared into life. Handing Edwin a life preserver he helped him aboard before casting off the mooring lines. The captain turned the cruisers bows towards the open sea against the incoming tide, and surged out of the Marina resulting in a huge bow wave to demonstrate its turn of speed.

Captain Bellis didn't need to check his compass bearing to find his way to Rodney Bay. He had fished in these waters for twenty odd years and recognised all the landmarks as he headed north towards the bay. As they approached, he cut the speed and slowly entered the bay checking his map and his compass bearings with landmarks on shore. Switching the engine to idle, he looked at

Edwin and said 'As far as I am concerned this was about the spot where the Sunray was found drifting in the bay.'

'What are your present map co-ordinate readings?' Edwin asked taking a piece of paper out of his pocket. When Captain Bellis gave him the readings Edwin nodded his acceptance as the readings were virtually similar to those written on his piece of paper. 'How far would the yacht Sunray drift once the anchor ropes were cut?' he asked.

'It depends on the tide on the night of the murder. If the tide was falling and the sea was calm she would drift about half a mile by the time she was found by the coastguard. If the tide was coming in she would have been very close to the other anchored yachts. Without checking my tide tables, I would guess the former, as Mrs Warren had to yell to catch the attention of one of the occupants on the other moored yachts.'

Edwin suggested the Captain check the facts and try and make a calculated guess where Sunray was moored. Pausing for a moment to consider other options he wished to explore, he asked the Captain if he could spare the time to do some detailed investigations for him. 'It will involve additional costs so I suggest you keep a detailed record and I will reimburse you when you have concluded the investigations.'

'I am at your disposal,' the captain reminded him. 'Just what have you in mind?'

'I would like you to track down the owners of all those yachts that were anchored in the bay and ask the Captain, and crew where applicable, to mark on a map of the bay where they were anchored on the night of the murder, and where they consider the Sunray was anchored the same night? Could you also ask them (a) if they had sight of where the Sunray had drifted to? (b) Whether they had seen any other boat in the vicinity of the Sunray? (c) Did any of them witness the arrival of the coastguard on the following morning? and (d) did they see the police sending down any divers?'

Captain Bellis noted down all the questions. 'What are you hoping to achieve?' he asked.

'This is strictly confidential and personal,' emphasized Edwin to the Captain.

When Captain Bellis nodded his acceptance, Edwin said he was hoping to find the spot where Julia's husband had been dumped overboard.

'May I ask with what purpose?' the captain asked.

'I really don't know at this stage, but if we find the body it could gave us some useful information that is currently only speculation by the authorities.'

Captain Bellis shrugged his shoulders as if suggesting that a decaying body would be of little help. Going back to the questions he had been posed, he made the observation that all of those yachts would have moved on as the majority of them would all be cruising the Caribbean.

Edwin nodded his acceptance of the observation 'Check the Harbour Master and the Coastguard for the name of each yacht, then widen your search to other islands with the same inquiry. Those boats must still be in the Caribbean. Find as many as you can and let me know when you run out of steam. The information you can glean from those people is vital if I am to find where the body was dumped overboard. Thanks for the help today, now take me back to Castries for I have a difficult court case to prepare before the end of this week.'

Ch.10

Edwin made another trip to Dennery prison two days later and was led into the interview room where he was told to take a seat while the wardress collected Julia from her cell.

When Julia was shown into the waiting room the wardress closed the door but remained inside leaning on the wall. 'Edwin pointed to the door and told the wardress the interview with his client was confidential. 'Would you please wait in the corridor until I call you and please don't attempt to listen at the door.'

When the wardress left, Edwin asked Julia if she had been moved from her cell. When she confirmed that she had been transferred to a new more acceptable cell immediately after the last visit. She told Edwin that the new cell was on the ground floor, and that she was the only occupant; confirming that the bribe had worked. When Julia also reported that her food had improved dramatically Edwin was very pleased.

Getting straight down to the reason for his visit, he told Julia he had carefully read and digested her statement. 'Is there anything you missed out of your statement and why? he asked. 'Tell me again what happened when you heard footsteps on the deck above you, and can you recall if anything was said by your husband, or by the two men who assaulted you?'

Julia told him that the two men demanded the combination of the safe but she told them that she didn't know. 'One of the men muttered that someone called Pascie or Pascoe would be mad if they didn't get the list. Then they raped me before dragging me onto the deck where I saw my husband trussed up like a chicken. They asked him something but I didn't hear what it was, then they..........' she paused for a moment, 'lifted him off the deck and threw him overboard with the anchor attached to his feet.'

'Did your husband say anything before he was thrown into the sea?'

Julia paused for a moment......... 'No, he cried out before he went under the water. But that is all.'

'Julia, I am going to ask you a few questions that could be both unusual and upsetting. You said in your statement that Walter was aware of what was about to happen to him as he was being thrown over the side of the yacht.'

Julia shuddered as she was reminded of the terrible scene she was forced to witness on the night of Walter's murder. A brief nod of her head confirmed that her husband was alive and well aware of the fate that awaited him.

'Did he say anything at all to you before he was lifted over the side?'

'No nothing at all. He was there one moment and the next he was gone.'

'Can you recall anything he said or boasted about during the years you were married? For example did he ever mention any system he used to authorise payments on his credit card? Did he sign any documents using the name W Warren or Walter Warren? Did you ever know the code he used to open his computer or his safe?'

Julia shook her head from side to side in a negative way before thinking deeply about the questions.

Edwin Crosby accepted that his questions were to say the least unusual. But he persisted. 'In order to get to the bottom of the reason your husband was killed I need to explore every avenue; every minute detail. Somewhere in his background is the key to unlock this mystery and you may be the only person who can open that secret door to his mind. Nearly every person uses a simple code for a password. Sometimes it's a birthday linked to a house number, or the year they were born.'

Julia suddenly realised what he was searching for. 'He never signed his name on letters using only an initial with an attached squiggle. I once asked him what was and he told me it was his initials expressed in a way only he could unravel.'

Edwin Crosby asked her to write in down and she wrote a large W with a squiggle attached to the top of the W. Looking at it closely he accepted that most people used a similar squiggle rather than the clear initials of their Christian and Surname. But he had to admit it didn't look like WW.

'What about birthdays?' he asked again.

Julia frowned at his persistence. 'Mine is on the 24th August and Walters on the 10th of May,' she said. He was ten years older than me and was born in 1980 so he could have used 1980 or 1080. The only person who can answer that is Walter and he is no longer here.' She added with a winsome shrug of her shoulders.

Edwin made notes of her comments and accepted that apart from clutching at straws there were literally dozens of permutations, maybe hundreds to be examined, if he was to find Walter's key to Pandora's Box. In the meantime the main key to Walter's murder were the names of the two men who had raped Julia.

'Julia, some parts of what you have told me was not included in the statement you made to the police why is that?'

'I didn't like the tone of the Inspector's questions and I wondered if they might turn up something that would incriminate my husband. Walter must have got into some devious deals in his import export business and I was not prepared to help the police damage his good name.'

Her observations caused Edwin's eyebrows to rise slightly in astonishment. It was not the reaction he expected from someone who recently witnessed the murder of her husband.

Before he left the prison he told Julia that she would be required to attend the hearing to request bail he had arranged for the following week. 'A prison warder will bring you over to the court and you need to be there by 9.45am. 'You must be prepared to be asked questions by the Judge, or the Prosecuting Attorney, but I would doubt it.'

When Edwin was driving back to the hotel he let his mind

wander as the traffic on the mountain road was quite light. Who the hell was the mystery man Pascie? And what was in that safe on the Sunray that was so important to the mysterious Pascie? Edwin thought he would give a king's ransom to get his hands on the two rapists. They would surely know the answers to some of his questions.

When he eventually got back to the hotel he sat with Marion and brought her up to date following his visit to her friend.

Marion too, expressed concern about the new problems that were now being added to Edwin's investigations. Although she was due to return to the UK in a few days, she envisaged Edwin spending months in the Bahamas with very little hope that his conclusions would help her friend.

– – –

He had not heard anything from Captain Bellis when the day of the hearing arrived. Edwin presented himself to the High Court and waited in the foyer for Julia to arrive. When she did, he ushered her into the courtroom and sat chatting to help her calm down before the Judge arrived. He noticed Inspector Bishop and Sergeant Totti sitting on a bench in the corridor glancing in his direction as he and Julia walked towards the courtroom. The Inspector glowered at him as he walked past the bench, but Edwin noticed that the sergeant gave a wan smile that seemed to indicate he was only here under sufferance to support his boss.

They both entered the courtroom and Edwin helped Julia into a chair alongside his own at the Defending Counsel's table.

As soon as she was seated Edwin told Julia to make no comment during the proceedings and if she was asked a question in the witness box by the Judge or the Defence Counsel, to glance at him for confirmation that she could answer. 'Keep your responses brief and try not to elaborate your answers with opinion. I know it is difficult to remain calm when in court but I will help you as much as I can.'

Julia was nodding that she understood when the court usher asked everyone to rise while the Judge entered.

The Judge bowed in Edwin's direction before taken his seat. The clerk of the court announced in a loud voice that 'His Honour Judge Francis Bell was presiding to hear the appeal on behalf of Mrs Julia Warren.'

Edwin remained standing and informed the Judge that he was counsel for Mrs Warren.

The Judge acknowledged the announcement with a nod, before making the comment to Mr Crosby that he was a long way from his chambers in England and hoped his journey would prove to be fruitful.

Edwin acknowledged the observation and wondered if the Judge's comment would turn out as indicated.

The Judge adjusted his bi-focal glasses that appeared to have slipped down his nose, before picking up his pen and indicating that he was ready for Mr Crosby to begin.

'Your honour, I appreciate that the application for bail for my client was refused at an earlier hearing in the Magistrates Court when my client was represented by a local lawyer appointed by the court. I am reapplying for bail to be allowed as it appears to me that no evidence was produced to defend my client's right to be granted bail. Now I think I have the evidence and wish to present it to your Honour in order that you can decide whether it now merits a change of mind by the court. May I call my first witness a Detective Sergeant Totti. May I draw the Judge's attention that both my witnesses are part of the prosecutor's team and should be regarded as hostile.'

'Point taken' said the Judge.

Detective Sergeant Totti was shown into the witness box and asked by the court clerk to take the oath.

When he was seated Edwin Crosby began his examination. 'Did you receive a message at police headquarters on the morning of the fourteenth of April that there had been a fatality on a yacht called the Sunray anchored in Rodney Bay?'

'Yes.'

'And did you accompany Detective Inspector Bishop aboard a Coastguard cutter to investigate the report?'

'Yes.'

'What did you find when you arrived at the scene?'

'A man called Fisher told me that he was from another yacht called Lion King anchored in the bay. He had heard Mrs Warren call out that she needed help as her boat was drifting seaward and her husband had been murdered. Mr Fisher told me his wife was down in the cabin with Mrs Warren, who claimed she had been raped by two men who had tossed her husband overboard with an anchor tied to his feet.'

'What did you do then?'

'The cutter placed us alongside and the Inspector and I climbed aboard.

'Did any of the cutters crew join you on the Sunray?'

'No.'

'Why was that?'

'Because the Inspector told them to remain on their own ship so that they would not contaminate any evidence.

'A very commendable instruction,' suggested Edwin

'What did you then do?'

'We boarded the yacht and went down into the cabin where we saw two ladies sitting at a table one of whom was Mrs Warren.'

'Did you take a statement from Mrs Warren?'

'No'

'Why not?'

'Because Mrs Warren looked seriously distressed and was crying.'

'What happened then?'

The Inspector who was with me, went back on deck and ordered the cutter to take Mrs Warren on board and to take the Sunray in tow back to Castries where it would be placed in police quarantine until a forensic team could check the yacht for evidence.'

'I assume that is exactly what happened?'

'Yes.'

'Sergeant, did you eventually take a statement the next day from Mrs Warren?'

'Yes.'

'Who else was present?'

'Detective Inspector Bishop.'

'Where did this occur?'

'We met her in the Adelphi Hotel where Mrs Warren was being temporally accommodated.'

'Where in the Adelphi was she questioned?'

'We met in the hotel's conference room.'

'Why was the statement not taken in a police station?'

'The Inspector decided otherwise.'

'Was she cautioned before making her statement?'

'No.'

'Why not, when a suspected murder had been committed?

'At the time I did not think it necessary all we were doing was gathering facts.'

'And yet you asked Mrs Warren to sign her statement to confirm she was telling the truth as she saw it?'

The sergeant made no reply.

'You had the statement typed and presented it via a prison administrator to Mrs Warren while she was being held in remand. Did you suspect that Mrs Warren's statement was false?'

'I had my doubts.'

'Then why didn't you caution Mrs Warren before she signed the typed copy and inform her that she could have legal advice?'

'I was busy with the Inspector on another case and we had no time available to go to the prison.'

'A rather lame excuse Sergeant.'

Again Sergeant Totti decided not to respond.

'Has the yacht Sunray been tested for evidence by the Forensic Team?'

'Yes.'

'And what are their conclusions?'

'They have not yet issued their findings.'

'Thank you sergeant, you have been most helpful.'

The court usher stood up and looked at the Judge who nodded.

'You can stand down sergeant but you may not leave the courtroom until the Judge grants you permission.'

Sergeant Totti looked slightly distressed before he sat down in the well of the court, hoping to God that he had not let his Inspector down. Life would be hell on earth for him if he had dropped a clanger during his examination by the English lawyer.

The Judge finished writing on his pad and looked across at Mr Crosby. 'I propose to adjourn for lunch. Detective Sergeant Totti will be accompanied by a court official during the lunch break to ensure he has no contact with the next witness.'

The Honourable Justice Bell rose and bowed to those assembled in his courtroom before retiring to his chambers at the rear of the court.

As soon as he retired, Julia asked Edwin who the other persons were who were sitting in the courtroom.

'Mainly members of the press, but some will be nosey members of the public who want to watch the contest and have a gander at the person who they think committed a murder.'

'But I am innocent.'

While Edwin clearly understood that Julia had still not accepted the seriousness of her predicament, he found it difficult, no impossible, to remind her that the local ghouls she could see in the gallery were gathering round the victim waiting for the Judge to literally place the hangman's noose around the delicate neck.

Inside the well of the courtroom, the journalists were having a field day. To have a juicy murder trial on the Island was a special bonus to be enjoyed to the full.

Ch.11

The court convened promptly at 2.0pm when the Judge resumed his seat on the raised dias facing the court room.

Turning to the Public Prosecutor he said 'Mr. Scott do you wish to cross exam the last witness?'

Raymond Scott remained seated and shook his head from side to side. He had been aware that the Detective Inspector had erred like a novice copper when he had not formally cautioned Mrs Warren. Personally he would have done so, and now the Defence Counsel was using the Inspector's vital slip to argue his case for bail. Things were not going too well at the moment, he thought.

'Mr Crosby call your next witness please.'

'I call Detective Inspector Harry Bishop.'

Harry Bishop took the oath but not before glaring at Edwin Crosby. Everyone in court that afternoon quickly realised that this youthful British lawyer was facing a very hostile witness.

However, this was not the first, nor would it be the last hostile witness he had been caused to examine. He quietly went through the same questions he had directed at the sergeant earlier in the day, receiving the same short answers he had noted that morning. At one stage the Judge looked at Edwin quizzically as if to ask why he required an answer to the same line of questioning he had pursued in the morning.

When Edward pressed on in the same vein the Judge continued noting the answers on his desk pad.

It was when Edwin got to the yacht Sunray that the Judge noted a slight change of tack by the lawyer.

'Inspector when you and the sergeant arrived at the Sunray on the Coast Guard Cutter you prevented any of the cutter's crew from going aboard, may I ask why?'

'Because I did not want any forensic evidence corrupted.'

'Why was that, when there were already two other persons

from a nearby yacht already aboard?'

'As far as I was concerned everyone on board the Sunray was a suspect until proven otherwise.'

'Were you aware at the time that two coloured men had boarded the Sunray and committed the murder?'

'I didn't get that information until I was informed by the Captain from the other Yacht.'

'So at the time you suspected that anyone or all of the three persons you found aboard could have committed the murder?'

'That is the first responsibility of a police officer involved in a murder case.'

'So at that stage did you suspect that Mrs Warren could have murdered her husband?'

There was a long pause while the Inspector tried to analyse the reason for the question.

His Honour the Judge became quite exasperated. 'Please answer the question.'

'I suppose I did.'

'What about her story that two coloured men raped her and threw her husband overboard?'

'I thought it was possible that she had paid the men to help her kill her husband, a course I would obviously pursue during the course of my inquiries.'

'Quite.'

The Judge who had been extremely patient during the long tedious day asked Edwin Crosby whether these questions had any real significance.

Edwin replied that they were relevant.

Which provided Edwin with the punch he was about to deliver.

'Inspector, if you, as you have just stated, suspected Mrs Warren of murder, or complicity to murder, can you explain why you interviewed her the following day in her hotel instead of your police headquarters?'......pause.

'Can you explain why she wasn't arrested? And can you explain why you failed to issue her with a verbal caution before making her statement and offer her a solicitor to advise her on her legal rights?'

Inspector Bishop knew for the first time in his long career, that he had grossly underestimated this young boyish looking lawyer from Britain. 'In retrospect, maybe I should have done so, but the lady I saw was extremely distressed and at the time all I was seeking was her initial short verbal statement to gather the facts. Similar statements were taken by another detective from the two persons who went to her aid.'

Edwin inclined his head towards the Judge, as if the reply was just as he expected.

'Inspector, this morning your sergeant informed his Honour that you were still awaiting forensic evidence to either support or change your viewpoint regarding this murder enquiry, is that still the case?'

'No.'

Edwin looked completely surprised. 'No?'

'The report was received before I left the station this morning and I had no time to discuss it with my staff. I only had time to glance at the contents before leaving for this hearing.'

At this point the Judge intervened. 'Inspector until Counsel for the defendant has had time to peruse the report in detail, anything you may say now is irrelevant to this hearing.'

Edwin who had remained standing told the Judge that he had no intention of pursuing this issue at the present time, adding that he had no more questions to ask the Inspector.'

The Prosecuting Attorney who had listened intently to the questions and noted the responses could see no reason why he should get involved in an application for bail. That responsibility could be left to the Judge.

When the Judge looked in his direction to see if he had any questions of the witness, Raymond Scott remained seated and continued writing.

'In that case' the Judge said to Edwin are you in a position to sum up?'

'Yes your Honour.'

'Will it be short?' asked the Judge glancing at the court clock.'

'Yes sir.'

'Then proceed.'

'Your Honour I asked for this hearing in the hope that you would grant bail to my client who is extremely distressed, not only with the tragic loss of her husband, but because she now finds herself in a remand prison suspected of either murder of complicity to murder. I am not challenging her guilt or innocence at this time, that will come at a later date. What I am challenging, is that she was asked to sign a statement by two supposedly competent police detectives without being cautioned, or with a solicitor being present to help her, as to what content she was prepared to disclose. In my view she was misled and her statement should now be declared invalid in a court of law.'

'There is no evidence that Mrs Warren had any differences with her husband to justify treating her as a suspect. In fact all the evidence is that not only was she deeply in love with her husband but she insists that they had intercourse only a short while before her husband was attacked.'

'I am asking your Honour to grant my client bail. She has no intention of leaving the Island until her innocence is confirmed. As her passport has already been confiscated she will have difficulty leaving St Lucia. If you agree to release her from the remand centre she promises to reside in the Adelphi Hotel until such time as the court orders her passport to be restored.'

'The Judge finished writing, put down his pen and only then realised he had not discharged the witness. Turning to the Inspector he told him he could stand down and leave the court as his services were no longer required.

Turning to Edwin he told him he would consider his application overnight and give his answer on the following morning at ten am. The Judge then bowed to the assembled people in court and retired to his room.

Julia was hustled off to the remand centre by the fiery little wardress, firmly convinced that the weekly income would continue.

Trying to cover any contingency, Edwin telephoned his father to update him with the situation he was in. 'If bail is granted tomorrow I may need a large sum rather quickly, say one hundred thousand pounds, to ensure my client doesn't have to go back to jail.'

His father reminded Edwin that funds of that size were always available and wished him luck on the morrow explaining what Edwin had to do to ensure funds were readily available.

Edwin, following his father's advice went straight to the Castries branch of HSBC and asked to speak to the manager. When the teller asked why he wished to see the manager Edwin bristled at the question. What he had to discuss was none of the Teller's business and the question he was about to ask could quickly get into the wrong hands. 'Inform him that I am Edwin Crosby a Lawyer and the matter is highly confidential.'

Edwin was quickly shown into the Branch Manager's office, who asked him to take a seat before getting down to business.

'I may urgently need considerable funds tomorrow morning. Can you contact my Branch Manager in Liverpool today, to confirm that he can arrange that I have adequate funds available to meet a large demand for bail from the Judge who I am seeing tomorrow?'

'What figure have you in mind asked the Branch Manager well aware of what was happening in the nearby High Court?'

'About one hundred and fifty thousand pounds,' replied Edwin, upping the ante just in case the Judge decided to value the bail bond high enough to placate the Prosecuting Attorney.

Taking note of his account number the Manager quickly found

the telephone number and put a long distance call through to the Branch in Liverpool.

The response from Liverpool was positive, so Edwin asked the manager sitting at his large desk if he could have a letter prepared to confirm that such funds were readily available on demand by the Lawyer.

With the letter in his hand, Edwin returned to the hotel to sweat it out overnight.

In the meantime, Julia travelling back to the prison accompanied by the wardress was having a hard time trying to convince Wardress Javendes that she was not in any trouble accepting a payment to ensure Julia was allocated a cell of her own.

'You never told me that your so called friend was in fact your attorney,' Javendes said angrily. 'If I had known he was your attorney, Rodney Bona and I would never have agreed to transfer you to a cell on the ground floor. Rodney will be as mad as hell when he finds out that you have put both our jobs at risk.'

Julia quietly pointed out that she was not present, or party to, the arrangement made by her Counsel. 'I didn't know at that stage that he was to become my counsel, 'she countered. 'My friends did not like to see me so distressed because I was sharing a cell and asked Mr Crosby to try and arrange my transfer to a cell on my own. I see no reason for you, or your warder friend to worry unduly. We agreed that it would cost money for me to be upgraded to a better cell and I see no reason why it shouldn't continue.'

Wardress Javendes calmed down somewhat before they arrived back at the prison, but as she locked the cell door on the ground floor she made her way quickly to the upper level to acquaint her partner in crime of the change in circumstances.

Rodney Bona was a greedy bastard and was not prepared to cancel the arrangement. 'Nothing is in writing,' he told her, 'and nothing can be proved, even by a smart arsed lawyer from the UK.

What we need to do in the future is make sure no one sees us accepting the weekly payment. I will arrange for a trustee prisoner to collect the cash directly from Mrs High and Mighty Warren. You tell her in the morning that future payments for the rent and food must be paid by her personally to the prisoner that cleans her cell. There are many ways to skin a cat, so stop worrying.

Ch.12

The court convened promptly at 10.0am, but on this occasion Julia was required to remain in jail as she was not required to be present to hear the Judge's ruling.

Judge Francis Bell wigged, and wearing his red robe with the ermine collar, entered the court, while everyone stood respectfully until he sat down. Looking directly at Mr. Crosby he smiled and said 'I presume you have had an unsettled night worrying about your client. I admit it is very rare to grant bail for such a serious charge that currently faces your client. Unfortunately it is quite easy for anyone without a passport to slip away to one of the many Islands in the Caribbean; some of whom have government's not well disposed to the United Kingdom.'

He paused and consulted his notes. 'In the case of Mrs Warren she has no previous criminal record, therefore I came to the conclusion she would not travel all the way to St Lucia to have her husband murdered in sight of possible witnesses on numerous other yachts anchored in the bay. When she eventually appears before the Central Criminal Court for the trial, a jury on that occasion, after hearing all the evidence put forward by the prosecution, may decide otherwise.

'I am prepared to grant your client bail for a surety of one hundred thousand pounds sterling and order her release from the Remand Centre when that bond has been paid into the court.'

Edwin's face registered relief as he handed the bank manager's signed letter, plus a signed cheque for the sum demanded.'

The Judge read the letter and glanced at the cheque before commenting. 'I am impressed Mr Crosby, your forward planning shows how confident you were regarding my finding on behalf of your client. I hope you continue to enjoy success when the case eventually comes to trial. The prison governor will now be informed to release your client.'

When the Judge retired, presumably to conduct another case, Edwin hurried from the court and returned to the hotel to inform Marion and Cara of the decision.

At Dennery Remand Centre similar enthusiasm was not so evident. The two warders were aware that their illegal backhanders would immediately cease, so the wardress released Julia from her cell, and conducted her to the reception desk without uttering a word of congratulations. Julia had a few personal belongings returned for which she had to sign. She was then led to the prison gates and unceremoniously dumped on the footpath outside to find her own way back to Castries.

Julia found a nearby phone box and rang the hotel to say she had been released. Casa overjoyed to receive the message, told Julia to hire a taxi and advised her that she would pay the driver when Julia arrived.

Marion was both overjoyed and excited that her friend would soon be among friends and able to sleep in a comfortable bed in the hotel without having nosey warders peeping into her cell every hour.

When Julia arrived at the Adelphi, both Cara and Marion expected her to be on a high now that she was temporarily free from the prison regime, but the sight of the expression on Julia's face said otherwise.

Marion clasped her arms round her dear friend and asked why she was looking so glum.

'I understand Mr Crosby paid one hundred thousand pounds into the court as a bail bond to effect my release. Where am I going to find that sum of money from? My husband's assets will be frozen until after the trial and I am not certain whether he made a Will, or if it will be in my favour. After all I am his second wife and his first wife is still alive.' With that she burst into tears.

Marion got Julia to sit down on a settee and as soon as she calmed down informed her that the bond would only be retained by the Court if Julia absconded while awaiting trial. 'Edwin has put his trust in you and I don't think for one minute you will let him down. The day you turn up in court for your trial Edwin will be refunded his money, (which was not quite true).....so stop worrying and concentrate on enjoying your freedom from that prison. In the meantime you must thank Edwin for his undeniable skill in obtaining your freedom. In the meantime I think we should open the bar and drink to your release.'

It was two hours later with the sun sinking over the 'yardarm' that Julia was helped up the stairs to her bedroom by Cara where she crashed down in a happier state of mind. Marion on the other hand was fast asleep in a chair in the corner of the bar, and would only be disturbed by Cara when the first of the hotel customers decided to have a drink before dinner was served.

Ch.13

In the meantime Edwin had arrived at the Marina expecting to see Captain Bellis and ask how he got on with his enquiries. To his dismay, neither Captain Bellis or his yacht, were in the Marina. When he enquired with another yacht owner he was told that Captain Bellis sailed two days ago and he had no idea where he was bound. 'Ask the harbour master he might have left a message there as to his whereabouts.'

When Edwin did just that, the harbour master told him most yachtsmen just cast off without leaving any word as to their sailing plans. 'It makes it bloody difficult for me if they get into any sort of trouble with a breakdown or storm damage, but that is the way with yachtsmen sailing the Caribbean. They don't give a damn until they have urgent need of the coastguard.'

There was not much Edwin could do except ask the harbour master if he saw Captain Bellis return to port to ask the Captain to get in touch.

Edwin headed back to the hotel mainly because he had promised to take Marion to the airport as her holiday was at an end and her flight back to Jamaica was due to leave at 5.0pm where she would transfer in Kingston to a long haul flight back to Heathrow.

He then decided to telephone his father to update him with the amount of bail demanded by the judge, and inform him that his client was now out of prison. In his own mind he decided to extend his visit for a few more days before returning to the UK. He intended to promise Julia that he would return in time for her trial and to assure her that there was nothing he could do in the interim except engage a local lawyer to try and obtain copies of any further evidence the police had gleaned from their investigations, including the report from the Forensic Laboratory.

On arrival at the hotel he was greeted with a message from the harbour master that Captain Bellis had just moored up in the

Marina and he had passed on the message for him to get in touch.

Although Edwin was anxious to find out what Captain Bellis had discovered, his first priority was to take Marion to the airport. As soon as Marion's plane had departed he headed for the Marina only to find that Captain Bellis had locked up his boat and left a written message pinned to the cabin door that he could be found, if required, at the Adelphi Hotel.

Cursing to himself for the frustration and wasted time he headed back to the hotel where he found the Captain snoozing in the lounge with a nearly empty glass of rum lying on the table next to him.

Giving the Captain a nudge, he awakened, rubbed his eyes and smiled as he saw Edwin standing in front of him.

'Any news?' demanded Edwin.

'I think so,' replied John Bellis. 'Sorry it has taken me so long but half of those bloody yacht's had sailed away and I had hell's own job finding the owners. I'll supply you with the details and costs incurred shortly that might make you blanch when you see the amount. However, I think you will be more interested in the end result that I have sketched on a rough plan.' With that he reached into his pocket and extracted a single sheet of paper that he placed on the small coffee table in front of the settee.

'The plan shows the anchored location of each yacht or cruiser on the night of the murder. I traced the owners who are as follows:-

A - Mr. Fisher owns Lion King - Still at St Lucia

B - Mr. Lawson owns Sea spray - Still at St Lucia

C - Mr. Antonis owns Anna - Now anchored at Guadeloupe

D - Mr Selwyn owns Amerigo - Now at Puerto Rico

E - Mr Garouch owns Texas B - Now back home in
    Texas.

F - Mr Enrico owns Swift Sure - Now in the Port-au
    Prince in the Dominican Republic

G - Mr Yenson owns Annette - Now sailing toward Panama.
    Yenson is Japanese and on his way home.'

'I contacted each owner who confirmed they saw the Sunray anchor on the day before the murder and each Captain gave me what they thought was the Sunray's position. The harbour master kindly gave its position the following morning after it drifted during the night.'

Rodney Bay – St Lucia

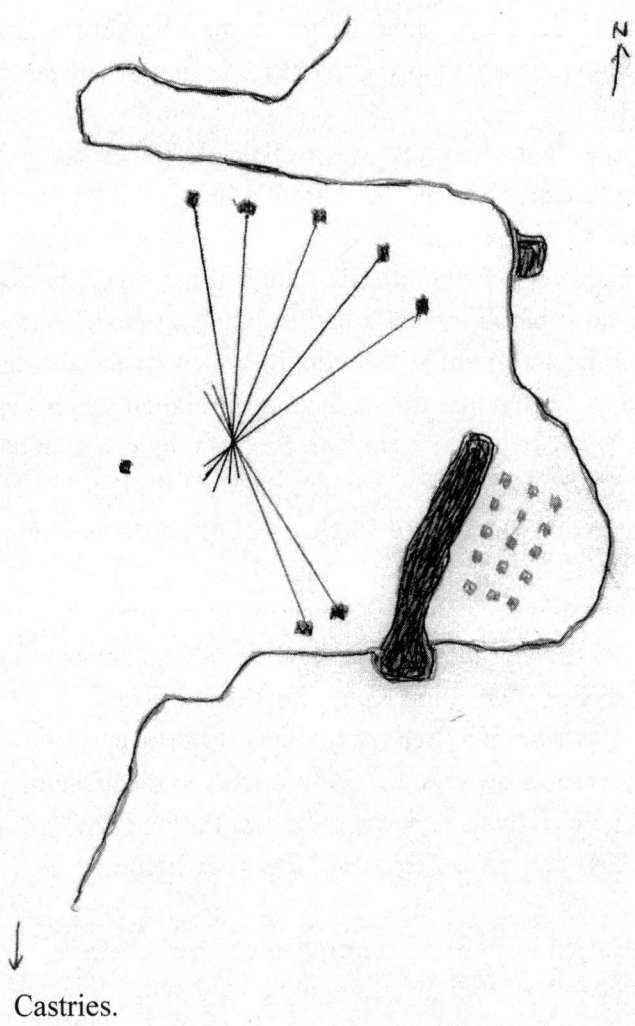

Castries.

'Starting with the first yacht at the top I drew a line to the position where Fisher saw the Sunray and so on until I got what all the yachtsmen thought was the location of the Warren yacht. According to the map that appears to be 57° North and 14° East. The outer square shows the position where the yacht was found by the coastguard. The other squares in the inner harbour show the location of the Marina. With houses in between them and the bay no one on those yachts would be able to see the Sunray.

Edwin was overwhelmed with John Bellis's detailed investigations. 'How in hell did you find the names and owners of the moored yachts?'

'From the harbour master; a few extra dollars in his back pocket got me their present locations and ship to shore radio bands. For the guy back in Texas I got his home number and found him sitting on his front porch contemplating his navel,' smiled Captain Bellis.

Studying the map for a few moments Edwin turned to Bellis. 'Could you find me two reliable divers who can use an underwater camera? I want them to try and find the body of Walter Warren in the area you have indicated. If they are successful they mustn't disturb the body, just take a few pictures then report their discovery to the police. They must not inform the police that they have taken pictures which must be handed to me. You may need some more cash to pay these guys to ensure they keep their mouths shut,' so Edwin handed over one thousand dollars.'

'You've done a brilliant job of research Mr. Bellis, let me know how much I owe you a.s.a.p. I don't think I will require your services any longer but thanks for your support over the past few days.'

Edwin heard Bellis mutter as he walked away from the boat, 'thank God I can now get back to some decent fishing.'

Ch.14

When Bellis left the hotel Edwin made no reference to Julia as to the plan he had seen, nor to the instructions he had given the Captain. Best kept confidential he thought in case nothing came of the search, or any mention to Julia of a possible outcome, as it would only add to the present stress she was suffering knowing she was facing a trial by jury in the not too distant future.

That evening over dinner he updated Julia and Cara with his intention to return home within a few days and reassured them both that he would return before the trial. 'After all,' he said, 'it only takes a few hours to get to St Lucia from the UK, and if there were any serious developments before the trial I will come back on the first available flight.'

What he didn't say, was that he found St Lucia not to his liking as it was grossly overloaded with tourists, especially brash Americans, camera toting Japanese, and Britons on holiday. They drank too much, dressed outrageously wearing as little as possible in disrespect to the local religious community who were appalled at the wilful display of flesh by females in bikinis, and men without shirts, who should have had the courtesy to cover themselves before leaving their beachside hotels to shop in town.

Every sidewalk was packed with holiday makers, making it difficult for locals to go about their business. Using your own car even though it was hired, continually frustrated Edwin when he was sitting impatiently in a traffic jam caused by tourists jaywalking across junctions even when traffic lights were on green.

He thought about Liverpool that had its own traffic problems, but it was not grossly overloaded with tourists, particularly in the city centre that was far from picturesque.

– – –

Three days later he received an urgent telephone call to go to the Marina as John Bellis had some news about his recent instructions.

Edwin hurried down to the Marina to find John Bellis leaning over the stern rail of his cruiser keeping a watchful eye on the end of the landing stage hopefully expecting Edwin to arrive within minutes of his telephone call.

As soon as he saw Edwin on the landing stage he jumped off his boat and strode towards him. 'The divers have found a trussed up body within yards of my calculations, still attached to an anchor. They did exactly as ordered and photographed the body before surfacing and calling the police, who are already at the spot and sending down their own divers to recover the cadaver.

Without seeing the divers' pics, Edwin was convinced the body was that of Walter Warren. That the press would soon latch on to the police presence in Rodney Bay was obvious. Before they sent out their evening papers he knew he needed to inform Julia a.s.a.p. He asked John Bellis if he would send copies of the divers' pics in a sealed envelope to the hotel as he may need them as evidence in the forthcoming trial. Whether they would be of help in his defence of Julia Warren was at this stage debatable.

In his view, the pathologist's report about the body could either prove Julia's statement was correct, or condemn her to life imprisonment. What he desperately needed was the names of the two men who committed the rape of his client. The chance of that happening appeared to be odds of thousands to one against.

One other thing that still bugged him was Julia's husband's cry as he was pitched into the water. What was the significance of remembering his school nickname and the numbers 1024? Was the nickname the key to getting access to his computer or laptop, and were the numbers a combination and the means of access to his safe, or safes; or was it the other way around?

Dashing back to the hotel he asked Cara if she would join him while he talked to Julia. They went up to her room and knocked on the door. Julia opened the door wearing her dressing gown looking a bit dishevelled as if she had been resting on the bed.

Looking alarmed at the sudden appearance of Edwin with Cara in tow, Julia asked if something was wrong. Waving the two of them to enter her room she closed the door and repeated the question?

Edwin quietly explained that information had been received from a number of the yachtsmen who were moored in the bay on the day her husband was murdered that led to divers finding the body of her husband that was presently being recovered from Rodney Bay by the police.

'Before you let your hopes build up, finding his body will not alter your position with regard to the charges against you. A pathologists report might help, but don't build your hopes up. What we really need are the names of the two men who raped you, so that they can be taken into custody and questioned as to why they were on your yacht.'

He paused to allow the situation to sink into Julia's befuddled brain. 'Those two villains are the key to the whole sordid story, but...' Shaking his head, he told her that miracles were a rare occurrence when you desperately needed one to happen.

As expected and the reason why he had asked Cara to accompany him to Julia's bedroom, Julia broke down and cried. 'On top of everything that has happened, now I will have to attend my husband's funeral, or get involved in the long drawn out process of having his body returned to the UK for burial. What am I supposed to do?'

Edwin was not quite sure how the law would progress. 'Walter's body will be retained until after due judicial process has been followed. That is unlikely to happen until after your trial unless a coroner's court decides otherwise. Before I leave for the UK I will arrange for a local lawyer to keep me informed of the court's decision. In the meantime Julia you must remain with Cara and hope that the court will allow you to remain at this hotel until your case comes up for trial.'

Cara nodded her head in agreement then gave Julia a comforting hug saying 'put your trust in Edwin and accept his advice. He's your main hope in proving your innocence.'

Ch.15

Having cancelled his previous flight back to the UK, Edwin checked with the International Airport Desk on St Lucia to try and rebook a flight via Jamaica back to Heathrow in the UK. The desk clerk expressed surprise that Edwin wanted to fly back by that route as it meant changing at Kingston where there was often long delays.

'I have a seat available on a long haul directly from this airport to Gatwick. Surely that would be quicker and more economical than the route you have selected.'

Edwin explained that on the outward route from London no spare seats to St Lucia were available for weeks, so he had little choice but to take the outward bound route via Jamaica. Accepting the offer, he paid for his seat by credit card and was told to be at the airport three days hence at 10.0am for a noon flight.

Three days later Edwin flew out of St Lucia bound for England and his father's practice in Liverpool.

On the plane he took the opportunity to re read Julia's statement that was now no longer acceptable to the court.

Edwin thought there were one or two aspects of her statement that would be very damning if they were ever read to a jury. Particularly the last few comments about how she had considered divorcing her husband because of his violent nature. Had a lawyer been present at the police interview, no lawyer worth his salt would have allowed her to make and sign a statement that could show reason for her to murder her husband.

It was possible that the prosecuting attorney might insist on a new statement being prepared this time under police caution. If that occurred Edwin would have to pre-brief Julia to make no comment on that score. He made a little note in his book to remind him should the need arise.

He made another note to ring Julia and ask her (a) if there was a safe in her house and if she had the combination? (b) What was the name of her late husband's bank in the UK? And (c) Could she speak to the Bank Manager and arrange for Edwin to have an interview?

Apart from those points Edwin was at a loss as to how he would find sufficient evidence to prevent Julia from going to prison. He had no illusion about how a jury would react when strong but circumstantial evidence was presented by the public prosecutor.

Tired after the prolonged pressure he had been put under during his short visit to the Island, Edwin drifted off to sleep and knew no more until the stewardess was touching his shoulder in an attempt to wake him before the plane began its long descent into Gatwick airport.

The thought of the long train journey from Gatwick and having to change at Euston Station made Edwin decided to take an internal flight to Liverpool airport.

After a delay following the time difference, he landed at Liverpool's airport and made the short journey to his father's chambers where he was warmly welcomed back by the staff and Marion in particular, who asked if she could be updated with the investigations so far.

Edwin gave her a brief résumé before walking into his father's office. Having already updated his father when he spoke to him on the telephone from St Lucia he decided he required his father's advice regarding Julia Warren and her future.

'Dad' he opened. 'Julia Warren has a real problem now she is the prime suspect in her husband's murder. All her husband's assets have been frozen by the court and it would seem that poor Julia has no finances of her own she can draw on. The bank have limited her credit to ten thousand pounds, and what with hotel bills and the fact she had no other clothes than the ones she was wearing when she was apprehended by the local police on St Lucia, those funds will soon run out. I would like to give her an interest free loan, but she has a stubborn streak and I think it will be refused. Have you any bright ideas how I can get round the problem?'

Dad looked at his young son with a twinkle in his eyes. 'I've got the distinct impression that Mrs Julia Warren has unknowingly caught you in her net. Is she pretty?'

Edwin blushed deeply. 'Julia is not pretty, she's beautiful, one hell of a looker, charming, lonely with no parents still alive, and desperately in need of someone to take care of her.'

Dad gave a deep sigh before replying. 'I have a feeling that one young man has fallen for a widow who has just lost her husband and comes across as very vulnerable. For you to be seen to be emotionally involved with her at this stage would be disastrous for both of you, presuming she feels the same way about you. Does she?'

Edwin shrugged his shoulders. 'I have no idea how she feels, but I do know how I feel. Can't we do something to help her?'

Edwin's dad thought about it for the moment. He was inclined to tell his son to grow up and find an unattached girl in Liverpool rather than saddle himself with a widow suspected of murder. But he knew how his son reacted to life in general. Edwin had spent the last few years dedicating his life to becoming a top lawyer like his dad and during that period had no time for romance. Now he appeared to have fallen hook line and sinker for this girl on St Lucia and nothing the father said would have any bearing on Edwin's future. He was no longer a boy to be manipulated by sound advice. He was a man with a strong personality and determined to make his own way in life.

'I have an idea that might solve your problem. Send a cheque for thirty thousand pounds to the HSBC Bank Manager in St Lucia and enclose a letter asking him to deposit the money in Mrs Warren's account without disclosing to her who had donated the funds. That way she could not refuse the donation because she has no idea who she should return the cheque to.' Edwin thought it was a brilliant idea, shook his dad's hand and dashed out of the office to deal with the problem that had troubled him for a few days.

Marion intercepted him on his way back to his office. 'I was so pleased to see you this morning that I forgot to give you some interesting news. The chambers applied for legal aid on behalf of Julia and yesterday we received a letter informing us that the application had been approved subject to the sum being refunded if Mrs. Warren wins her case; the embargo on her assets is lifted; and that she is granted title to her late husband's estate.'

Edwin thanked her for the news. 'Julia will be relieved to hear that her court costs will be covered. Would you please ring the hotel and speak to either Julia or Cara and give them the welcome news.'

Once he was seated at his desk he wondered whether the pathologist had completed her autopsy and what damning evidence she had presented to the prosecuting attorney. He had applied for a copy of the report before leaving St Lucia but was not holding his breath, knowing how devious the Detective Inspector could be, by attempting to keep the report confidential until a few days before the trial to give Edwin little time to challenge the content.

Sipping his morning coffee he tried to concentrate his mind on the list of cases piled in his in tray now requiring his urgent attention. Having to deal with cases of petty theft, marital disharmony, and three cases of affray, seemed positively mundane compared to the case of suspected murder resting quietly in the Caribbean while awaiting a slot in the court's calendar for later in the year.

Ch.16

Professor Christina Vos was busy examining the remains of the late Walter Warren. Her department smelled strongly of formaldehyde that made occasional visitors either retch or faint, but the Professor and her assistant were immune as they concentrated on preparing a report for the Coroner and Director of Public Prosecutions.

She photographed the naked remains of the corpse lying on the dissecting table while she dictated her findings onto a disc spinning slowly in a machine placed on a table next to where she was absorbed in the challenge facing her.

The cadaver had been slit from sternum to naval and rear of the neck to the base of the spine as she examined the lungs, liver, heart and spleen and stomach.

'The cadaver appears to have died from drowning while secured by ropes around the arms and ankles. The knots in the ropes appear to have been tied by someone with seagoing experience. The arms were secured behind the ....back, and the anchor and rope securing the feet ensured the victim died quickly when submerged in the sea.'

'Prior to death the cadaver appears to have been soundly beaten by something heavy, either by a baseball bat, or metal rod. Both knee caps had been splintered and five ribs broken in the assault. Five toes on one foot were crushed and the ankle bone broken in two places. There were several stab wounds in the stomach area; and one nostril had been mutilated by a sharp instrument.'

She went on to describe the contents of the stomach; the fact that the liver was affected by early signs of cirrhosis; the lungs were filled with sea water; and the heart showed no signs of cardiac problems.

'It is my considered view that the person had been tortured before being consigned to the sea to be forcibly drowned.'

'In summary, the body recovered from Rodney Bay had been partially eaten by fish and shell fish and had been dead for several days before being recovered by the police.'

The report was typed by a typist who had become immune to the graphic dissection of the body and analysis of contents described by her boss.

— — —

The forensic report and the pathologist's report arrived by hand at the coroner's office within days of each other, with copies sent to the public prosecutor.

Forensic tests taken on the yacht Sunray as requested by Detective Inspector Bishop from Police HQ Castries were inconclusive. There was evidence that Mrs Julia Warren had had some sexual activity within twenty four hours of the test. However, due to the use of a douche in the vagina and a body shower using a shower gel, it was impossible to determine with whom she had sexual activity.

Both Captain Fisher and his wife Ann who had been invited aboard the yacht by Mrs Warren, provided specimens from nose and mouth that only proved conclusively that they had been on the yacht.

Two other specimens showed that two men of coloured origin had left specimens in the cabin, on the bed linen; and on the aft well deck; the engine housing; and starboard side seat and rail.

Following the recovery the body reported to be that of a Walter Warren, further forensic tests from the cadaver proved that he had been present in various parts of the yacht including the engine housing, thus confirming that he was on the boat and possibly crewing.

When Detective Inspector Bishop was given sight of both reports he screwed his mouth to one side. A facial expression that showed he was pleased with the reports. He turned to his sergeant and muttered 'I can't see how that bitch can wriggle her way out of these conclusions.'

He telephoned the Director of Public Prosecutions, asked if he had read the reports and confirmed they were on his desk, and that he had read them. Harry Bishop asked if the DPP now had sufficient evidence to prosecute Mrs Warren.

The DPP replied. 'A lot of the evidence is circumstantial and I would be happier if we had the two suspected rapists in custody. But beggars can't be choosers; I feel I could convince a jury that Mrs Warren is as guilty as hell. One thing I am certain of, is that the Defence Attorney will have greater difficulty proving her innocence.'

Inspector Bishop put down the phone, clasped his hands together as he leaned his elbows on the desk and thought that Mrs Warren's statement would wrap the case up tight, before he remembered that it could not be used in the trial. He then realised that he could draw attention to the now defunct statement and suggested to the Prosecutor once he got her on the stand, that he could drag the information out of Mrs Warren that she was considering divorcing her late husband for assaulting her on several occasions.

The fact that she had stated she had no idea what her husband did as an importer/exporter would fail to convince any jury. No woman could be married to a man for three years and claim she had no knowledge of what he did for a living.

This case could be wrapped up and put to bed within days, he thought.

Ch.17

Crosby and Welland were ordinary everyday attorneys at law. They had no desire to specialise like other law offices in cities such as Liverpool, Newcastle on Tyne, Glasgow, Southampton and London who where specialisation in shipping law that had been both rewarding and lucrative. Shipping was now on the decline on the river Mersey and most of these vast companies had to move some of their staff abroad to try and capture the changing market. In the meantime Crosby and Welland continued taking insignificant cases such as marriage disputes, common assault, grievous bodily harm, and speeding fines, to Magistrates Courts and occasionally to Crown Courts, where the majority of their business costs were supported by grants for legal aid.

Their business was thriving and the two senior partners James Crosby and Oscar Welland were now extremely wealthy lawyers and well respected in the upper echelons of Liverpool's moneyed class.

James had moved his family to Southport a number of years ago and bought a property near the Royal Birkdale Golf Club where he was not only a member but a past captain. Golf was his passion and struggling to maintain his handicap of four one of his serious challenges in life.

As he reached sixty years of age he found regular practice to keep his competitive swing lined up with the fairways a chore. He had tried to encourage Edwin to take up golf and become a member of his club, but sons hated being manipulated by parents and always chose a different route to concentration and physical fitness.

Edwin had joined the local tennis club, enjoyed football, and one of the most dangerous sports of all rock climbing. Dad and mum nearly had fits when on a holiday in the Lake District National Park to discover Edwin half way up the perpendicular rock face on Pavey Arc, leading two other climbers in a race to the top of the sheer cliff, a well known challenge at the head of the Langdale Valley.

However, in the office, father and son worked like a well oiled machine, each complementing the other in their desire to be the leading family lawyers in Liverpool.

Breaking away from parental control, Edwin bought a modest semi detached house in nearby Hillside, another upmarket estate with a mixture of late Victorian semis and post war detached residences, where the price ranged from around four hundred thousand to three quarters of a million pounds. In his father's area, house values seemed to start at a million pounds.

Edwin with his bachelor pad required a housekeeper come cook and a part time gardener, while mum and dad employed a butler and all the other service workers that kept their house running smoothly.

Attending courts on a daily basis, while holding meetings with clients, meant each day was fully occupied. Even weekends were not always free to enjoy their respective sports, as Saturdays and sometimes Sundays were taken up reading briefs ready for the next battle with prosecuting counsels, whose job it was to win cases, seek costs, and top up the Liverpool Council's treasure chest.

All this activity for the Crosby/Welland chambers was rewarding and obviously lucrative, but Edwin's interest and the need to meet the daily challenges had waned somewhat after his excursion to the warm climes of the Caribbean Islands. What he really wanted to do at this moment in time was to get his teeth into the Julia Warren mystery. To prove to her that he was competent enough to provide her with the best legal advice money could buy; and to ultimately win her heart by his endeavours and charm.

What he hoped for each day as he walked out of the magistrates court in a grey skied, fog bound Liverpool, was to hear her cry for help in his direction as the date approached for her coming trial. He arrived back at the office after a frustrating morning in court where the sitting Magistrate extended one of his cases by dwelling time and time again on the fine detail, until it became necessary to delay hearing the remainder of Edwin's case until the following day. The Magistrate's clerk apologised to Edwin for the delay, ignoring the fact that the extra morning was an expense Edwin could well have done without.

Marion collared him as he walked into the office. 'I have had a call from Julia who wanted to speak to you. When she said it was urgent, I put her through to your father who offered to deal with it.'

Edwin took the short journey to his father's office, who told him that Julia had called earlier to inform Edwin that the Coroner's Inquest into her late husband's death had been scheduled two days hence. Julia had been asked to attend and wondered (a) if she should go and, (b) whether she should have someone to advise her.

'I advised her to attend and told her I would find a local lawyer to accompany her,' Edwin's father explained. 'I contacted a lawyer called Franklin Jenson, whom I met on two occasions at a conference at Grays Inn of Court in London. His practice is on St Lucia and he impressed me with his attention to detail and willingness to gain experience by coming to London to attend a number of cases being held in the Criminal Courts. He has agreed to accompany Julia and has given an undertaking to advise her in your absence should she be pressurised by that Detective Inspector you dislike so much.'

'Knowing how English people react when meeting coloured professionals for the first time, I spoke to her and told her that Mr. Jenson was a seasoned professional lawyer and would ensure she was protected from any offensive questions.'

James paused for a moment to see how his son would react. When Edwin nodded his head to acknowledge that his father had acted wisely, James continued. 'While we are on the subject of representation, you can't keep dashing backwards and forwards to St Lucia to represent Mrs Warren every time she has a problem. You have enough cases here that require your attention, and I don't have the resources in this office to constantly put a substitute in your place while you are gallivanting off to the Caribbean every few weeks.'

'I think we should ask Franklin Jenson to act on our behalf, including when Mrs Warren's case comes to trial. Murder cases can take month's before a jury reaches a decision, and to be perfectly honest I can't spare you to be away from here for such a long time.'

Edwin initially looked shocked that his father would regard the trivial cases he had to represent as of greater importance than seeking evidence to prevent an innocent woman from going to prison for many years.

However on reflection, he had to agree with his father's observations. Although he would dearly like to be present at Julia's trial, one experienced lawyer was as good as another when it came to disseminating witnesses statements and attacking flaws in the prosecutions presentations.

His father reminded Edwin that as the titular head of the business, he had a responsibility to his partners to ensure they all made a comfortable living from working out of his chambers. In addition there was the added responsibility of ensuring enough income was available at all times to pay the salaries of non qualified staff like his secretary Marion, and still be able to pay the rent, rates, liability insurance, and all the other on costs that even small businesses have to meet.

A very chastened Edwin returned to his office and took the next folder out of the pile in his in tray and commenced to digest the content of another mundane case.

Ch.18

The inquest was attended by Detective Inspector Bishop, Sergeant Totti, Professor Christina Vos, Doctor Mendosa from the Forensic Laboratory, and other persons either directly or like the press, indirectly involved.

The Coroner opened the inquest advising all those assembled, and particularly the local press, that a jury had been appointed whose duty it was to determine the cause of death in the case of one Walter Warren deceased. 'They are not here to determine who, if anyone caused that death. That process is for the criminal courts to decide.' He explained.

Julia, sitting at the back of the court room with Mr Jenson sitting alongside, wondered how she was going to react when the gory details of her husband's death was read out and examined in detail.

The Captain of the Coast Guard Cutter was the first to give evidence. He explained how he had been called out by the harbour master to recover a body found on the sea bed in the bay between Gros Islet and Rodney Bay, approximately longitude 57° and latitude 14°. When his cutter arrived at the scene two local divers were waiting on their dive boat to point out where the body lay. 'Divers from my Cutter recovered the body believed to be that of Walter Warren that had been missing for a number of days from the yacht Sunray, presumed drowned.'

'Detective Inspector Bishop accompanied by Sergeant Totti who had also been informed of the discovery, were on my Cutter and gave instructions to my men to take the body ashore and hand it over to the harbour master where an ambulance was waiting to take the body to the Department of Pathology.'

Detective Inspector Bishop was called and confirmed the Captain's statement. 'I asked the two divers what they were doing in that area and they told me they regularly dived in the bay for lobsters, crabs and octopuses and that they sold their catch to local restaurants who paid good rates for freshly caught shellfish. I checked their diving certificates of competence and licence to take fish from the bay and was satisfied they were genuine. I asked how they came upon the body and they said it was purely by accident. They were aware a yachtsman was missing so they radioed the harbour master who asked them to remain at the scene until the Coast Guard arrived. 'When I saw that the body was bound with rope and'.......

The Coroner intervened. 'Inspector what you saw after the body was recovered is for a criminal court. Have you anything further to add?'

'No.'

'Then you may sit down.'

The pathologist was called. She said her examination showed that the body of Walter Warren had been alive when it entered the water and death had been by drowning. She too was rebuked by the Coroner when she went on to say that several stab wounds and other bodily damage had been found.

The Doctor in charge of investigative forensic medicine confirmed that the body was male and from information given earlier by the police regarding height and weight, it appeared to be that of one Walter Warren reported missing from a yacht in the vicinity of where the body was recovered.

Mrs Warren was asked if she was prepared to take the stand. Mr Jenson stood up and said he represented Mrs Warren who was currently awaiting trial in the Crown Court. 'Mrs Warren is prepared to give evidence providing I accompany her to the stand to advise her how to answer questions that may be asked.'

The Coroner agreed.

When Mrs Warren was seated he asked her to confirm that her husband was on board the Sunray on the night he went missing? When she nodded her head in affirmation, he asked her to answer the question for the sake of the jury members who may not have noticed her gesture.

She said 'yes'.

'Did your husband suffer from any medical problems that may have caused him to fall overboard?'

'No.'

'Have you any idea how he went overboard into the sea?'

Franklin Jenson touched Mrs Warrens arm. 'I suggest you do not answer that,' he said.

The Coroner accepted his point of view. 'Mrs Warren please accept the condolences of this court. It must be very distressing for you to attend this inquest.'

Turning to the jury he told them that sufficient evidence had been provided for them to come to a decision. Either death was by 'misadventure' or it was 'open' to further enquiry by the police.

The appointed foreperson of the jury muttered to the other members before standing up. 'We the jury are unanimous that the verdict should be 'open'.'

The jury was discharged and the Coroner told those assembled that he concurred with their decision. 'It is now up to the police to continue with their enquiries into this sad death,' he said.

– – –

When they left the grim building Franklin suggested they adjourn to a nearby coffee bar where they could sit down and get acquainted. When Julia still feeling slightly giddy after the morbid proceedings acquiesced, Franklin took her to a well known coffee house where they were guaranteed peace and quiet and an excellent choice of blended coffees.

As soon as they were shown into a rich leather booth with high backed seats to ensure their privacy he explained to Julia that he was a Barrister rather than a run of the mill lawyer. 'I worked in Britain for a number of years and cut my teeth on a number of dodgy cases that ended up in the High Courts in London. Some of my clients had committed most serious offences and hoped I could get them off with a light sentence. However the law does not work that way. If you're guilty as hell there was nothing much I could do about it, particularly if I couldn't find a loophole in the prosecution's case. I am making the point because Edwin's father has asked me, subject to your approval, to represent you at the forthcoming trial. In his opinion he thinks that Edwin is too far removed in the UK to devote sufficient time to preparing your defence.'

Taking a sip of his coffee he gave Julia time to digest what he was suggesting. 'You may not like a coloured stranger taking over from Edwin, but let me assure you I know all the senior police officers, the coast guard service, the Crown Prosecution team, and all the magistrates and judges on St Lucia and the adjoining Islands. I know their strengths and weaknesses and in many case's their temperament. For example I know that Detective Inspector Bishop is confident he can win his case and expects you to be given life imprisonment.'

Julia's eyebrows shot up in a mixture of amazement and horror.

Franklin continued, while Julia was so shocked she allowed her coffee to go cold. 'Edwin and his father are totally convinced of your innocence and having had sight of a copy of your statement kindly sent to me by Edwin's father. I have also managed to obtain a copy of the Pathologist's report being a close friend of Professor Christina Vos that in my opinion supports father and son's viewpoint. I have tried to obtain a copy of the forensic report but the Inspector is proving to be very cagey. He has promised to release it before the trial that gives me the impression he is not as sure of himself as he professes.'

'I expect Edwin to fly out to see you before the trial date, but to be perfectly honest if you prefer to put your trust in him the odds are not in your favour. Neither Edwin, nor I, can guarantee we will win, but between us you will have the best legal brains available outside London.' Seeing the questionable frown on Julia's face he told her he would order fresh cups of coffee while she pondered over his advice.

When the coffees arrived she told him she had made up her mind. 'I am pleased you have been so forthright and I am happy for you to represent me. What further information do you need to help you with my case?'

'None at the moment,' Franklin Jenson replied before continuing. 'Before he left the Island, Edwin has asked me to hire a top class private investigator to see if we can track down this elusive Pascie you referred to in your statement. I know the very man who has a bloodhound's nose for sniffing out criminals, and those who are powerful and rich enough to bend the laws in their territory. I have a feeling that my ex detective friend will run this Pascie to earth in due course. Once we find this mysterious man we'll soon track down the two rapists and murderers and put them behind bars for the rest of their natural.'

Franklin could see from the expression on Julia's face that she was finding the discussion about her future very upsetting. 'Let's change the subject,' he said and tell me what you think of Cara and her little hotel?'

Before parting company Franklin Jenson gave Mrs Warren his business card and told her his chambers were virtually next door to the Law Courts. 'I can walk there in five minutes' he told her, so if you want me at any time telephone to make sure I am not in court before you get a taxi to the High Street.'

Ch.19

The hurricane season arrived in the Caribbean before Julia knew the date of her trial. Ferocious winds with enormous power whipped across the Islands causing serious damage. The accompanying rain particularly on St Lucia resulted in the tourists scuttling for cover in the many shops and cafes across the Island, much to the delight of the owners whose takings during any wet season rose quite dramatically.

Cara's hotel was only half full, mainly with commercial travellers and the occasional back packers, who preferred a comfortable bed at a reasonable rate rather than attempt to sleep in a soggy bed roll on a wet camp site. This mix of people, were Cara's bread and butter, rather than tourists who located themselves in the more expensive beach side hotels.

Julia and Cara spent many hours in the evening discussing Julia's future which for the time being was unpredictable, yet still required long discussions to assess the pros and cons that may result from the final outcome. It was a case of what if, rather than when, as hopes were built up and suddenly dashed as the dreaded date arrived. Julia was convinced that no court could find an innocent person guilty of such a serious offence without substantial proof. While Cara was of the opinion, although she didn't express it to her friend that the police needed a scapegoat to put the murder case on their books to bed, and Julia was that scapegoat.

The storm abated as the second hurricane passed the Island without causing much damage. Two yachts sank in the bay after they broke from their mooring lines, a few palm trees were uprooted on the sea front, and one or two shops lost their folded parasols as the fierce winds sweeping in off the Caribbean sea were no respecter of loose tables and chairs outside the shop fronts.

It was a sunless day with black storm clouds scudding across the Island when the local postman delivered a recorded delivery letter to Julia care of the Adelphi Hotel informing her that she was required to present herself at 0800 hours on Monday six weeks hence, to the court bailiff at the Crown Court to stand trial for the murder of Walter Warren. Failure to confirm that she would attend as directed would result in a warrant being issued for her arrest and subsequent detention in Dennery Remand Centre.

Julia immediately telephoned her barrister Franklin Jenson who told her he had also been informed of the date. 'I have just spoken to Edwin Crosby in the UK who intends to fly over to St Lucia as soon as he has cleared his current backlog of local cases. He hopes to arrive about two weeks before your trial but cannot guarantee to remain on the Island for the duration of your trial which may last several months.'

Julia had been feeling low for some days but this latest news that Edwin was handing over the defence to Franklin Jenson rather than defending her in person left her very depressed that even Cara couldn't uplift with cheerful rejoinders 'that innocent persons like Julia had nothing to fear.'

Franklin told her he had already confirmed to the court bailiff that his client would be present in court on the due date. 'So there is nothing you need to do other than patiently wait and try to reassure yourself that you will be represented by the best legal team on the Island.'

Poor Julia was not impressed. She had spent several days in the Remand Centre at Dennery and realised the level of corruption that pertained there. It would cost her dearly not to be housed with some female perverts who would enjoy having a murderess in their midst to relieve their pent up emotions by making said murderess's life a living hell. Julia shed many tears during the next few days.

One night she and Cara were watching the weather forecast on the late evening news when it was announced that Hurricane Tosca was approaching the Caribbean from the South Atlantic with winds expected to reach one hundred and twenty miles per hour causing enormous destruction and deaths as it crossed the Caribbean affecting the Dominican Republic, Cuba, and Florida. The report indicated that St Lucia and the Windward Isles would be slightly affected. Never the less everyone should be prepared in case the wind changed direction.

Julia was thankful she was on land. If she had been on her late husband's hired yacht she would have been terrified, but not as terrified as she waited for her trial to commence.

As luck would have it, the hurricane decided to give St Lucia a reprieve. Instead, it concentrated its enormous power on the Island of the Dominican Republic resulting in several deaths and destroying hundreds of properties in its path. Not only were many yachts swept from their moorings and destroyed, but a visiting cruise ship was swept ashore and badly damaged. Fortunately no crews were aboard the yachts due to the weather forecast warning them to find somewhere ashore to live, but several deaths and many accidents occurred when the cruise ship struck the rocks.

Ch.20

The private detective hired by Franklin Jenson on behalf of Edwin Crosby was getting concerned about the amount of money he was spending and his mounting hire charges as he vainly searched for some semblance of a name that resembled Pascie, Pasken, or Pusken. He had obtained a list of voters at the last elections from most of the Islands as far as the Dominican Republic to the north west and to Venezuela. Most of his requests were met with the question of why he wanted them and when he gave a truthful reply was told that they were available on payment of a small fee plus postage. The small fee in some of the cases was an exorbitant extortion on a grand scale leaving him frustrated when he received the copy days later only to find no one resembling that name on the lists.

Jamaica, Cuba and the Cayman Islands had refused his request but told him he could have sight of the lists if he personally visited the local government offices, presented his credentials and paid the appropriate fee in cash. He anticipated that Cuba with its seriously far left government would want blood money before they parted with any names. While the Cayman Islands would never let him have access to their list of residents as they were handsomely rewarded by some of their affluent residents to keep their names secret. The official did say that if he had a name, they may.....only may, disclose that the person was resident on the Island. The payment they required for disclosure would make even a bank manager blush.

Private Detective Roberto Sanchez totted up his costs and had a sneaking suspicion that he would have to make a very strong case to obtain his money and to remain in charge of the search for the elusive Pascie. He called Franklin Jenson, told him what his costs were to date, and explained how they would escalate if he was to fly to the northern islands in the Caribbean to carry on his search.

He was surprised when the barrister seemed unperturbed by the size of his bill. 'The client's lawyers in the UK need to track down this man, so carry on with your search and keep me constantly up to date. We could do with some success within the next few weeks or their client who I am representing in court may finish up in prison.'

Roberto Sanchez was not a private detective without brains. He was well aware that the client was a Mrs Warren who was fast becoming a much hated celebrity on the Island now that she was free to wander round Castries, when many citizens were of the opinion she should be kept in prison.

However that was not his problem. Each day he scoured the lists looking particularly down the 'P's. There was a Pascoe who surprisingly turned out to be a Scot from Edinburgh who lived on Guadeloupe. He was over eighty and he and his wife had retired to the Island nearly thirty years ago. He was in a wheel chair and according to a local had been something in the city before retiring.

A man on the list named Pascali made Roberto's temperature pick up, only to find him residing on Puerto Rico where he owned an ice cream parlour and had been back home to Italy on the dates immediately prior to the murder.

There were Palmer's, Perry's, Penny's, Pitts, Potts, Parrish's, Pentlee's, Plover's, even a Putné who was French, while the others were either British, American, or bloody Australian. It was most frustrating.

One other problem that bothered Roberto was the number of illegal immigrants who found their way onto the Islands. Mainly from Mexico, Costa Rica and Panama; mostly poor people with no possibility of finding work in their own country, who were prepared to work for a pittance in the rich holiday resorts surrounding the Caribbean. It was possible two of those male immigrants received enough dollars to persuade them to commit murder for this mysterious Pascie who was intent on finding a list that contained information he appeared to be desperately seeking.

Roberto decided the only other avenues he could explore required a plane journey north. So he booked his seat to Cuba where he expected little help from the Castro family and their communist block, but it was all he had, because he was scratching the bottom of the barrel and coming up with zilch.

As expected, he met every obstacle imaginable as he tried to obtain access to the lists of people who were registered to vote. Doing a quick assessment of the number of sheets in the register he calculated that about one third the people of the island were not deemed to be eligible to vote, so any search for a 'Pascie' or 'Pascal' would prove to be fruitless.

In any case, the offer of a substantial bribe to view the 'approved' lists proved to be a waste of time. The officials turned out to be more frightened of repercussions from on high than lining their pockets.

Ch.21

Edwin true to his word arrived on St Lucia one week before the trial was due to commence. He made a courtesy call on Julia and Cara, the latter of whom offered him the bedroom he had used during his previous stay.

He explained to Julia that time was of the essence and he had no time to spare for socialising. He intended to spend most of the period before the trial going through the evidence available, such as the detailed report from the Pathologist, and the report that Franklin had only recently obtained from the scientific laboratory that had carried out the forensic tests.

'Franklin and I need to spend several hours preparing our defence strategy, bearing in mind some guesswork is involved anticipating the Prosecuting Attorney's strategy. Our big problem is not being able to trace the names, or whereabouts, of the two rogues who boarded your yacht.'

With Julia listening intently he carried on. 'The first two or three days of the trial are normally spent sorting out the jury and setting the stall for the witnesses. After the court gets that out of the way, the Judge will start to listen to the real nitty gritty. That is where Franklin and I have to be on our toes and dig out weaknesses in the prosecution's case.' He took hold of Julia's hands and told her that she must remain strong even if she feels the evidence is against her. 'Most of this case against you is based on circumstantial evidence rather than fact. The unknown quantity is how the jury will interpret the information placed before them. Personally I am going to rely on the Judge who is more qualified to sort the wheat from the chaff and direct the jury accordingly.'

He paused for a moment to draw breath. 'It may all go pear shaped and out of our control, but you can be assured we will never give up until your are declared innocent and have the sword of Damocles removed from hanging over your head forever.'

Julia had sat quietly listening to Edwin pontificating without showing that she accepted anything he had said. Nothing she had heard over the past few weeks had convinced her that she had a strong case. She was resigned to being sent to prison for at least twenty years. The only redeeming feature was that she would only be forty three years old when she was released. Time to find another man willing to co-habit with a murderess and live the rest of her life avoiding so called business men who constantly live life on a razors edge, as they manipulate the markets to fill their greedy pockets.

– – –

The first day of any trial by jury is full of expectation, drama, and downright curiosity. Camera operators with their heavy burdens either on three legged pedestals, or hanging over shoulders, jostle with each other to get the best focusing site outside the main entrance to the court. The pen pushing journalists with their court passes pinned to lapels, sat on hard seats at the side of the court sweating profusely, even though the fans above their heads were whirring with the sound of a slight hiss as the blades cut through the heavy atmosphere.

The public, only interested in the gory bits, crowded the rear balcony having queued since dawn to make sure they got a prime seat in the ghouls' gallery.

In the well of the court the Clerk of the Court, a qualified solicitor, wearing his black gown and a grey wig sat at his desk awaiting the entry of the judge. He looked disdainfully up at the noisy crowd in the gallery, then across the room at the Crown Prosecuting Attorney at Law also in a wig and gown, before turning his attention to the star of the show.

Julia in a plain green and stylish two piece suit sat between Franklin Jenson and Edwin Crosby similarly attired as the Prosecutor as they sat behind a large mahogany table also awaiting the arrival of the Judge.

The jury of twelve men and women sat restlessly wondering whether their tenure would be for as little as two weeks, or as long as three months; all hoping for the former, because they were not here by choice, but by written command of the court.

Precisely at ten of the clock the bailiff called for all to stand while his Honour Justice Francis Bell took his seat on the high dais facing the courtroom.

Bowing towards the two lower tables containing the opposing barristers at law he took his seat. Looking around the mass of people filling the courtroom he announced in a loud voice to remind all, that this was Her Majesty's courtroom and not a bar room, and he expected everyone to conduct themselves accordingly. He warned them that Court Ushers will remove anyone who interrupts the proceedings, as he wished to hear and record every word uttered by the witnesses who had yet to take the stand.

'My first duty is to swear in the jury unless there are any legal objections to any person waiting to be sworn in.' He looked at the prosecutor and defence counsel and when they both shook their heads he commenced.

When the jury was seated, having been briefed as to their responsibilities, he asked Barrister Jenson and Mrs Warren to stand.

'Under normal circumstances the accused of such a serious crime would be brought before me directly from prison and sit between two warders in the dock. However, in this instance, you Mrs Warren have adhered to the terms of bail, so I will allow you to sit with your counsel who will be able to advise you as the trial proceeds. But first we must hear how you plead. Please pay attention to the Clerk of the Court.'

The bewigged Clerk of the Court rose to his feet holding a piece of paper recording the charges. 'Mrs. Julia Warren you charged (1) with complicity to premeditated murder of one Walter Warren (2) using persons as yet unknown to dispose of Walter

Warren's body and (3) attempting to conceal said body by using weighted objects to dispose of said body in the sea. How do you plead to each charge?'

Julia drew in a deep breath before saying in a low voice. 'Not guilty to all three charges.'

The Court retired for lunch at 1.0pm prompt.

As Julia with her two legal advisers were leaving the courtroom she saw Detective Inspector Bishop, Sergeant Totti, and the Captain of the Coastguard Cutter, sitting chatting amiably on a wooden seat placed in the corridor for witnesses waiting to be called into the court room.

Their relaxed light hearted attitude annoyed Julia greatly, who thought everyone involved in her trial for murder should act accordingly and remain sombre throughout the case

When they saw Julia leaving with her two escorts, the Inspector appeared to smile in her direction, but Julia regarded it as a smirk rather than a smile.

— — —

For the next few nights Julia slept fitfully, her over active mind busy reminding her of various witnesses being examined in depth by the Public Prosecutor and cross examined by her Barrister Franklin Jenson without her having a clue as to whether the points made by each Barrister were proving her guilt, or in favour of her innocence.

Each morning she struggled into the courtroom and by the end of the day wished the whole complicated procedure would soon come to an end so that she could be put out of her continual state of nervous distress.

Even though both Franklin and Edwin tried to reassure her that nothing of import had been said so far by any witness and they were confident all would be well in the end; that proved some time later, that those Barristers at court, like Valuers at auctions, can get it wrong at times.

Julia tried extremely hard to show an interest in the proceedings, but the court process was so slow and ponderous and the prosecuting attorney so pedantic on unimportant issues that she found it hard to stay awake after losing so much sleep at night.

She was told by Edwin that the Detective Inspector had received a hard time from the judge who criticised his bulldozing method of policing as unacceptable to the public at large, and incomprehensible when presenting his evidence in court.

One day Julia was pleased to see Mr and Mrs Fisher from the yacht Lion King waiting to give evidence. She took the opportunity to thank them once again for coming to her aid and introduced them to her Barristers.

Mr Fisher gave his evidence and was followed by the remaining witnesses for the prosecution.

During the period Barrister Jessop was up and down like a jack-in-the-box challenging various points and particularly those that were not related to fact. He spent some time cross examining Dr Christine Vos, drawing attention that the Prosecuting Attorney had made little reference to the pre drowning injuries to Walter Warren. He asked Dr Vos if she thought Walter Warren had been tortured before being heaved over the side of the yacht.

When she replied in the affirmative he thanked her and said he had no more questions.

When the Judge asked Mr. Jenson if he had any witnesses he came to the conclusion that as the Prosecutor had not made a strong case against his client he would leave well alone, and not provide the prosecutor with any opportunity to challenge any defence witnesses as he too had little to offer in defence of his client.

With nearly three weeks of purgatory endured, Julia suddenly realised that the Judge had announced that as no more witnesses were to be seen he called upon the two main protagonists, the opposing barristers, to present their closing address to the jury. Hastily calling the day's proceedings to an end, the Judge explained to the jury that on the morrow after they had heard the closing addresses, they would retire to the jury room and try and reach a unanimous decision. 'I am sorry that you cannot be allowed to go back to your homes and family until you reach a decision. In the meantime you will be accommodated in the nearby hotel where a room has also been made available for you to discuss the case. A court bailiff will remain in attendance at the hotel to ensure you have no communication with anyone other than the rest of the jury members. Should you require any further explanation on any legal point you will return to the court and your foreman will put the issue to me for clarification.'

Rising to his feet he announced that the court was adjourned until 10.0am on the following day when counsels would address the jury.

Ch.22

The following morning low cloud had descended overnight across the Island. The air was humid with a cloying heat making any movement unpleasant. Cara, who had not been able to attend any of the trial days due to her responsibilities at the hotel, had tried to encourage Julia to update her with progress reports and hopefully to hear that the case was very much in favour of Julia rather than the depressing situation that it was nip and tuck for either side.

When Edwin joined in the discussion he told Cara that the next few hours would be very critical, particularly when the jury returned to the court to give their decision.

Cara asked Edwin if he was confident that Julia would be declared innocent and be released from the burden she carried daily across her shoulders.

Edwin shrugged his shoulders. 'The Prosecuting Attorney has worked very hard to emphasize a number of issues that have troubled him about this case. All very circumstantial, but it depends how the jury react and whether they are convinced by the strength of his arguments.'

Cara reacted angrily. 'So you don't think Julia has a chance of winning?'

Edwin suggested she calmed down and try not to get too involved as she had not heard any part of the case and was therefore not qualified to make observations about the impending result. 'I didn't say that Julia would lose. I'm only pointing out that juries are notoriously fickle. One or two members with strong personalities and predetermined views can pressurise weaker members into changing their viewpoint because they are not strong enough to argue their side of the case.'

'All we can do is await their decision. If, and I only say if, the verdict is not in our favour then our work will really begin in earnest for there is only one chance to appeal.'

They all retired to bed early, knowing the next few hours could be critical.

– – –

In a smart town house at the other side of Castries, Franklin Jenson was burning the midnight oil. The night air had remained oppressive and he was sweating profusely. Hands clammy, as he clutched a pen in his right hand while trying to form the right words that would impress not only the jury, but the learned judge who would have the final word before the jury retired to consider their verdict.

He knew at heart that he was concerned about how the jury, or the judge, would react to his summation. Joining him next morning was a young but vastly experienced lawyer from the United Kingdom of Great Britain. Franklin was aware the Edwin Crosby would absorb every word he uttered; analyse it in his active brain; and look for loopholes that he, Edwin Crosby, would never have made.

On the morrow Franklin knew that he too would be on trial by his English counterpart. He critically re-examined his notes and after making a few final alterations, hoped he would not let the side down at this crucial moment in Julia's trial.

– – –

Promptly at 10.0am the court reconvened to a packed audience, some of whom had not bothered to attend the weeks of skirmishing between the opposing parties. They were only here to relish and see the Judge don the black cap and utter the words that would condemn the murderess to be hung by the neck until she was dead (literally speaking of course because the Island followed British law and banned executions). Never the less, having already reached their own sad conclusions they would smirk openly when the bitch was sentenced to life imprisonment. Exactly what she deserved, they would think, as they watched the jury file into the court and take their seats.

The Prosecuting Attorney, having received a nod from the judge rose to his feet and without any reference to notes began to present the reason he was expecting a guilty verdict.

'Members of the jury, I, like defence counsel, accept that some of the evidence you have heard over the last three weeks is circumstantial. However, that circumstantial evidence is part of a sizeable jigsaw puzzle that presents a picture of that happened on the yacht Sunray on the night Walter Warren was brutally murdered at the instigation of his wife Julia Franklin. You have heard how Mr and Mrs Warren were in bed and asleep before Mrs Warren claimed she was woken when she heard movements on deck not realising that two coloured men had boarded the yacht.'

'Although Mrs Warren has never been put on the stand to allow me to cross examine her, we have a statement from a reputable and a highly trained Detective Inspector that Mrs Warren gave him that information when he boarded the yacht early the next morning having received a distress call from the local harbourmaster. The same statement Mrs Warren made to the Inspector was confirmed by the master of the yacht Lion King, a Mr Fisher and his wife who were called to the yacht Sunray by Mrs Warren around 6am the following morning.'

'There remain several issues that remain unanswered that would have been put by me to Mrs Warren had the defence counsel thought it necessary to put her on the stand. In my considered view they were aware that Mrs Warren would be embarrassed by having to answer my questions so they refrained from putting their client the accused under any test of the validity of her statement.'

'First, no one on any other yacht anchored in the vicinity of the Sunray saw any other strange vessel in the bay that night, or the following morning. No one on any other yacht saw two men approach the Sunray. Most of those yachts contain people who are holidaying in the Caribbean and are known to hold parties aboard until the early hours of the morning as they enjoyed the barmy evenings of this tropical paradise. So I ask you to consider how could the two men actually get aboard that yacht late in the evening of the murder without being seen by at least the occupants of one yacht?' How could they row from the shore in a small dinghy and sneak aboard, or as Mrs Warren has inferred in her statement to the police, they must have boarded the yacht from another darkened cruiser?'

'I accept the Police Doctor's report that Mrs Warren on her own could never have tied up her husband, and inflicted so many injuries, before physically pushing her husband overboard. There must have been another person or persons to assist her in committing the murder. The questions remaining unanswered are why those two persons attacked Mr Warren, and how those persons got back to the shore without being seen by anyone? You are all aware that on this exotic holiday Isle many young couples wander the beach during the night enjoying the romantic swish as the sea rolls up the sand. Surely someone would have seen a small dinghy being launched in the bay containing two men?'

You heard from other witnesses that Mrs Warren after seeing her husband trussed by his hands and feet dropped over the side of the yacht with an anchor attached to weight him down, returned to the cabin below deck, used a douche and took a shower, thereby preventing the Police Doctor from taking a forensic sample to prove conclusively that she had, as stated by her, been raped by two unknown coloured men. I suggest that Mrs Warren never used a douche, and was never raped by the men she employed to kill her husband.'

'Mrs Warren also claims, according to more than one witness who spoke to her after her husband died, that having got dressed, she waited until after daylight to hail the yacht Lion King when she saw the owner arrive on deck. I ask you to consider why she failed to use the ship to shore radio to alert the coastguard after the supposed rapists had left the boat?'

'The Forensic team have confirmed that two male persons were on the yacht some time before, or during the period of the murder. Extensive police enquiries have failed to discover those persons and a search of the known criminal elements known to the police have cast iron alibis to confirm they were nowhere near the yacht at the time of the murder. It is feasible that only one man was needed to assist in helping Mrs Warren to lift her husband over the side. It is also quite feasible that a man wearing a life preserver could actually swim ashore after assisting Mrs Warren to commit the murder.'

'Mrs Warren was married quite young, at twenty three years of age to Walter Warren who was ten years older than her. He was a rich business man with assets worth well over two million pounds. I ask you to consider whether this was the prime motive for killing her husband.'

The Prosecutor paused for a moment before turning to the judge and saying 'I rest my case your honour.'

The judge gave the jury a few minutes to digest all that had been said by the Prosecutor. When he was sure they had completed taking notes he turned to Franklin Jenson and asked 'are you ready to present your response, Mr Jenson?'

Franklin nodded and got to his feet. Walking in his casual gait he passed the Prosecutor's bench without a glance at his opponent.

Approaching the jury of twelve, he glanced from the foreman to the lady in the end seat of the front row and gave a slight bow to acknowledge that he respected their presence in the courtroom.

Pausing for a moment before opening his final summation of what he had absorbed during the three weeks of the trial of his client he spoke in a quiet but authoritative voice.

'Ladies and gentlemen of the jury;' again he paused. 'When you retire to consider your verdict, I want you to consider carefully, as I am sure you will, that during the whole period of this trial you have you heard only two pieces of evidence that are proven facts.

One, that Walter Warren was bound hand and foot and weighted down with an anchor when his body was recovered from the bay and two, that my client Mrs Warren was rescued from the yacht where she was marooned. Everything else put before you by the Prosecutor has been a mixture of supposition and conjecture and the statements of hostile witnesses with their version of what they think happened on the Sunray on the evening of the murder of Walter Warren.'

'Let me put it more forcibly to you ladies in the jury. Try and imagine yourself in Mrs Warren's position of being savagely raped by two coloured men she had never seen in her life before that night. If you had a shower room handy, complete with a douche, what would you do in the middle of the night before calling for help, when the only people able to assist you would most likely be sound asleep in their bunks or beds?'

'The Prosecuting Attorney put forward a wild suggestion that most of the yachts in the bay hold parties until the early hours of the morning. It is as I have just stated "a wild suggestion" and not a proven fact so I ask you to disregard his observation.'

'As for the Prosecutor's late tactic of suggesting that Mrs Warren should have used the ship to shore radio; please remember that this was the first time Mrs Warren had sailed on a yacht. She had no previous experience of how to start the engine, put up sail, or how, or where, to drop the anchor to moor the boat. Not only could she not use the ship to shore radio, she had no idea such a complicated piece of equipment existed.'

'The defence acknowledges that two men, whom forensic officers claim to be of coloured origin, were on board and more than capable of putting Mr Warren over the side weighted down with an anchor. I ask you to seriously consider the alternative opportunities Mrs Warren had to murder her husband. (1) She could have subdued her husband possibly with either drugs or alcohol, tie him up, then paid the two men to attach the anchor to his feet before throwing him over the side; or (2) she could have subdued her husband by getting him drunk and when he was unable to defend himself assist him over the side where he would eventually drown. Assuming that in either event the police would eventually recover his body, the former would obviously prove a murder had been committed, while the latter could be explained away that her husband in a drunken state had fallen overboard. There is only one of the alternatives that would allow her to get away with the death of her husband.'

There was a suggestion from one witness that Mrs Warren was at odds with her husband to justify the murder. She had only been married for three years and it *is* possible she regretted marrying a man much older than herself, assuming that his wealth was the real reason she married Mr Warren. Every married couple have differences of opinion and the occasional row even in the early days of marriage. The question of how she felt about her husband is irrelevant. These days it is a simple matter to apply to the courts for a divorce and for the courts to decide how the party's wealth is distributed.'

'Would any intelligent person commit a dastardly murder knowing that the first thing the court would do is freeze the assets of the murdered person until the question of guilt has been established.'

'Over the last three weeks you have been bombarded with suggestions of what might have happened, and not one feasible fact that proved conclusively that Mrs Warren pre-planned the death of her husband. I trust in your deliberations during the next few hours that you find my client not guilty.'

Turning to the judge he said he rested his case.

It was the turn of the judge to direct the jury.

'Members of the jury you have patiently endure three weeks listening to testimony from a number of witnesses. The Public Prosecutor has summed up his case against the accused. The Defence Attorney decided not to put the accused on the stand, but you must not assume that by not doing so, he was trying to hide some relevant facts that could have been brought to light by the Prosecutor. In law, a person is innocent until proven guilty and the Defence Counsel has every right to look after the interests of his client.'

'Assuming that Mrs Warren is innocent of any crime, it is right that her Defence Counsel does his utmost to save his client from any pressures she would have to endure by being cross examined.'

'Now you must retire and consider your verdict. I will accept a majority verdict if there is some disagreement, but a unanimous verdict would be more appropriate in a murder trial. Please retire and when you have reached a verdict inform the bailiff so that I can recall everyone who awaits your decision.'

The Judge rose to his feet, bowed and retired to his chambers.

Ch.23

The proverbial fly on the wall in the jury room would have been aghast at the scene taking place below as the foreman of twelve 'men' and true opened the discussion.

'Ladies and gentlemen let me begin by asking each person sitting round the table to express their view on how they interpreted the proceedings over the last three weeks, or if you have any questions that need answering before you can come to a decision.'

The first of the ladies, a timid young thing was about to speak when she was interrupted by one of the rather large men sitting at the bottom end of the table.

'Hold your horses Mr Foreman. Before we get into a lot of useless tripe, I call for a show of hands as to who thinks the dolly bird on trial is guilty. If we get a vote in favour by ten of us then we can get back into that flaming hot court room this afternoon and tell the judge to get on with the sentencing.'

The foreman of the jury didn't know quite how to react to the proposal, so he bowed to the pressure. 'Please let us have a show of hands of those in favour of the motion.'

Eight hands went up.

'Right that settles that. How many of you are in favour of a guilty verdict?'

There was a pause for a moment before only four hands went up and they were all men.

The foreman looked around the room before responding. 'As we do not have a majority I think we should proceed as I directed.'

The overweight Timothy Hollenburg again interrupted. Turning to the young lady who was about to put her views forward, he bellowed 'It's as clear as can be that the Warren woman did her husband in for his dosh. Why would two coloured blokes kill this guy Warren and expect to get away with it. All they needed to do was tie him up; pinch anything loose; and the ship to shore radio that they could sell to another sailor seeking a cheap radio. I ask you lot, what does a ship to shore radio cost?' Without waiting for an answer he told them that if it was new it would cost around five thousand dollars. 'These guys could sell it on for five hundred dollars and have enough dosh to keep them in dope for weeks.'

He glowered at the timid jury member until tears appeared in her eyes. 'Put your hand up if you now think the Warren woman is guilty. Two of the women on the jury who had just voted against the proposal reluctantly raised their hands.

'Now we are six against six,' Tim Hollenburgh gloated. 'By the end of the day I reckon I can get a majority in favour,' he said, looking directly at the foreman.

The foreman slowly losing his patience with the bombastic approach of the male at the other end of the table suddenly banged the table with his fist. 'I have been appointed as foreman by all of you; therefore *I* am in charge of the proceedings. As I directed earlier, there will be no more counter proposals until everyone has had their say and there will be no more voting unless I as chairman call for a vote; is that clear to all?'

A silence descended on the jury room until Tim Hollenburgh could contain himself no longer. 'We appointed you as foreman only to count our votes and tell the judge our decision. Nobody elected you as chairman so shut up and let us get on with coming to a decision.'

The response from around the table was surprising. Everyone reacted angrily to Tim Hollenburgh's outburst. One of the assembled male jurors told him to be quiet for once in his life, and stop trying to bully everyone into his way of thinking. 'Chairman or Foreman; the title is irrelevant. We appointed Charles to keep us in order and that is what he is trying to do. Over to you Charles it is up to you to sort us out.'

Charles Avery thanked the member for his support and began again.

'Let us begin as I directed. Miss Rodwyll you first.'

The fly flew out of the window disgusted.

— — —

At the end of two long and tiring days the Foreman sent a request to address the judge.

Judge Francis Bell asked the bailiff to recall everyone waiting in the hall and lobby to hear the jury's verdict.

When everyone was assembled, the reporters waited anxiously with their pens and tape recorders poised hoping to hell that they would be in time to catch the late edition of their newspaper waited as the jury returned.

The Public Prosecutor was only interested in a 'guilty' verdict that would gain him several brownie points with his immediate boss and the possibility of further promotion, or at the very least, a rise in salary for his investigative and legal excellence.

On the other hand, Defence Counsel couldn't prevent himself from nibbling at the end of his index finger while wondering if a 'guilty' verdict would be the decision of the jury. Like the Prosecuting Attorney such a verdict would have the opposite effect. It would not enhance his reputation as a highly capable attorney and not necessarily guarantee he would continue to be engaged by the client to present an appeal on her behalf.

The Judge asked the foreman of the jury if they had reached a verdict, knowing by the note he had received from the foreman that it was unlikely, but court procedures had to be followed.

The foreman stood up. 'Your Honour, we have debated the issues before us for two long days and I have to report that it appears that we cannot reach a majority verdict.'

The Judge lowered his head and was seen to blow air out of his mouth in what appeared to be frustration. 'Members of the jury, you will retire to your hotel with a member of the court bailiff's in attendance and you will continue to debate the issues for the next twenty four hours, or until you reach a majority decision if that comes earlier. Please let the bailiff know when you have reached a decision, so that I can reconvene the court to hear your verdict.'

The following day the court was reconvened when the foreman informed the Judge that not only had they failed to reach a majority decision, but it was his opinion that jury were equally divided and he could see no way that that viewpoint would change.

The Judge was left with no option but to declare that the jury would be discharged and a new trial be convened with a new jury at a later date.

Rising from his seat on the dais he bowed to the three Barristers and asked if they would join him in his chambers.

When Edwin, Franklin and the Prosecuting Attorney Raymond Scott were seated round the Judge's desk, the Judge gave them a quizzical look before expressing his opinion. Shaking his head he told them he was not surprised at the outcome. 'Unfortunately we appear to have collected together a jury, some of whom appear to have preconceived opinions as to how the outcome should have ended. Let us hope that the next jury will come to a firm decision reasonably quickly. Everyone should be aware that trial by jury is to say the least, a very expensive business, and a retrial is extremely unfair on the accused, who must remain on bail until later in the year, or even next year.'

Franklin Jenson raised his hand and when the judge nodded, he asked if Mrs Warren could have her passport returned to allow her to return to the UK to deal with personal issues that required her presence. 'I can give a firm assurance he told the Judge that Mrs Warren will return for the trial. The laws in the UK are similar to those on this Island and if Mrs Warren changed her mind and refused to return she could quickly be rearrested and returned to the Island.'

The Judge gave a negative nod. 'I appreciate your confidence in Mrs Warren's acceptance of the situation she is now in, but once she has her passport she can disappear into any country she selects knowing she will be protected from our joint laws. Permission denied.'

The Prosecuting Attorney nodded his head in agreement because had the Judge agreed to the request, he was already prepared to oppose the application.

Wishing all the Barristers 'good day,' they rose from their seats and left his chamber. The Prosecuting Attorney knowing he would live to fight another day. The Defence Barristers wondering how they could inform Mrs Warren as delicately as possible, that her stay on the Island was going to be a long and expensive one.

Ch.24

The sun had graced St Lucia since shortly after dawn, turning the Island into a boiling caldron that eventually made the population seek the shaded areas, or the cooling air from the air conditioning vents in shops and hotels. Even in the early evening it was still humid and oppressive when Julia returned to the hotel accompanied by Edwin, who had pre warned her that with the trial being brought to an abrupt end he had no alternative but to return to the UK and resume his practice.

Julia was in a low depressive state by the time they entered the foyer, only to be greeted by a beaming Cara who was pleased to see Julia return, hoping against all the odds stacked against her friend that she would not be sent to prison.

'I assume you have been successful,' she cried throwing her arms around Julia, only for Julia to burst into tears.

'The jury failed to agree and I have to face another trial,' she cried. Bowing her head as if in shame, she told Cara; 'the judge wouldn't let me return to the UK, even though I gave a solemn undertaking that I would return for the retrial when the date was known. I'm not sure what I can do now; how can I continue to survive the next few months?'

Cara was shocked to the core. 'You can continue to live here for a start,' she said. 'Give yourself a few days to get over the shock of hearing how the jury vote was split. Why don't administrators select people for jury duty who have a semblance of intelligence, instead of picking people at random some of whom possess nothing between their ears than sawdust?' As no one responded to her question she continued. 'Between us I'm confident we'll find a solution to your problem.'

Julia wiped her eyes and gave a little sniff before responding. 'My Barrister gave a remarkable closing address and I was confident that the jury would find me not guilty, because there was nothing in the evidence that proved conclusively that I had murdered my husband. The fact that they failed to agree either way, proves that at least some of them considered me guilty. How could they?'

Edwin put his arm around Julia, while it entered his mind that his father would strongly disagree with the gesture. 'I entirely agree with you, but......and it's always but when you are left hanging in the air so to speak. As Cara has pointed out, those people selected for jury service have no legal training, which is a great shame and many have preconceived ideas of what they intend to do even before they have heard the evidence. I can't suggest for one moment that you grin and bear it. All I can suggest that you continue to put your trust in Franklin and me, because we will fight the opposition all the way until you are able to go home again without a stain on your character.'

Cara poured a triple measure of dry martini and handed it to Julia. 'Drink that down and you'll sleep like a log. Tomorrow we'll sort out your future.'

— — —

When Julia rose from a deep sleep the following morning and descended to the dining room, she discovered that Edwin had left the hotel before dawn to catch an early morning flight to Gatwick.

Cara was waiting for her when she had finished breakfast. 'I've got an idea to put to you that will help solve your problem over the coming months. I'm sure you don't want to sit moping around the hotel all day, and jobs are scarce during the autumn and winter months when most of the tourists depart.'

'This hotel doesn't get many tourists but we do have a regular clientele of business people so we are always quite busy. Why not join the staff as a chamber maid. You can surely change beds and use a vacuum cleaner on the carpets and I will pay you the basic rate of pay. It entitles you to share a staff bedroom but you can stay in your own room and I'll charge you ten dollars a week so the staff will not think you are being shown any favours.'

Julia gave Cara a great big hug and a kiss on both cheeks. 'I accept with gratitude. I'll never be able to repay our kindness.'

One more brick was placed on the foundation of what would become a lifelong friendship.

– – –

Julia was busying about the hotel when Cara told her Franklin Jenson was in the foyer wanting to talk to her.

Arriving in the foyer still wearing rubber gloves and a patterned pinafore she asked him why he had called when she was so busy. Cara poo pooed her haughty stance and told her Franklin had something very important to discuss with her 'So sit down and hear what he has to say.'

Franklin explained that Edwin and he had had a lengthy meeting the night before to discuss future plans and policy prior to the next trial.

'Edwin is very concerned about your husband's last remarks before he was killed and wants to make some discreet enquiries when he gets back to the UK. Obviously he can't just blunder into your past life without causing a furore. What he requires is for you to give him written authority to act on your behalf when he starts probing into your late husband's past life before you left for the supposed holiday on this Island. I recall you told me that your husband cried out to you before he was thrown overboard. Edwin has a note of what he said and intends to try and unravel those words with various people in the UK.'

Franklin produced a typed letter headed with the name and address of his chambers. 'This will make it look legal and give Edwin licence to probe into your husband's past.'

Julia signed the letter without asking any questions as she was trying so hard to prove to Cara that she was no slacker and wanted to get back to cleaning the rooms on the first floor which was her allotted task each day. Julia had to admit to herself that her husband's past observations that she was an idle slut was probably true. She accepted that she had left most of the housekeeping chores to the cleaner while she spent her days discovering new ways to spend her husband's money.

Now she was gainfully employed she was enjoying the experience of helping to keep the hotel in tip top order while meeting deadlines to prepare for incoming guests. It was while she was dusting the bedside tables in one of the bedrooms that she also accepted that it was also a lovely feeling to have an inexhaustible supply of funds to indulge her love for designer clothes and shoes and eat in the best restaurants at up market hotels.

Putting aside the dream, she carried on with the task at hand knowing that those days of living the life of leisure were now behind her and she must now look to the uncertain future.

Ch.25

Edwin was enthused when he received the signed legal authority five days after he arrived home. Having thought about the problems he may have to face, he asked Marion to telephone Julia and ask some pertinent questions. The address of her house in Merseyside?, whether the house had a safe and did she know the combination? the number of occupants?, the name and address of her UK bank?, did her late husband have a bank vault security box?, what was his mother's maiden name?, and the name of Walters school when he was 14?

Marion thought that some of the questions were rather weird, never the less she did as she was asked and took the opportunity to have a brief but friendly chat with Julia; sympathising with her dilemma and the fact that she was unable to leave the Island.

When Edwin was given a list of the answers he had requested he listed them in order of priority and visited Walter's school after arranging an appointment with the Head Teacher. He told her the reason for his visit and when she laughed he immediately took offence. 'This is no laughing matter' he explained. 'I am investigating the murder of one of your ex pupils.'

The head teacher apologised and said she was surprised he had not worked out the answer. 'Did you study algebra and formulae at school?'

Edwin admitted he had, but found it very confusing.'

She asked if he remembered the formula $A = \pi \cdot r^2$ or pi R Squared?

When he nodded in the affirmative, she told him all the boys with the same initials were very rarely addressed by their name by the maths teacher. 'Walter Warren would normally be called W Squared or use the initial and number W^2 when asked to sign his initials on a document. Peter Patterson was P Squared. (The author was R^2 at his school).

Edwin muttered that the maths teacher must be a weirdo to make life for his pupils so complicated. What the hell was wrong in calling his pupils Smith, Jones, Warren etc. However, if Walter Warren used this convoluted system of protecting his assets it could be one useful step forward in Edwin's search for the reason why he was killed.

The Head Teacher told him she had heard him use the expression weirdo. 'It may sound weird to you Mr Crosby, but the maths teacher used a number of techniques to make his boys remember formulae. Even those without the double letter names mocked the boys by calling them 'square head' etc. But ask any boy in his class how to find the area of a circle and they would instantly say pi = 22/7 x the radius squared. So please don't form judgements until you understand the motive.

Edwin felt suitably chastened.

— — —

Edwin's next port of call was the Warren home situated in Formby, an upmarket conurbation of expensive looking houses and the residential homes of rich footballers belonging to either Liverpool FC or Everton FC, business executives from the nearby city, and in a number of cases Directors of large departmental stores in Southport and other surrounding towns.

The Warren house, looking similar to a small mansion, was a six bedroom modern brick built building surrounded by a high wall and large automated iron gates. The house and grounds were far too large for two persons, so Edwin assumed it was image related than the desire of Walter Warren to produce a large family.

When Edwin pressed the house communication button to announce his arrival, a man in gardening attire pressed a button to open the two gates. Driving into a pebbled drive to the front of the house an elderly gentleman in a dark blue suit was waiting at the top of the four steps leading up to the open front door. Introducing himself as Mr Warren's butler he led Edwin into a large lounge with French windows giving a panoramic view of the large rear garden, beautifully maintained, with a striped lawn and wide flower beds planted alongside a mixture of semi tropical shrubs.

Edwin showed the butler his letter of identification as he asked how many persons were present on the site.

'There are only four of us' the butler replied; 'myself, the cook, the housekeeper and the gardener who let you through the gate. The house keeper and gardener are a married couple who live a short journey away. The cook lives like me in the garret in two single rooms' he hastened to add. 'We read in the newspaper about the tragic death of Mr Warren and have kept the house in good order pending the return of Mrs Warren. May I add sir that none of the staff has been paid for a number of weeks since Mr and Mrs Warren left on holiday. Mr Warren did inform us that an agent from the bank would call weekly to pay the staff but no one has turned up as yet. Although I am normally paid monthly into my bank account, I have not received any payment since my employer was murdered.'

Edwin nodded his acceptance of the situation. I will deal with that issue a.s.a.p. but at the moment I am anxious to look into Mr Warren's affairs. I would like to see the location of the house safe; his computer or laptop; his study; any keys he may have left here; and I need to examine his master bedroom and the cellar.

The butler looked puzzled by the requests, so Edwin explained that Mrs Warren had a number of issues that needed resolving. 'So I need to carry out a detailed search to see if I can find any clues to aid her solve those problems.'

The butler showed Edwin into the study where a large leather bound desk dominated a room heavily panelled in dark oak, with a large window with little outlook other than a small border of shrubs, and one of the high walls surrounding the house. A computer was placed at the side of the desk, alongside a keyboard and a telephone. On one wall, a collection of leather bound books was stored on shelves and one reproductive oil painting in a gilt frame hung from another. The butler touched the side of the picture which swung open to reveal a small wall safe fitted with a combination lock.

'The master kept his keys on the top left hand drawer but the desk was always kept locked and only he possessed the keys for that desk.'

Edwin told him he needed access to the desk and asked the butler if he could find either a big screw driver or some strong scissors so that he could gain access.

The butler blanched at the request. 'The master will go spare if he finds the drawer has been tampered with.'

Edwin shook his head in despair. 'Your master is dead and this house belongs to his wife who has given me written authority to examine any aspect that will help her defend her case. So please get me some tools to open the drawer'

The butler scuttled off, no doubt to inform the rest of the staff that the visiting Lawyer had no respect for someone else's property.

Edwin switched on the computer and waited for it to boot up.

As soon as the screen showed the contents of the desk top, he tried to open the programme for 'documents' only to be informed by a small window that a password was required.

Without any hesitation he typed in 'wsquared' and hit enter. He gave a quiet whoop of excitement when the alphabetical list of the contents of 'documents' flashed onto the screen. He realised that what he urgently needed from his father was their computer wiz kid to search the contents for what he was looking for. He decided to arrange that when he got back to the office so he switched off the computer and waited for the butler to return.

A screw driver soon forced the top left hand drawer open for Edwin to find a number of keys that presumably opened other drawers in the desk. One key in particular caught his attention. It was small and had a metal disc attached. He lifted it out of the drawer and examined the attached disk. It had the number 1024 imprinted in the metal. 'Bingo' cried Edwin, as he put the key into his brief case. He transferred the contents of the drawer he had forcibly opened, into another drawer in the desk which he locked with one of the keys before rejoining the staff in the lounge.

They all stood up when he entered the lounge so he told them to sit as he had something important to say. When they were seated he told them that he was prepared to see each person individually if that is what they preferred, or collectively, so there would be no misunderstanding between them.

When they affirmed that they would remain together, he commenced with the news they were collectively dreading to hear.

'As you are all clearly aware your employer is now deceased. What you may not know is that all his assets were frozen by the Supreme Court until either a Will is discovered and cleared by probate, or Mrs Warren is found innocent of murder at her rehearing in St Lucia. Those are the reasons why you have not been paid. Once her innocence has been proved she will return to her home and employ a lawyer to sort out the technical difficulties regarding her future.'

In the interim, due to the Court freezing all the late Mr Warren's assets, Mrs Warren can no longer afford to keep all the staff running this house. I am directed by her to terminate the butler's employment with immediate effect and pay any redundancy money due.' Turning to the butler he told him that he would not be surprised at the decision now that his employer was deceased. 'I would be pleased if you would collect your personal belongings and leave me an address to which I can send your cheque,' Edwin said adding how sympathetic he was that the decision had to be made by Mrs Warren,

'As Mrs Warren will be detained in St Lucia for a few months she has no need for a cook so the same applies to you madam,' he said turning to the cook whose eyes filled with tears. I'm sure Mrs

Warren will write directly to you both within the next few days expressing her sadness at having to make such a difficult decision.'

'Mrs Warren indicated that she still requires the house and garden to be maintained in good order pending her return, so Mr and Mrs Goodfellow you are welcome to remain, and my office will continue to pay your salaries until Mrs Warren has had time to resolve her financial state and decide her future. Should you decide to leave her employment please let my secretary know and I will arrange for your severance pay.'

— — —

Edwin couldn't get to sleep that night, as his mind was over active trying to find solutions to the many problems facing him since he visited the Warren residence. Was the small key he had found in the drawer a key to a safe deposit box, or was it the key to a strong box stored somewhere in Walter Warren's warehouse? Could the numbers 1024 be a secret code? Or the password to his credit or debit cards that were still unaccounted for? Or was it for some other purpose he had failed to consider?

Sleep eventually claimed him, but the following morning over breakfast his mind was still hyper active. Later that morning, he decided to make another visit to the Warren house and phoned the housekeeper to say he was on his way. He took the Chamber's computer buff with him to try and extract some useful information from Walter Warren's desk top lists and his lap top.

Once they were let into the house he was informed that a very disgruntled butler had left that morning and the cook had not turned up to collect one or two things that she left in the kitchen.

His computer man was quickly seated with eyes glued to the screen deeply absorbed in his search. Edwin decided to have another look in the desk for a diary, or bank statements. Both brought a blank result. He then turned to the safe and looked at the combination. Twiddling idly with the knob he tried 1024 turning it to one on the right and 2 to the left and so on without a result, although he thought he heard the click as he tried each number. He zeroed the combination and tried again with 1024 only this time he continued turning the tumbler and reversed the numbers using 2410. There was a loud click and the door swung open. He was convinced that the numbers were birthday dates so the reversal was the first obvious choice.

Inside he found a file with many months of bank statements showing that Walter kept only a limited but healthy working cash balance of thirty thousand pounds. Another file listed stocks and shares investments, amounting to roughly three million pounds as he totted up the values in his head. It appeared from the addresses that Walter used four Brokers to control his wealth, obviously not trusting any one Broker to know his true wealth.

On a shelf was a stack of bank notes in bundles of £50, £20 and £10; obviously ready cash for immediate use if required.

In one lower draw was a diary full of times and numbers that Edwin could only assume were appointments with customers or dealers. Being a shrewd business man he was not prepared to have the diary fall into the wrong hands and give them a list of the business men he dealt with. Each person obviously had a code number and the list to open the code was somewhere else.

It is said that the unexpected can quite often shock. At the back of the safe wrapped in a piece soft felt, Edwin found a well oiled Blood Hawk Machine Pistol with six magazines filled with cartridges, obviously ready for immediate use as one magazine was already slotted into the gun.

Locking the safe by spinning the combination barrel Edwin asked his computer buff if he was finished. When he told him there was more to do, Edwin told him to dismantle the computer and put it in the car so he could carry on with his search once they were back at base.

Ch.26

The following day Edwin visited the HSBC Branch in Liverpool having made an appointment with the Bank Manager. As it was the same bank used by Crosby and Welland, the manager assumed the purpose of the visit was to discuss some financial arrangement. When Edwin explained he was representing the widow of the late Walter Warren the Bank Manager literally speaking pulled down the shutters.

'I am sure you are aware that the late Mr Warren's assets have been frozen by the Court and I am not allowed to release any asset until I have the authority of the court.'

Edwin confirmed the observation with a nod of the head. 'He produced the small key with the tag 1024 and showed it to the manager. 'I am informed by Walter Warren's widow that this is the key to a safe deposit box that contains some expensive pieces of jewellery belonging to Mrs Warren. I appreciate that Mrs Warren cannot have them back until the Court lifts its ban, but Mrs Warren has asked me to check that her jewels are still in your vault. She has a suspicion that her husband may have sold some of the pieces without her knowledge. All I am required to do is check that they are still in the box.'

'One of your staff can accompany me and search me before I leave. I have her written authority to act on her behalf if you wish to see it.'

Knowing Mr Crosby both as a customer and a well respected lawyer in Liverpool, the manager agreed that as Edwin held the second key to the safe deposit box he would arrange for one of the staff to accompany Edwin to the Strong Room while he checked the contents of the box.

Edwin was shown into the array of boxes and the location of box 1024. The member of staff used her key to unlock the first lock leaving Edwin to insert his key into the second lock. The staff member then retired to the end of the room and waited for Edwin to examine the contents.

The box did contain several pieces of what looked to be jewellery. It also contained a typed list in an envelope and surprise surprise, another small Sig automatic pistol and two magazines of rounds.

Edwin lifted out the jewellery and placed it on the table as he photographed each piece. As he was returning them to the box he glanced in the direction of the girl who had accompanied him to the strong room and noticed she was fiddling with her hair and not looking in his direction. He quickly palmed the envelope into his side pocket as he replaced the gems in the box. When he asked her if she would like to check that nothing had been removed she nodded her head from side to side indicating she was not really interested. Edwin locked the box which in turn was then locked by the girl and they both went back upstairs where he thanked the manager for his kind assistance. 'Mrs Warren will be so relieved to see the pictures I have taken of her jewellery. Someday soon she may be able to wear them for a special occasion.'

Returning to the chambers Edwin thought it about time he consulted his dad. Going into his father's office he wondered how his father would react to his son breaking the law.

Putting all his cards on the table he awaited his father's reaction.

James Crosby was never one to give sudden judgements. 'I read a copy of Mrs Warren's statement obtained by the police, and I have to admit that the fact that she stated she was disillusioned with her husband and was considering her options was enough to condemn her in the eyes of the law. However the fact that the local plod failed to caution her, did mean they could not use her written statement as evidence. However, the Prosecutor has used every devious means he could to get the message over to the Judge that Mrs Warren was considering leaving her husband. The evidence you have uncovered recently, tends to confirm the Prosecutor's theory that Mrs Warren had come to a conclusion that she had married a man who was steeped in criminal activities. She may even have had serious thoughts that his vast wealth was not generated from any legal import and export business.'

'In my view son, you have opened Pandora's box. Somewhere in that box of tricks is the real answer as to why Walter Warren was murdered. The list you obtained from the safe deposit box could be the answer, but first you and I have to unravel the code. Walter Warren didn't go the Caribbean for a holiday; he went to sort out some of his illegal activities in that area that must have gone pear shaped. The fact that he asked his wife accompany him was obviously a smoke screen. What we need to do is a bit of lateral thinking to see if we can solve this bloody puzzle.'

Edwin heaved a sigh of relief. No mention or criticism from his dad that he had broken the law. The whole team, including Franklin Jenson on St Lucia were trying to grasp at straws that kept blowing away in the wind. This list must be what the two thugs were after, but what did it mean?

That night Edwin burnt the midnight oil trying hard to think laterally without much success. He looked again at the sheet of paper and shook his head. It was a whole list of gibberish as far as he was concerned.

J -25k Mon 2200 San Pedro Pete L.
C -250k Tue 1100 Bk Jorden.
PR -50k Thur 2100 Coral Island Javié B.
SL -30k Sun 0400 Lido S Rafael B.
BT -0k Tue 2230 B Caf El Dey Tibo S rfl?
V -120k Thur 0200 Wharf 7D Enr C
MXC - ? Tue? DPF ?

Edwin emailed the list to Franklin Jenson and asked him to pass a copy on to the detective Roberto Sanchez they had hired to see if either of them could offer any solution.

One week later Edwin received telephone call from Franklin. 'You'll never believe this. 'Roberto and I wracked our brains and came up with zilch. For some unknown reason I decided to show the list to Mrs Warren so I called at the hotel only to discover she was out shopping at the hypermarket on behalf of the chef.

I showed the list to Cara and asked her if she would give it to Mrs Warren when she returned. Cara looked at the list and asked who it belonged to. When I told her it belonged to the late Mr Warren she said it looked like a travel itinerary.

'Julia told me they flew to Jamaica on a Monday and her husband left her on her own for a full day when he flew to the Cayman Islands for a business meeting. Does that help?' she asked innocently hitting the nail on the head.

'I called Roberto into my office and the two of us sat down and came up with some possible solutions. Have you got your list handy?'

When Edwin told Franklin it was in front of him he said 'look at your computer for I have just sent you an email. Adding I think Cara deserves a huge bonus for pointing us in the right direction.'

Edwin called up his emails and there was one from frankj@law.com.

The email read as follows

'J could be Jamaica and San Pedro is hotel in Kingston. Waiter in hotel named Peter Lorenzo who is known to handle drugs; possibly paid £25,000 by Warren for supplies. Known to have an expensive sports car he could not afford on his hotel salary.

C could be Cayman Islands and a meeting Warren had arranged with a Bank Manager called Jorden at the Butterfield Bank where he withdrew £250,000.

PR could be Puerto Rica and the hotel is the Coral Island. The Assistant Manager is one Javié Batista who must have been paid £50,000 for services rendered. We could put the police on to that one, but Roberto advises we leave it to him to put some pressure on JB before we involve the police.

Next one is easy as it refers to St Lucia where we have a hotel called the Lido Star where the Head Chef is one Rafael Bonico an Italian immigrant known to the police as someone with Mafia connections. Assume he was paid £30,000 by Warren but for what? Narcotics I suppose.

BT according to Julia, was Bridgetown in Barbados on the following Tuesday, so we assume Warren intended to Island hop during the intervening days. Roberto and I thought the Ok was an acceptance that there was no problem there, but we then realised the Ok was in the money column so it really read nil payment. Roberto's enquiries with the local police confirmed it was a small bar come café on the beach called El Dey and owned by a black Nigerian called Tibo Simba. The police say they are aware that the bar is a magnet for young holiday makers where illegal drugs are readily available. It is only a guess on my part but I think Simba owed money to Warren and he was going to have a visit to sort him out. The rfl with a question mark could mean 'remove from list' or in other words 'kill' if he failed to pay up. If I am right Walter Warren was far from being a loving husband, but a serious killer and enforcer for his Mafia boss.

V could be for Venezuela and according to Mrs Warren they were due to arrive in the Capital Caracas in two days, that was impossible in a sailing boat that would require at the very least two weeks with good sailing weather. Roberto discovered that a wharf 7D was in fact in that port so we presume Warren proposed to fly there leaving his wife looking after the yacht in Barbados. Enrico Castello owns warehouse 7D and while the police suspect more than normal export goods leave the warehouse, they have not enough proof to obtain a warrant to carry out a search of the building. Walter Warren expected to pay out £120.000. The question remains was it for export goods, or narcotics?

Finally MXC proved to be more difficult to interpret. Roberto and I did a map scan of the southern Caribbean, Venezuela and Columbia because of their narcotics record and it came up blank.

Moving north to places like Panama, it was Roberto who came up with Mexico City.....MXC. He has a friend there in the National Police HQ and contacted him to see if he could help.

His contact scanned his computer for known criminals and came up with local Mafia boss called Don Frederico Pascal. The Officer told Roberto they have tried umpteen times to try and find evidence to arrest him without success. He is known to bribe officials at the highest level to ensure he stays out of prison. The question against the payment and date remains a mystery.

There are many questions waiting to be resolved. One that seems worth investigating thoroughly was the Pascie mentioned by one of the murderer's, it could be the Mafia Boss Don Pascal?

I await your instructions. Franklin.'

Ch.27

Edwin printed the long email and dashed into his father's office, fortunately finding him without a client. Then his father was running down his clientele prior to retiring after nearly fifty years in the legal profession and the last thirty as senior partner. James Crosby would like his son to take over the reins, but the other senior partner Mr Welland, had other intentions as he still had four years to go to retirement and his eldest son Roland was competing with Edwin for the upgrading.

James Crosby did a quick scan of the email as he raised his eyebrows higher and higher. When he got to the last interpretation of the coded list he gave out a 'bloody hell' before putting the document on his desk.

'We both thought Warren's import export business was a bit of a sham because very few business men can acquire so much wealth in such a short a time. If he really was into illicit drugs that answers part of the conundrum as to why he was killed. The fact that he may have been involved with the Mafia, at least gives us a clue as to where to look for those two thugs who are the key to Mrs Warren's proof of innocence.'

James paused for a moment as he sorted out a myriad of thoughts bouncing round his brain like the hard ball in a squash court. Don Pascal is obviously the top man in Mexico. 'Dons usually reign with a rod of iron, he thought, and if they have sons they too can be as bloody ruthless as the father. Their domains are usually impregnable living in Haciendas surrounded by high walls; a sophisticated security system; and enough armed guards to frighten off the police who tend to keep their distance. Learned judges in that country, with political ambitions, have tried for many years to clean up their territory only to be found dead with a bullet wound in the back of the neck to send a message to other politicos to keep their noses out of Mafia business.'

'We as a family tend to go where other angels fear to tread, but crossing swords with the Mafioso is something we have never had cause to challenge. However, there is a first time for everything, so you and I need to think carefully how we propose to enter the lion's den without being ripped to pieces in the process. What I suggest is you book yourself on the first available flight to St Lucia to meet up with Franklin and Roberto and formulate a plan for my approval. In the meantime I will sit down with the rest of the partners and see what we can come up with. I don't for one moment think Don Pascal will be quaking in his boots it he discovers we are hot on his heels,' he added with a rather cynical laugh.

– – –

Edwin left it to his secretary to make the necessary arrangements and to inform Franklin and Julia Warren of his time of arrival on the Island.

The last few weeks he had been literally snowed under with cases and the impending trial in St Lucia that he had had no time for the fading romance he was involved in. Two or three times he had rung his girl friend only to have her mother answer the telephone. When he left a message for her daughter to ring him back, nothing happened, so he presumed that she had either not got the message, or was so pissed off with him that she was playing hard to get.

Needing to visit the barbers shop for a hair cut before he left for St Lucia, he walked into the city centre from his office. He was half way down the main street when he spotted his girl friend on the arm of a debonair young man who was in earnest conversation with her, completely oblivious to the other people on the sidewalk.

Susan spotted him as he crossed the road for a head on meeting. There was no sign of confusion on her face as she dragged her partner to a halt. 'Hello Edwin,' she said. 'I thought you had somehow left this planet and found a beautiful Martian to keep your bed warm. May I introduce Howard Price who has asked me to marry him.' Waving her left hand she showed Edwin the enormous diamond engagement ring on the third finger.

All Edwin could do was shake the fellows hand and wish him the best of luck before he turned and walked away. The sigh of relief from them both was reserved until he had his back to the pair of lovers.

– – –

The flight from Gatwick to St Lucia was once again delayed by unforeseen problems at the airport until 0200 hours leaving Edwin furious and frustrated as there was nothing he could do about the delay. When the plane eventually took off, Edwin had the opportunity to snooze as he never could sleep deeply on a plane. The stewardess disturbed him at five in the morning offering tea or coffee and a light snack. He declined all, knowing coffee or tea would keep him awake and any form of hot drink made his trips to the loo too often to be tempted.

The flight ended with a squeal of tyres on the runway in hot sultry weather that suggested thunder storms were in the offing sometime during the coming day.

He was met at the airport at 6.0am St Lucia time, by a bleary eyed Franklin in his genuine antique Oldsmobile that bore a similar resemblance to interior decor of a British Rolls Royce Coupé. It possessed a walnut facia board; tan leather seats; and an engine that ticked over silently while awaiting the order to smoothly pull away from the airports arrivals lounge.

Franklin commented that Edwin should time his arrival on St Lucia at a more reasonable hour so that he could enjoy a good night's sleep. Once they were on the move he told his passenger that nothing knew had developed since he had sent the email, but he and Roberto the Private 'Dick' had worked out a plan of action for Edwin's approval.

'I thought it advisable to avoid the Hotel Adelphi until we have had a chat as we don't want any distractions with Julia or Cara offering advice. We will stop for breakfast at a café on the sea front where Roberto will be waiting for us.'

This was the last thing Edwin wanted, having left his home in the UK at 5.0pm the previous day to allow sufficient time for him to get to Gatwick for his 10pm flight to St Lucia, only to find the flight delayed for four hours. If he had arrived on the Island at 1am Caribbean time, there would have been sufficient time for him to grab a few hours sleep before this meeting.

Now he was being forced to make decisions while his mind was still cloudy from lack of solid sleep. In future he decided to arrange from someone at the office to ferry him to Liverpool airport and fly him to Gatwick.

He could never understand how a plane's flight could suddenly be aborted, having been recently checked by experienced engineers and deemed fit to fly. Then he had no experience of the complex situations that could develop at airports that could result in flight delays and cancellations that had nothing to do with the technical side of a plane's ability to fly.

Ch.28

The sea front café was empty at this time in the morning as most tourists enjoyed having breakfast in their hotel dining room. Franklin and Edwin joined Roberto who had his nose so buried in the morning newspaper that he failed to see them arrive.

Over a light breakfast Roberto Sanchez opened the conversation. 'There is no way I would fly to Mexico City and demand an audience with Don Frederico Pascal. The Caribbean is full of dead corpses and I have no desire to join them for a game of four handed whist.'

'Some four years ago during my long service in the Mexican Police I was privileged to work under a Lieutenant Arturo Vegas and his assistant the late Sergeant Tomas Carrillo who were both determined to put Don Frederico Pascal behind bars for life. Unfortunately Sergeant Carillo was later killed in the line of duty. I will always remember how dedicated a team they were, and how frustrated they became at the failure to bring the arch criminal and his cohorts to justice. Bribery and corruption is rife in that country, but when anyone crosses the path of the mighty Don they are apt to die a violent death and I for one will not put my life on the line. Before you arrived I made some discreet enquiries to one of my contacts in the Mexican Police and discovered that the Lieutenant had been promoted to Captain and transferred to head a team investigating police corruption.'*

'In order to facilitate our entry into Mexico and carry out investigations into the mysterious Pascie, I took the opportunity to speak to Captain Vegas and told him a little of the background as to why we needed to enter Mexico. The Captain was most helpful and is prepared to meet us as soon as we confirm time of arrival in Mexico City. He did as I expected, and warned us not to attempt to make contact with any undercover private investigators for

*(See the author's novel 'Journey into Fear')

assistance, as they may already be getting backhanders from the Don to keep him informed of anyone investigating his activities. He also reminded me of Don Pascal's formidable heavy back up mob and said on no account should we make overtures to anyone in his pay asking for a meeting without sufficient police backup that he, the Captain, will be happy to provide.'

Edwin had to admit he was very impressed with the local private investigator who Franklin had hired. While on the plane last night his mind dwelt on the email he had received and how it could be of use. 'This Mafia Don appears to be a very unpleasant character and we would be wise to accept the help and advice of this experienced Mexican officer,' he said with a frown on his face.

That made Roberto smile, who thought how naive this English lawyer is about the way the mafia work. Dons the world over, head a family who terrorise the local community and make millions, no billions, using extortion, corruption, brutality, and anything else they can use to achieve one object in their miserable self centred lives; to be recognised as the Don, the head man of the Mafioso, one to be feared and obeyed without question.

Edwin continued. 'This Pascal must be the person who ordered the two men to extract by using force if necessary, the secret list that Walter Warren kept secure. We could offer that list back to Pascal in exchange for the names and addresses of the two men we want to get Julia free of the murder wrap hanging about her neck, while we promise to walk away and not inform anyone including the police that we knew a list existed.'

Both Franklin and Roberto shook their heads in amazement. 'Apart from signing the death warrants for the two men, do you think for one moment that as soon as you hand over the list to Don Pascal, he will allow you to leave his hacienda, except of course in a plain wooden box?' Franklin commented.

Roberto was slightly more receptive to the idea even though he thought it a mad idea. 'Let us discuss our problem with Captain Vegas and see how he reacts.'

Returning to Edwin's idea he decided to add his six pennyworth for what it was worth. 'No way is the Don going to give you their names, assuming he knows who they are. Once they were handed over to us, any admission from these two men that their orders came directly from the Don, or his immediate underlings, would bring the Mexican Police into the frame, who have been dying to get their hands on Pascal for years.

– – –

It was two very frustrating days before they could obtain three seats on a plane to Mexico City. In the meantime the three spent some time sitting round an outside table at a bar on the beach, where they could speak without being heard and at the same time enjoy the onshore breeze coming off the Caribbean Sea.

'I wonder how Detective Inspector Bishop will react when we eventually decide to inform him that his patch is part of a chain of drug handlers controlled by a wealthy Mexican Don, and organised by the late Walter Warren,' muttered the ex detective Roberto with a devilish grin on his face. 'For years the Inspector has been aware that there were drugs available on the Island, but he dismissed the idea that it was widespread and organised by drug barons. He was always of the opinion that narcotics were brought onto the Island by one or two well known locals using small boats from Venezuela. When he finds out that one of the up market hotels on the Island is a major distribution centre he'll not only go spare, he'll blame everyone but himself in his department for gross incompetence.'

Franklin was more positive. 'When the police on each Island are provided with the name of the narcotic importer the local and the national press will have a field day, blaming the police for the growth in drug addicts. The question I want the answer to, is who does the dirty on the police? I certainly don't want to be on the other end of their vendetta when it starts. I have a living to make on this Island.

Edwin aware that he was no longer tied to Susan his now ex girl friend, ignored his father's warning about not getting involved with a client. He left the two men sitting talking about accommodation in Mexico City and left it to them to arrange the hotel booking.

It was only a pleasant stroll to the Adelphi and when he entered the foyer was greeted with a welcoming hug by Cara who told him his room had already been prepared by Julia who was also looking forward to seeing him once again.

With a puzzled look showing on his face, Cara explained how Julia was being kept active by doing chores around the hotel. 'She's a little short on funds until the court releases assets, so she is paying her hotel bill by helping out.'

Julia suddenly appeared in the foyer and like Cara flung her arms round his neck and gave him a peck on the cheek. 'Any welcome news?' she asked. 'Or is it all doom and gloom?'

Without disclosing how the investigations were proceeding he told her that the purpose of his sudden visit was to have further discussions with her Lawyer. I also have some business to attend to in Mexico but I expect to return here for a few days. I am entitled to some holidays so dad told me to count this visit as part of my holiday entitlement. Dad doesn't miss a trick, no wonder his staff 'love' him' he added with a smile on his face.

Edwin spent the rest of the day relaxing and catching up on his jet lag. He invited Julia to join him for the evening meal, and when Julia declined, by reminding him that she was an employee and not allowed in the main dining room, Edwin then invited her to join him for dinner at a nearby restaurant so she cleared with Cara before accepting.

Although Edwin was his usual charming self and delighted that Julia had welcomed him back with open arms, he recognised he was on delicate ground while Julia was awaiting retrial so he confined his conversation to what was going on in the UK; how Her Majesty the Queen had enjoyed her diamond jubilee year; and the crazy political manoeuvres' taking place between the three political parties that was causing real concern with the electorate.

After dinner they strolled along the promenade making a leisurely way back to the hotel where he bid her goodnight in the foyer without exchanging a kiss before retiring to his room. When he undressed and lay on the bed Edwin was convinced he and Julia had already formed a mutual bond that could eventually lead to something much more permanent.

The following morning the trio flew to Mexico City wondering what was in store for three amateurs venturing into the seedy world of the Mafioso.

Ch.29

They were met at the airport by Arturo Vegas dressed in light weight khaki tropical shorts and shirt due to the oppressive heat. Sweat marks already showing under both his arm pits suggested high humidity levels waiting to welcome the newcomers as they descended the stairs from the coolness of the air conditioned aircraft.

His delight at meeting up with Roberto again was a joy to behold. 'You've put on a bit of weight since I last saw you Robo,' he said. 'Being a private eye must have some benefits,' he added with a huge boyish grin on his face.

Roberto was just as delighted to see his old boss again. 'One of the perks is having a free meal with the potential customer. Perhaps on reflection I've had one too many,' he added shaking Arturo's hand vigorously.

Captain Vegas got down to business straight away. 'I am now in charge of the department dealing with police officers up to the highest level who are involved in corruption, or other criminal activities. As such, technically I should not get involved in your case.' He paused drew in a sharp breath. 'However, I have never been concerned about 'technical responsibilities'. Don Pascal has been my bêt noire for as long as I can remember. I nearly had the old bugger in cuffs three years ago with the necessary warrant in my hands when some miserable sod in my station warned him in advance so he quickly scarpered off to South America until the heat died down.'

'The officer who replaced my old boss as Capitano, appears to have conveniently lost the warrant for Don Pascal, who is back to his old ways and living in Mexico City without a care in the world. I often wonder how many dollars changed hands between the two. When Roberto called and told me the whole grisly story about the Warren murder and the possibility of Pascal's involvement it rekindled my appetite to bring him to justice and put him where he belongs.......in one of our hard labour prisons until he departs this world.'

Turning to Edwin he got to the reason for their visit. 'Now if you can fill me in with what crazy idea you have in mind, perhaps I can be of help. I understand you are booked into a hotel in the centre of the city. I would have suggested somewhere a little more discreet, but we can discuss that during our first meeting that I have arranged for after the dinner I have organised for this evening.

Dinner was a bit of a sombre affair as the three visitors to Mexico were well aware that their venture might turn out to be a tragedy as they planned to enter a dark tunnel without knowing the location of the exit.

As soon as dinner was over, Arturo led the trio into a small lounge area where they could sit nursing a drink while contemplating the next phase of their journey into the unknown.

Arturo opened the discussion. 'First let me spell out the dangers of what you are proposing. You can't just walk into the lion's den and expect the shaggy host to welcome you with open arms. Pascal's fortress is on the outskirts of Mexico City. His hacienda is situated on a hill top overlooking acres of vineyards, plantations of olive groves, and lemon bushes, and is without an invitation, virtually impregnable. There are armed guards all over the estate and there is only one road into the hacienda and that is protected by a manned guard post behind a metal barrier to prevent anyone approaching the hacienda without permission.'

'The hacienda has a high outer wall patrolled twenty four hours each day by armed guards. There is a large heavy metal gate giving access to the inner courtyard where according to reports savage dogs roam freely at night.'

'Armed guards patrol the inner walkways and Don Pascal has several enforcers available when required to remove any unwelcome visitors. His senior enforcer, who remains virtually at his side at all times, is a Japanese martial arts expert. He is reported to be sixteen or seventeen stone, all of which is hard muscle and is over six feet in height; a formidable and dangerous mixture. We have reports that when the Don sends an invitation to persons who have incurred his displeasure the invitation is accompanied by two enforcers who point out that the invite requires immediate attendance. None of the invitees who enter the hacienda are rarely seen again and the bodies are never found. That scenario is what you suggest becoming involved in to put before the Don a proposal he can't refuse. In my opinion gentlemen you are off your heads to consider such a proposal.'

'However, because you are here, I assume nothing is going to deter you from attempting the impossible, so I will explain my plan in an attempt to checkmate the formidable opposition.'

'I recommend that Senor Crosby accompanied by Roberto request an interview with Don Pascal, while Franklin remains unnamed outside the outer guard post. The reason I suggest Franklin remains outside and unnamed as he could easily become a target for reprisal on St Lucia should the operation become pear shaped. Roberto on the other hand, is authorised to carry a hand gun and has the experience to take care of himself.'

'I, accompanied by my deputy will wait in a radio operated police vehicle on the main highway as back up, but in sight of the hacienda. Should the Don turn nasty he will be aware that I am able to call for reinforcements at the drop of a hat, so I think my plan will ensure your safe return after or if, you gain admission to his castle. If there are any objections to my plan then say so now and I will insist the operation is called off.'

Edwin glanced at his colleagues who showed no sign of lodging an objection so he nodded his acquiesce to Arturo's plan.

The next day at 0800 hours the team met again and listened to Arturo Vegas repeat his planned operation so that there would be no misunderstanding what each person had to do.

– – –

When the back up team was in place, Edwin and Roberto drove up to the barrier where two armed guards waved their vehicle to stop.

Edwin wound down his window and explained to the guard that he wished to see the Senor Pascal on a business matter.

The guard informed him that Senor Pascal was not at home and next time he should telephone for an appointment.

Edwin asked the guard to contact whoever was in charge at the hacienda and inform that person that he possessed the list Senor Pascal was urgently seeking.

Tapping impatiently on the steering wheel with his fingers he waited for an answer.

The other guard asked both Edwin and Roberto to exit the car where he methodically searched them both. Finding no offensive weapons he slowly raised the barrier and waved them through on the inner road to the hacienda. Both of them breathed a sigh of relief that they had passed the first barrier.

At the main gate another guard carried out the same search procedure before opening a small wicker gate for them to gain access to the inner court yard, instructing them to leave their vehicle parked on the road outside.

Inside the courtyard no dogs were evident but another armed guard escorted them to the main entrance to the Don's residence.

The formidable Japanese giant awaited them and indicated without words that they should follow him. They were then shown into a large open lounge with French style windows that were open onto an inner courtyard where a fountain gushed into the air giving a feeling of inner coolness to the viewers.

Another person with Latin American features was sitting on one of the settees eyeing his visitors up and down. 'I am Don Pascal's advisor and I want to know how you came to acquire this so called list and what you want in payment before you hand it over.'

Edwin shook his head from side to side. 'My name is Edwin

Crosby and I am a lawyer from England representing a client who is currently being charged with the murder of her husband, a man named Warren. As to being informed that you are the Don's advisor, do you think I would have come unprepared. I've seen your photograph at the Central Police Headquarters and know for a fact that you are Don Pascal in person, so let's stop playing silly buggers and get down to the reason why I am here.'

'I possess the list you so urgently want and I am not interested in selling it to you for dollars. I want information that will clear my client of a murder charge and you possess that information.'

The enormous Jap moved quickly forward for such a large frame and positioned himself directly behind Roberto.

Don Pascal eyes turned to slits showing how much venom was waiting to strike. 'Who states I am interested in these so called lists you say you possess?'

'The men who murdered Walter Warren stated that Pascal would be angry if they failed to obtain the list.'

'Do I look angry Senor?'

'You may be concerned now that you know I possess the list you so desperately seek.'

'If I wanted the list you possess, what's to stop me having you taken down to the cellars and making you hand over the list?'

Edwin didn't flinch. 'First, I don't have the list. Second, the person who now possesses the list is in the United Kingdom and even I don't know where it is currently being guarded. Third, your main door is currently being covered from two angles with binoculars, and if I and my colleague don't leave within the next few minutes a police Captain who possesses a search warrant (a little white lie) will call for reinforcements to ensure my release. If I or my colleague is harmed in any way, you will be the first to be arrested and the earlier warrant for your arrest for extortion and murder will be reactivated.'

Don Pascal waved his hand in the direction of his Japanese protector to indicate he should step back and await further instructions. 'You are well informed Mr Crosby, but I have other means of obtaining what I require, now that I know it is in your possession. You may leave my house unharmed, but rest assured we will meet again when the shoe will be on the other foot as you British regularly claim.'

Edwin was determined to have the last word before leaving. 'Her Majesty the Queen has never taken kindly to her citizens being abused when they are perfectly innocent of any wrong doing. You may have a bevy of armed guards around your hacienda protecting you from Mexican law, she can call on hundreds of highly trained soldiers who could open your door with a small can opener and your Mexican police would never know they have been in this cursed country. Good day to you Senor.....I am as sure as you are that we will meet again and quite soon.'

Captain Vegas was relieved when he saw Edwin and Roberto stroll back to their car and drive away from the hacienda.

Ch.30

Back at the car they told Arturo how the exchange of words, threats and counter threats had developed into a standoff.

Arturo asked for a near verbatim of what had transpired. 'At least Don Pascal accepted that he had been recognised. For many months anyone in authority be it police, local government inspector, or the water authorities who asked to see Senor Pascal were informed he was out of the country and any matter would be dealt with by his legal advisor.'

'I always thought the old bugger was secure in his cage. Now we know for sure he's at home to visitors. Unfortunately, with our police chief, judges and town mayors firmly in his pocket it is going to be very difficult to winkle him out of that fortress.'

Arturo glanced down at the notes he had made while listening to Edwin's discourse. 'One issue that seriously concerns me is the Don's threat that he would find an alternative way to obtain the list. I have a feeling he would use his usual tactics and either abduct, or threaten someone close to you, to achieve his objective. The obvious person that comes to mind is Mrs Warren.'

Edwin's face looked aghast. It was one aspect he had not considered.

Arturo had noted the expression. 'In my view you should get Mrs Warren out of the hotel where she is now staying and into an apartment under an assumed name, with you Roberto and anyone of your ex colleagues you can trust implicitly, to watch over her twenty four hours a day until she either comes to trial or we get the perpetrators of this murder behind bars.'

'In the meantime I'll exert some pressure on a couple of past colleagues of mine in the police department to let it be known that sufficient evidence is now available to issue a warrant for the arrest of Don Pascal. He's bound to be told by someone high up in the police department and hopefully will decide to take another long holiday in South America. It might relieve the pressure and buy us time.'

Edwin agreed and said he would telephone the hotel and ask Cara to set the move in operation immediately stressing how dangerous it could be if Julia remained in the hotel. 'I'll warn her that Roberto is on the way to guard her, but insist she moves Julia out of Castries immediately. 'I'm sure Cara will have somewhere in mind, where Julia will be safe until Roberto takes over.'

Roberto was already out of his seat ready to make a move for the airport and bribe an airport official to find him a seat on the next plane to St Lucia.

Producing a copy of the list, Edwin handed it to Arturo on their return to Mexico City. He explained that having seen the code unravelled there was one aspect that could be used in their favour. 'It appears to me that Tibo Simba was in trouble with the syndicate and Walter Warren in particular. He may be unaware that he was a marked man. However if he was made aware that someone in the Mafioso was displeased and became a worried man, we may be able to get him to talk in order to save his neck. If we could promise to get him safely out of Barbados and the Caribbean area in general, he might tell us who his boss is, and what in hell he had done to incur their displeasure.'

Arturo nodded his head to concur.

At the same time, Edwin was pleased that he had the Captain rooting for him. Arturo Vegas was a man to be admired for his brilliant assessment of the changing pattern put before him. In Edwin's view, Roberto was going to be extremely busy once he landed in St Lucia.

Ch.31

On the flight back to St Lucia, Edwin and Franklin held a long discussion assessing all the problems that were suddenly rearing before them. They had entered the lion's den and found him unhelpful and threatening. Now the lion was stalking them and they needed to be ultra cautious once they were back on the Island.

What they and no other member of the enlarged team could have anticipated was an unexpected breakthrough in their unquestionable thirst for help from any quarter.

It arrived as a result of a telephone call one week later from Captain Vegas. 'I received a call from a colleague in the Jamaican Police with whom I maintain regular contact. Apparently two days ago a known Jamaican criminal called Enriqué Castello was arrested after stabbing a man in a downtown bar who has since died. When he was told the charge of wounding with intent would be changed to murder, he offered the investigating officer that he would provide information about a murder on the Island of St Lucia if the charge against him was reduced to manslaughter. He offered to plead guilty to the lesser charge, in the hope that this would bring about a reduced sentence.'

There was a brief pause while Arturo allowed the news to sink in. 'I suggest Edwin that you fly to Jamaica with Franklin and meet my contact who I am assured will allow you to question his prisoner to see what he knows about the murder. Best of luck to you both; keep me informed.'

During the intervening period Edwin and Franklin kept well clear of Julia's new address in case they were already under observation by the Don's team of enforcers.

Cara, wearing a wig and older clothes to disguise her age and bearing, had visited Julia twice, but not immediately after leaving the hotel. Edwin had warned her to do a bit of shopping and sight seeing while checking over her shoulder that she was not being followed. She reported back to Edwin that Julia was very frustrated at being confined to the flat, so Cara bought a dark wig for Julia and they both took evening walks, double checking that no one was interested in them during their perambulations. Cara had the pleasurable opportunity to inform Julia that there appeared to be a breakthrough in the murder investigation and there was renewed hope that the investigating team could at long last prove Julia's innocence. 'Keep your pecker up' she told Julia. 'Edwin has always been confident that he would find proof of your innocence. He's off to Jamaica with Franklin to follow up a lead.'

– – –

When their plane landed at Jamaica's International Airport outside Kingston, Edwin realised he had never visited the Island other than to change planes at the airport.

The Island was not unlike other Islands in the Caribbean, but his first impression on leaving the airport was that there was more poverty than on St Lucia, possibly because of the Island's independence from Britain over 60 years ago.

More interested in the purpose of their visit, Edwin and Franklin made their way to the Capital's Police Department and asked to see Superintendent Oliver Laneson. Edwin found the name alien to the local population until he discovered that the Superintendent was Danish and had lived in Jamaica for many years.

Welcoming them to his office, the Superintendant told them how pleased he was to talk to his old friend Arturo in Mexico. 'Arturo and I go back many years from my time in the FBI when I was based in Florida. I scratched his back and he scratched mine when we had problems with Mexican citizens boating across the Caribbean intent on reaching the Promised Land.'

'I'll take you down to Enriqué's cell and leave one of my officer's with you to ensure he behaves while you interview him.

Please come back to my office after you conclude the interview because I am interested in what he has to say.'

Enriqué was lying on his bed when the two lawyers were admitted to his cell. They introduced themselves and explained to Enriqué that they could do nothing to help him with his request for a change of plea. 'What we want is a statement from you about how you found out about the murder on St Lucia. We promise that anything you tell us will remain strictly confidential. In order to protect your current situation we guarantee your name will never be used by us.' Franklin took a small recorder from his brief case and put it on the little table in the cell. 'Please tell us what you know about the murder.'

Enriqué got up and sat on the end of his bed before starting to speak. 'You must realise that talking to you and providing information about my friend Emille Segura is putting my life on the line. I would prefer to keep my mouth shut but I need to do anything to ensure I am not charged with murder.'

He then continued to speak into the recorder. Emille had been beaten up by two enforcers from the Mafioso and called me for help, asking me to hide him for a few weeks. His right knee cap had been broken by a blow from a baseball bat and one eye had been removed when he refused to answer their questions about someone being killed on a yacht outside St Lucia. When they threatened to remove his other eye, he had no alternative but to betray the other man who he claimed committed the murder.'

Because his injuries were serious I immediately took him to hospital and told the authorities that he had fallen off a wall we were climbing over to get into a park that was closed. He caught his head on a bush in the border and one of the branches pieced his eye. He is still in hospital with his leg in plaster and I used to visit him every day until I was arrested and brought here. If you go and visit Emille and ask him questions about the murder the Mafioso will soon find out and I don't believe they will allow him to leave the hospital except in a box. I have never been to St Lucia in my life and had no idea my friend was involved in Mafia business. If I had known I would have warned him off and made sure he stayed on Jamaica and stuck to what he was good at......pushing dope to the tourists. I have nothing else to add.'

Franklin switched off the recorder. 'What hospital is your friend in and what is the ward number?'

'Kings Memorial Hospital Ward 11'

Thanking Enriqué for being so helpful Edwin told him he would have a word with the police superintendent to see if he could do anything to alleviate the worries of his prisoner.'

They shook hands and left for the hospital, forgetting until they were half way to the hospital that they were expected to report back to the superintendent

Edwin decided there was no point in returning and decided he would make contact with the Super., at the earliest opportunity and offer his apologies.

Ch.32

On arrival at the hospital and presenting their credentials they were initially refused admission. They asked the clerk behind the desk to telephone Superintendent Laneson at Police HQ and give him their names. After a brief pause she told them that the visit was approved and added that there was a message from the Superintendent to call and see him at HQ after their chat with the patient. They were shown up to Ward 11 and to the bedside of Emille Segura who was lying on his bed with the right leg in plaster from ankle to hip and a bandage over one eye.

Emille not only looked puzzled by the strangers suddenly appearing at his bedside, but here was a tinge of fear in his remaining eye.

Edwin introduced Franklin and himself and explained quietly to Emille that they had recently seen his friend Enriqué in a prison cell and had recorded a statement that his friend had given voluntarily. 'You can check our credentials with Superintendent Laneson at police headquarters, but before you do so, you had better hear the reason why we have come to see you.'

Franklin gave him a detailed run down of their long search for witnesses to the murder. 'Your friend has already confirmed that you and another unnamed person were involved and that you have been tortured by the Mafioso to reveal the present whereabouts of your associate. We noticed the fear in your eye and appreciate that you may feel the Mafia's enforcers will return once they have finished questioning your friend.'

'There is no doubt that while you are in this public hospital you are in great danger and we are both surprised that the police have not had you transferred to a private room and placed a twenty four hour guard on your door.'

'My colleague and I are prepared to arrange your immediate transfer to a private hospital, have you made comfortable in a private room, and will arrange for a guard to be placed outside your door twenty four hours each day. The costs of your care and security will be met by Mr Crosby,' he added, nodding to Edwin who was still standing at the foot of the bed looking rather surprised as they had not discussed this arrangement prior to this meeting.

Emille looked wide eyed and anxious. 'And what do you want from me?' he asked knowing full well what the two visitors required.

Edwin intervened. 'I am well aware that any information you give us about the murder of Walter Warren on the Sunray will put your life in danger; not that it will be any different from your current situation. 'If you agree to the move my colleague has suggested, we will remain with you until you are safely in bed in the hospital of our choice. As soon as you have made and signed a written statement I will arrange for it to be countersigned by a local Notary who will not be allowed to read your statement. His only obligation is to witness your signature on the document. Once that has been achieved I promise to place you on the first flight out of Jamaica to England, where my staff will ensure your safety and ultimately find you a permanent home in the country of your choice; although I might add that you will be much safer in England than most countries.'

'If you are not prepared to make a statement then we will say goodbye and leave you in God's hands.'

Emille's face was a mass of confusion but he knew his life was on the line and that the hospital would not have let these two lawyers access to his bedside unless it had been approved by a high ranking police officer. 'When will you move me, if I agree to your request?'

'As soon as I can arrange transport we will leave together' said Edwin, opening his mobile to ring the Superintendent.

Oliver Laneson, although firmly committed to bring the murderers of Walter Warren to justice, with the added hope that there may a lead from this investigation to help him bring certain Mafia leaders to justice, accepted the reality that the young man's life was also at risk from Mafia justice. He quickly organised a police vehicle to move Emille while arranging a private room at the St Clements Private Hospital some miles from Kingston and near enough to the airport if required.

The Superintendent contacted the senior consultant in charge of Emille's treatment and explained the reason for moving him to a more secure locality. Arrangements were made with the night Sister and Emille was made ready for the transfer without anyone in the hospital being made aware of his new location.

The move was made that night in the dark and Edwin and Franklin accompanied by two police officers ensured everything ran smoothly.

Ch.33

As soon as Emille was settled into his new location, it was obvious he was out of his depth, much like a fish out of water. A private room with views over immaculate gardens and nurses obviously caring about his condition was something he had never experienced in the past. From a rough family background this new experience of how those with the ability to pay for private health insurance was a little overpowering for the young man.

Edwin tried to put Emille at his ease, but it was obvious that he was going to take time to get used to this new environment. However, time was not on the side of Edwin. He urgently needed a solution to the current stalemate being experienced by his client who was still convinced that she was going to prison for many years.

His top priority at the moment was to convince Emille Segura that a statement was required that would hopefully prove the innocence of his client.

With an overnight comfortable sleep in his new environment Emille gave his consent to make a recording of his statement.

Edwin and Franklin waited with bated breath for Emille to speak into the microphone linked to the recorder.

Emille took a deep breath before he spoke. Putting his hand under his chin while clasping his jaw he pondered over how he would approach his opening remarks. In a rather broad Jamaican local accent he started to speak and shocked Edwin with his opening remark.

'My friend of many years Carlos Jacelin is, like me, a drug addict. In order to finance our habit we were both prepared to take on any work that funded our need for a snort. We were recruited by a Mafia enforcer who never revealed his name and instructed to board the yacht Sunray and obtain by any means a list held by an Englishman who was called Warren.'

'We were taken to the location of Warren's yacht anchored in Rodney Bay by the Captain of a large powerful cruiser called Northern Star. The cruiser sailed close to the Sunray in the dark and Carlos and I used a small air inflated boat to creep up on Sunray. We boarded the yacht without incident and were suddenly surprised when this stark naked man appeared on deck. Carlos was the first to react and used his cosh to knock the man unconscious. We tied him up and fastened him to the cockpit rail until he recovered. Once the man came to, Carlos asked him if he was called Warren and where the list we were seeing was kept. The man told us in no uncertain terms to ef off. Carlos coshed him again and broke his arm. When he still refused to tell us where the list was, Carlos broke his knee cap and his nose with two violent blows.'

'We left Warren to recover from his initial beating and went below to the cabin to see if we could find his safe. To our surprise and my mates delight we found Warren's bird lying naked on the bed. Carlos was the first to react and grabbed the frightened woman before raping her. I was not sure that I liked what happened because Mrs Warren, if that was who she was, was crying like a baby and pleaded with us to leave her alone.'

'Carlos asked me if I wanted a free shag with a white bimbo and when I declined he told me if I didn't give her the old one two, he would be obliged to cut off my dick and show it to the boss as a souvenir. Not wanting to lose my manhood I mounted the bird and did my bit to keep him happy.'

We dragged the bird up on deck to let her husband see how we had treated his wife hoping he would tell us where he had hidden the list, or give us the combination to his safe. The bugger was still obstinate even though he knew we had ravished his wife. Carlos was always a hothead and unpredictable and I was surprised and frightened when he suggested we tip the man overboard as he was refusing to cooperate. I told him that the boss would be very upset if we returned without the list but he had already made up his mind. He attached the anchor to the man's feet and asked me to help him throw the geezer overboard. I admit I was frightened because I knew the man would drown and we were committing a murder. With no choice but to agree, I did as Carlos asked and took the man by his arms and chucked him over the side. As soon as he submerged we left the yacht and rowed back to the cruiser where the captain gave us a right bollocking for chucking Warren overboard, before warning us that the Don would be more than angry at our failure to recover the list.'

'It was two weeks later when I was walking home back to my wife when a car pulled up at the curb and a man with an automatic waved me into the back seat. They took me to scrap yard outside the town where it was quiet and made me tell them where my friend Carlos was hiding. I didn't think Carlos was hiding from anybody, he had just dumped his partner for another more attractive bird and was staying in her flat.'

'The enforcer and his mate set about me with a baseball bat and a flick knife until I could hold out no longer and gave them his address. I have not heard from him all the time I have been in hospital and am worried about what they will have done to him when they found him at his bird's address.'

Emille shook his head indicating he had nothing else to add.

Franklin left the recorder disc rolling. 'What is Carlos's new address?'

'Flat 32A Benfica Walk'

'Have you got a picture of him?'

'No.'

'You were taken to St Lucia in a Cruiser?'

'Yes'

'How long did it take?'

'About three days'

'Where did you board the cruiser?'

'Savanna La Mar Marina.'

'Is that where it is normally moored?'

'I expect so. Carlos and I helped to crew the boat and that was where we used to go aboard.'

'Does it have a regular Captain?'

'Yes.'

'His name please?'

'Hulio Stanza.'

'What colour is the cruiser?'

'Dark Blue, with a white stripe at the water line.'

'Its name?'

'Northern Star'

'How many crew does it normally have?'

'Sometimes there are only two; but four of us for a long journey, because we have to sleep using a rota system.'

'Do you know if the captain and the other crew men are armed?'

'Always.'

'Finally, why did you kill Walter Warren?'

'I didn't want to. We couldn't get him to tell us where the list was hidden. We could have reported back that we were unsuccessful and the boss would have sent two others to try again. Carlos has always been a hot head and when he is coked up he is unpredictable.'

Edwin decided to take control. 'Emille, my colleague needs to find a computer terminal in the hospital to type out your statement. He will have to leave us for about twenty minutes. When he returns you must check your statement. You can ask me to alter anything you disagree with, but once the statement is signed by you in the presence of a Notary, I will make arrangements for you to be flown to England accompanied by a guard to ensure your safety all the way to your new home.'

While Franklin was away from the beside and before he commenced to prepare the statement for signature he telephoned a local Notary he knew personally and promised him five hundred

Carib dollars in cash if he would come post haste to the hospital to witness a patient signing an important statement.

Franklin was away for just over half an hour, and by the time he arrived back at the bedside the Notary had arrived and was waiting to witness Emille's signature on each page of the statement. The 500 dollars quickly disappeared into his pocket as the highest fee he had ever earned in his life.

The following evening Emille, who had never been in an aeroplane in his life, flew out of St Lucia seated next to the armed air marshal who accompanied flights to and from the UK as a normal routine to combat terrorism.

Ch.34

Roberto worked his butt off dealing with all the problems facing him. Getting to Barbados was never easy due to the lack of flights from St Lucia. The daily ferry appeared to be the best option so he booked passage and had to admit he enjoyed the short journey across the bay. Once on the Island he asked to be directed to the popular pleasure beach and soon saw the beach bar where Tibo Samba was supposed to work.

The bar was typical of beach bars being constructed of timber with a thatched roof. Three sides were open to the sea and tall bar seats were placed around each side of the bar on a wooden platform. Nearly all were occupied by sea worshipers, the ladies in skimpy bikinis with all over tans, and the men, Adonis types, dark brown and wearing those long knee length swimming trunks that are currently the fashion. All were chatting to each other amiably, while drinking a range of powerful cocktails, guaranteed to ensure that couples ended up in bed irrespective of sex.

Tibo Samba was easily recognised as he moved quickly from customer to customer, dispensing drinks as if they were going out of fashion. With only one vacant seat in the corner of the bar Roberto climbed onto the stool and ordered a Pino Colader, a mixture of rum, cream of coconut and pineapple. It was too sweet for his taste but with the rum being diluted by fruit juices, he reckoned he could while the time away and repeat the order to fill in time if Tibo was unable to get away from his duties.

When Tibo served him with his next drink Roberto asked him if he would be free soon to have a quiet talk.

'Who wants to know and why should I be interested?' he demanded.

Roberto looked him directly in the eyes, hopefully to show he was not threatening. 'I am a private detective currently employed by a British Lawyer defending a murder case. I suggest we discuss the problem somewhere more private than across this bar, but if you are worried about being overheard we can sit on the sand a few yards away.'

Tibor nodded his head an acceptance. 'Give me a few minutes to tell my assistant where I will be if she needs my help.'

Ten minutes later, Roberto and Tibo Simba were sitting on the hot sand within calling distance of the bar staff.

'What the hell is this all about?' he demanded. 'And what has it got to do with me?'

Roberto assured him that his client was not directly interested in Tibo's 'extra curricular activities' as he put it. 'What you do outside managing a beach side bar is not our concern. But the information that has come into my possession is definitely your concern, and you have my client to thank for arranging for me to come to Barbados and warn you.'

Now that that he had Tibo Simba's full attention, Roberto continued. 'The person who employs me is in possession of a coded list of visits to persons who may be involved in a number of illegal deals. Some of those persons were to receive considerable sums of money in exchange for goods. Others were required to pay lesser sums for services received from the same source. After further discreet enquiries we are fairly sure that the person involved in doing deals, was linked to the Mafia and could have been one of their heavy mob of enforcers.'

'In your case the list showed that no money was expected to change hands. You were listed for a visit to El Dey, the name of your beach bar at 2230 on a Tuesday some weeks ago.'

Although heavily tanned by the tropical sun Tibo' face turned a distinct pale colour and he looked as if he was about to be sick.

Roberto finished what he was about to say. 'The last bits of the code were the letters rfl. Tibo's tension was obvious when he puffed out his cheeks and exploded air from his mouth in an attempt to relax his tort muscles.

Roberto performed the coup de gràce. 'We think, but are not absolutely sure that the letters 'rfl' mean 'remove from list'. If this list is Mafia inspired, then we know the name of the person scheduled to visit you and that he was instructed to remove you from the list. Assuming that this person is a Mafia enforcer then there would be only way he would carry out the instruction, and I don't think from the look on your face that you have any doubts what that would be.'

'The thing is Tibo, I have an offer you may find hard to refuse.'

When Tibo looked as if he was ready to grasp at any straw on offer, Roberto continued. 'Fortunately for you, the man whom we think was sent to arrange your death has himself been murdered, so you have been granted a temporary reprieve. You can of course ignore what I have just imparted to you and get up and return to your nice little bar, while I will disappear into the crowd on the sea front. Then you can wait for the same people to deal with their obvious problem at a later date.'

Tibo never moved. The question in his troubled mind remained unasked.

'I assume,' Roberto said, 'that this has all to do with the drugs you have been selling at inflated prices to the young holiday makers swarming round your bar. Have you failed to pay the Cartel for the drugs they supplied you? Or have you sold their last consignment, or consignments, on to another Cartel prepared to cut you up if you try to prevent them taking over this lucrative territory?'

Tibo remained silent.

'Obviously you now realise that you need to beat a hasty retreat from this area, or your body will disappear into the deep waters of the Caribbean and only your nearest and dearest will shed any tears. Assuming you have a valid passport and not too much of the readies available, my client is prepared to offer you five hundred Caribbean Dollars here and now in cash, to allow you to take a ferry away from this island as far as the cash will take you. From there you will be on your own, although I have little doubt you have funds tucked away in one of those offshore banks from your drug activities that will allow you to relocate to South America, or any other Continent willing to accept you.'

'In return for the generosity of my client in allowing you to escape from Neptune's welcoming Parlour, my client and other interested parties need to know who supplied you with drugs, and who you paid, or owed money to.'

Roberto, ever able to assess the look of relief on a villains face when he is given a way out of his dilemma told Tibo it was decision making time. 'I'll give you five minutes,' he said glancing at his watch; 'then I'm off to the ferry.'

When Tibo immediately started to respond it was Roberto's turn to be surprised. 'I received my drugs from a runner who never gave me his name, but I paid the cash directly to the police sergeant who is secretary to the Commissioner. The sergeant came once a month to the bar to collect what he called a large percentage of my indirect takings from the young crowd that are aware what I keep under the counter. I was allowed to keep ten percent, but the sergeant insisted I give him two separate payments of five percent and eighty five percent; obviously putting the five percent into his own back pocket. Every bugger is on the take around here.'

Roberto found it hard to believe that a senior government official was linked to the Mafia and taking his cut from their nefarious activities. Knowing how the mafia ensnared its wide net it seemed to Roberto that the Police Commissioner would be allowed to deduct five per cent for himself for turning a blind eye to the narcotics entering the Island, before paying the balance over to people like Walter Warren who now appeared to be a member of the cartel; albeit a small fish in a very large pond.

With his recorder running in his pocket Roberto handed over five hundred dollars to Tibo Samba and walked away, not the least bit interested whether this scum bag lived or died. On the other hand, the Police Commissioner and his sergeant were in for a shock when the Drug Enforcement Agency eventually paid them a surprise visit.

Tibo Simba sat on the sand for a further few minutes contemplating what action he needed to take to prevent his early demise. Having provided this stranger with the names of the local drug controllers he reckoned his life could be measured in hours rather than days.

He got up from the sand told his staff to stop serving drinks and instructed them to pull down the shutters as soon as the last drink had been consumed. Leaving all his worldly goods behind in the bar, he made his way to the ferry terminal and booked a passage to Panama. On arrival at the canal he discovered there was a vacancy for an assistant cook on a large freighter bound for the Far East. He impressed the chef and the captain at his interview and was accepted.

Tibo accepted that his new position would keep him out of the limelight for months, and provide him with a companion at all times to ensure the mafia could not get their hands on him as long as he was at sea.

His rapid disappearance into thin air left his small staff temporarily unemployed and his unavailability to be called by the DEA as a witness when they eventually arrested the drug smugglers.

Ch.35

With the recording from Emille now in his possession, Edwin thought it sensible to involve Superintendent Oliver Laneson. Now that he was aware that the men manning the cruiser Northern Star were armed, it would be foolhardy for him to pursue a course of action that might result in him ending on the sea bed, already it seems, littered with the bodies of anyone attempting to cross swords with the dreaded Mafia.

Entering the Police Headquarters he was shown directly to the Superintendent's rather sparse office. After shaking hands Edwin was immediately taken to task for leaving the hospital without first making contact with Oliver Laneson.

'I can understand your need to spirit away Emille Segura as his life was already in great danger,' said the Superintendent. Fortunately your reckless decision to get him out of the hospital turned out to be successful, but without police protection the result could have been very different and you could have been prosecuted and found guilty on a number of charges; culpable homicide being the most serious. Next time you think about trying to outwit the Mafia talk to me first. I get extremely angry when novices try to become professional policemen and interfere with the due processes of the law.'

Edwin accepting the rollicking he so richly deserved, expressed his most sincere apologies whilst adding that he thought making contact with the police and waiting for help would put his most important witness in possibly jeopardy. 'The fact that I acted promptly, means my witness is now out of the reach of the Mafia,' he explained to the Superintendent.

Oliver Laneson shook his head in despair. 'No one is ever out of the reach of the Mafia anywhere in the world. If they want someone dead they will even use bribed police officers to carry out their order. Don't be so bloody naive Mr. Crosby, the Cosa Nostra is way out of your league. I hate to draw your attention to incompetence in issues that should only be handled by trustworthy police officers, but your Enrigué Costello was found hanged in his cell this morning. He was prepared to do a deal in an attempt to reduce his sentence. Unfortunately the Mafia must have paid one or two prison officers a handsome sum of money to ensure he was not around to act as a witness. Their web is so wide that someone at the hospital must have reported your interview. Now you know why I am so bloody angry with you. Now tell me why you want to see me so urgently?'

Edwin played the recording of Emille's statement and when it was finished he told Oliver that he accepted he was now out of his depth and wondered if the Superintendent could offer advice on how to deal with the Captain of the Northern Star, who according to Emille was implicated in the death of Walter Warren.

When Oliver Laneson smiled, his face registered that he appreciated someone recognising his expertise in criminology. 'I will take the captain by surprise and have him and his crew arrested and his boat placed in quarantine. I will interview him on the cruiser as soon as he has been formally cautioned, before his Mafia boss can call on 'legal advisors' to warn the captain to keep his mouth shut.'

Edwin's legal brain went into overdrive. 'Surely once you caution the captain he can demand legal representation of his choice to be in attendance during your interview.'

Again Oliver smiled. 'The captain will realise his situation is rather delicate once the arrest warrant has been served. His boss will not accept that the captain can be trusted to keep his mouth shut even with 'legal assistance'. He will take immediate steps to ensure the captain and the crew are not able to talk about the secret visit to St Lucia. I am confident that the captain will accept *my* offer to provide legal representation while *I* try to discover why he went to St Lucia and for what purpose.'

The Superintendent spent some time on the phone issuing instructions before replacing the receiver and turning back to Edwin. 'In thirty minutes my car will be waiting at the rear door accompanied by an unmarked police van with six armed police officers. I intend to drive down to Montego Bay and join a coastguard cutter. The Officer in charge of the cutter will take us across to the yacht marina at Savanna-la-Mar where I will detain the Northern Star and her crew. You are invited to join me at your own risk of course, because we know the crew are armed and may resist. Once the crew have been detained by my team, you may question the Captain about his part in the murder. I think on this occasion your colleague Mr Jenson should remain here. I can't afford to endanger two civilians if the going gets rough. It's not good for my ego.'

The drive to Montego Bay along the busy coast road took nearly an hour and a half with the hot sun baking the armed officers in the rear of the large van, while the Superintendent and Edwin enjoyed the cool breeze from the air conditioning fitted to the car.

The Cutter was moored to the quayside awaiting the arrival of the boarding team. The Captain saluted and pointed out to his superior officer that his own crew were equally capable of handling three armed men.

Returning the salute, Oliver pointed out that once the men were arrested and cuffed they had to be taken back to the cells in Kingston for questioning, while the Cutter's crew would need to get back to sea should there be another emergency requiring their services.

Arriving at the Savanna Marina two hours later, the Captain was informed by the manager, that the Northern Star had put to sea not thirty minutes earlier heading north towards Cuba. Oliver turned to Edwin fuming. 'Someone on my staff got a message to the Captain of the cruiser that we were on our way to arrest him. When I get back to the office I'll track who made the phone call and woe betide that officer when I get my hands on him'......he hesitated. 'Or her. Whatever monthly bribe they received for keeping the mafia informed on the movements of my team will be of little use to them in prison.'

The Coastguard Cutter with its marine engines on full power thrust its way out to sea with the radar officer scanning his screen as he searched for a pin prick that would tell him that a small ship was heading in a northerly direction and its current speed.

The Captain was well aware that the Northern Star could match his own ship for speed but he doubted if the cruisers captain would burn fuel in an effort to get to Cuba. Once clear of Jamaica he would not expect the coast guard patrol to be aware of his intended route once he was out of sight of the marina.

The Cutter maintained its present maximum speed and soon had the Northern Star in sight through powerful binoculars. Although the ship in front increased its speed when it saw the coastguard appear out of the sea mist it was too late, and when the cutter ordered it to heave too, the captain had little alternative knowing the cutter had a powerful gun mounted on the foredeck that could rip his cruiser to shreds within minutes.

Switching off the powerful engine the Captain of the cruiser waited patiently for the Coastguard Cutter to come alongside. The Captain of the cutter had been pre-warned that the men onboard were armed so he kept his ship well away from trouble. Using a tannoy he ordered the cruiser's crew to move from the cockpit to the stem with their hands on the heads.

As soon as they were assembled he closed the gap allowing two of his crew to jump aboard and handcuff them behind their backs. Securing the two boats together he told the Superintendent that he could take his team onto the cruiser.

Leaving the two crewmen sitting on the front deck the Captain of the cruiser was led into the main saloon and made to sit down opposite the Super and Edwin.

Receiving a nod from the Superintendent, Edwin placed his recording device on the table top and switched it on.

Superintendent Laneson wasted no time on formalities. 'I'm a police officer and the man with the recorder is a lawyer. You and your crew are under arrest. The charges will be listed later. One of my men will issue the appropriate caution before you are all taken into protective custody. I am aware you are Hulio Stanza captain of the Northern Star and that this boat is owned and registered by Federated Industries Inc., a company registered in Panama.'

He paused for a moment as one of officers entered the cabin with a piece of paper that he handed over to his chief. Oliver glanced at the note and looked at the Captain of the cruiser. 'My team of officers have recovered three automatic Glock 18's and three hand guns in the for'ard cabin together with approximately twenty pounds of pure cocaine. I feel sure more drugs will be found when my officers' commence to search the rest of this tub. My friend has a number of questions he wishes to ask you, but before he does so I have one or two pertinent points to make.'

'You must be aware that you don't have to answer any questions put to you without a lawyer of your choice being present. You may recall I said I was taking you and your crew into protective custody. When your boss discovers as he soon will, that you have been arrested and that his cruiser has been impounded, every effort will be made to ensure you and the two men on the foredeck are silenced one way or another.'

'You can of course forgo your right to legal representation and voluntarily answer some questions that will be put before you. I cannot of course guarantee your safety one hundred per cent, but I will put you in a safe house, guarded by some of my own officers who I would trust with my life.'

Captain Stanza took no time to ponder over his reply. He had already concluded that his life was about to be cut short and readily accepted the Superintendent's offer.

The questioning began. 'We are aware that Federated Industries is only a cover to give you a degree of legitimacy as you trade between various ports in the Caribbean, but who is the real owner of this expensive tub?'

The Captain gave a terrified look. 'If I tell you I am a dead man.'

'Captain your life was on the line as soon as two of your crew murdered a man on a yacht outside Rodney Bay.'

'What makes you suggest that they were from my boat?' he asked.

'I have a witness in custody who has already admitted he was put aboard a certain yacht from your boat. That is why we detained you. Now you have gun running and drugs to add to the offence that can put you inside for at least thirty years.'

'They were not supposed to kill him; they acted outside their instructions and have since paid the ultimate penalty.'

'So you admit you are aware of their deaths?'

'Everyone involved with the Mafia is made aware of the consequences of failure which is why I could never resign from my position as captain.'

'So who is your boss?'

'I don't really know. All my instructions come from various enforcers who remain nameless. I can only guess that they get their instructions from whoever is head of the Mafia in this area.'

'We are seeking one of the two men who killed Walter Warren a man named Carlos Jacelin. Do you know where he is?'

Again the captain blanched. 'You know the names of both of the two men?' he asked, looking astonished.

'As I explained, we have one of them in protective custody. Now tell me where I can find your other crewman Carlos.'

'I suspect he's now at the bottom of the Caribbean with a heavy chain round his ankles. He was taken off my boat by two big enforcers and carried to another cruiser before it headed out into the bay. I assumed he was in serious trouble but whatever he did wrong was not my concern.'

'There you are wrong captain. You were in charge when you took these two men on your cruiser to St Lucia. The fact that they committed a murder becomes your responsibility. You must have been aware when you approached the Sunray just before midnight that they intended to commit a serious crime. You may not have expected it to be a murder, but you were the man in charge at the time so you became an accomplice.'

'Will I be tried for the murder?' asked the Captain.

The Superintendent ignored the question. 'How did your two crewmen get aboard the Sunray without being observed by other yachtsmen anchored in the bay?

'My cruiser is painted a dark blue partly to make my boat undetectable in the dark. I approached the Sunray from the seaward side, with the engine just holding the boat against the current so it was unlikely I would be spotted in the dark. When the men returned in the dinghy I crept away on low engine revs.'

'Have you ever heard the name Pascal mentioned by anyone visiting your boat?'

'No.'

'You seem very positive. If I find out later that you have lied it will be added to the charges and I feel any judge will add on a further number of years for protecting your boss.'

The Captain of the cruiser blanched for a moment before replying. 'I repeat I have never heard the name mentioned.'

'One final question before I hand you over to this lawyer. Why didn't you leave this boat when you knew it belonged to the Mafia?'

'I was invited to become the Captain when I was interviewed by someone from Federated Industries after I had been shown around the cruiser. The pay was way above anything I had previously earned so I was delighted to accept. On my second trip to Venezuela I witnessed drugs being smuggled aboard. When I objected I was 'advised' that I either did the job I was being overpaid to do without question, or my contract would be terminated. The message was loud and clear. Since that day I have carried drugs, guns, and illegal passengers, always hoping that someday I would have enough money to disappear to Canada and the northern wilderness where I would never be found.'

Oliver Laneson looked at Edwin. 'Over to you,' he muttered.

Edwin looked angrily in the direction of the Captain. 'Did you know that there was a woman on board the yacht when you sent the two men to board the Sunray?'

'Yes, I was told that Warren had a wife who was most likely to be on board.'

'When the two crew men returned to your boat did they tell you they had raped the captain's wife before killing him?'

'I heard one of them boasting she was icing on the cake lying naked on the bed in the cabin.'

'Did you know they had killed her husband by dumping him overboard while still alive?'

'No, Carlos muttered that the job had been done, but the boss would not be pleased with the result.'

'Did you know they were trying to recover a list from Warren?'

'Yes.'

'And who were you expected to give the list to when it was recovered?'

'I have no idea; that was Carlos's responsibility.'

'Do you honestly expect me to believe that?' asked Edwin. 'As the senior officer on board the Northern Star, surely you were given the responsibility to collect and hand over the list to whosoever came aboard later to collect it?'

'I still insist Carlos was responsible for handing the list over.'

'I doubt if a jury would believe that.'

Edwin made a note on a pad before continuing. 'My client Mrs Warren, has been charged with her husband's murder. Do you think she was involved in having her husband killed?'

The Captain thought briefly before responding to the question. 'I honestly have never heard her name mentioned by anyone until I saw her name in the local newspaper.'

'Thank you captain for being so candid; I'm not really sorry to hear of your dilemma and to be quite candid I would hate to be in your shoes. The Cosa Nostra and all its tentacles have a very long arm and I doubt if you would be safe even in Canada. May God go with you, because He above seems to be the only one who can offer you salvation from the terrible crimes you have committed in the past.'

Edwin switched off the recorder and watched as the captain and his two crewmen were transferred to the Coastguard Cutter with their hands handcuffed behind their backs.

Turning to Oliver Laneson he asked what would happen once the three men were locked away in Kingston?

'They'll be dead long before they can come to trial,' he replied, shrugging his shoulders as if it was nothing to do with him.

'You promised the Captain you would keep him safe.'

Oliver shrugged his shoulders again. 'Yes, I did promise,' he replied, with a woeful smile on his face.

Ch.36

Edwin was convinced that somehow or other he and Franklin had inadvertently opened a can of worms.

This thought was confirmed when the Royal Barbados Defence Force including their Department of Customs and Excise, supported by the American Drug Enforcement Agency raided the home and office of the Police Commissioner and placed him and his personal assistant under arrest.

For two days the two civil servants were questioned about their links with the Mafia that they initially strongly denied. When they were informed that their activities in the drug trade had been monitored for months, it eventually broke their stubborn resistance when each one blamed the other.

As both faced a long term in imprisonment their individual plea for clemency brought to light some startling developments. The Commissioner claimed he was enrolled into the Mafia organisation for the distribution of narcotics by the friend of a friend. Further intensive questioning by Customs and Excise Officers brought to light that a police officer on the neighbouring island of St Lucia was his main contact for the import of narcotics from Columbia and Venezuela. A Detective Sergeant Totti was named.

The Customs Enforcement Agency on St Lucia claimed they had no knowledge of anyone in the police force being involved in narcotics but they would investigate and take positive action against any offenders.

While Edwin was unaware of the ongoing investigations, Roberto's friendly contacts in the police department admitted that information had been received from the Customs and Excise Department in Barbados that certain police officers' on St Lucia were believed to be in the pay of the Mafioso to turn a blind eye to the import of narcotics to the Island.

– – –

Everything was happening so quickly before Edwin realised that he had a client to consider who would be worried sick about the coming retrial. Now that he had something more substantial to present to a jury, he accepted that he had not brought his client up to date with the improvement in her prospects of an acquittal.

On second thoughts, he accepted the possibility that the Mafia would be trying to track her down after she had disappeared unexpectedly from the Adelphi Hotel and that he was the most likely person other than Franklin to be followed. In addition he couldn't attempt to speak to her on the telephone because his phone might also be tapped.

Maybe he was becoming a bit paranoid he thought, but one should never under estimate the Mafia and particularly Don Pascal whose recent instructions to his minions had been ignored with disastrous consequences. There were lots of sea creatures on the bed of the Caribbean, but if the initial count over the last few weeks was anything to go by, Neptune's Parlour over the years had become a vast repository for more victims of Mafia vendettas than would fill all the public cemeteries on the Caribbean Islands.

Edwin spoke to Franklin about his concern about Julia's security being breached. Franklin suggested Edwin write Julia a letter explaining the circumstances and the reason he has not made a visit. Franklin said he would use a friend to push the letter through her letter box. Edwin hated writing letters and generally used the recorder, or took one his secretaries into court to note in shorthand a record of the proceedings. On this occasion he had no option but to sit down and set out some brief facts about what had occurred during his visit to Mexico and Jamaica.

One aspect of the famous list that puzzled him was the fact that Detective Sergeant Totti was not mentioned, so Raphael Bonico who worked at the Lido Star Hotel must be in cahoots with Sergeant Totti. The plot thickens, thought Edwin. Never the less he was acutely aware that if Detective Inspector Bishop turned nasty he now had Sergeant Totti's name as a weapon he could use ruthlessly to protect his client.

He was contemplating how to arrange a meeting with the Prosecuting Attorney to convince him that in the best interests of justice, he, the Public Prosecutor should seriously consider withdrawing the charges against Mrs Warren; (a) to avoid the unnecessary costs of a retrial and (b) avoid the embarrassment of holding a lengthy court case and having a jury find Mrs Warren not guilty. His telephone rang giving him a brief startle at the unexpected interruption to his thoughts.

Superintendent Laneson was on the line from Jamaica. 'Hi Edwin, how are you coping with your pre trial paper work?' Without waiting for a response he added, 'I'm afraid it's bad news from this end. I arranged for the Captain of the Northern Star to be placed in a safe house under the watchful eyes of some of my staff before his case came to court. The rules for the team watching him were specific, or so I thought. Everywhere in the house Captain Stanza went, someone was to accompany him. If he went to bed the bedroom door had to be left open; same with the toilet. However one of my team let Stanza close the toilet door after he complained that it was embarrassing for him to sit and shit with someone watching him. The officer allowed him to close the door and Stanza escaped through a small window. He left a piece of flesh behind squeezing through the window, but he managed to escape.'

'I put out an 'all parties search' but he has disappeared into the blue. He has to be somewhere on the island because every avenue of escape is blocked but so far there has been no sight of him. I know Edwin that you have the recording he made which will assist you at the retrial of your client, but getting him into court in Jamaica would have strengthened your case. I'll keep you posted when we apprehend him. My officer at the flat is in deep shit and it could wreck his career. I have put my trust in these men and one has let me down by making a simple mistake.'

There was a lengthy pause that caused Edwin some disquiet before Oliver continued. 'More bad news I'm afraid. The two crew members were locked in cells prior to being conveyed to prison. One was found dead in his cell this morning and the coroner suspects poison was placed in his food. The other man is nearly out of his mind and refuses anything to eat or drink until we promise to transport him off the Island to somewhere safe....if there is such a place. I am sorry to ruin your day Edwin, but I can assure you my current situation is far worse. The Commissioner is set to hang me out to dry over this sad debacle.

Before Edwin could make any comment Oliver replaced the phone on its cage. Obviously someone else was in his office listening to this call.

Ch.37

Franklin and Edwin had a council of war to decide their next move and both agreed a meeting with the Public Prosecutor should be next on the agenda. However events during the next few minutes called for a rethink.

A long distance call from Edwin's father took precedence when he demanded to know how much longer Edwin expected to remain on St Lucia as legal issues at home requiring his son's presence where piling up. He pointed out that looking after Edwin's only witness who was still alive was becoming a major problem. 'The man is missing his family and friends and we are unable to convince him of the dangers facing him if he returns to the Caribbean. Unsurprisingly, he has not adapted to the Liverpool way of life, and constantly complains about the cold, even though our staff have done their best to keep him entertained and seen that he has adequate clothing to meet the change in climatic conditions. Unless the retrial of our client is in the offing, I cannot see how we can prevent him from returning to his homeland where he will quickly become a target for the Mafia. Your observations would be helpful.'

Edwin explained to his father how the research to help Julia Warren had turned into a massive enquiry into the distribution of narcotics in the Caribbean, localised drug abuse, and the implication that the late Walter Warren was no longer the Importer/Exporter they had envisaged. That was before his untimely death as a leading figure in the movement of narcotics between the Caribbean and the United Kingdom.

He explained to his father of his plan to arrange a meeting with the local Prosecutor in an attempt to get the charges against Julia Warren withdrawn. 'I will also try to discover when or if the retrial will be held. Should the date be somewhere in the distance, I promise to return home by the next available flight.'

With his father appeased, Edwin attempted to make contact with the Public Prosecutor who seemed to be most obstructive at any attempt to arrange a meeting, or suggest a date for the retrial to be held.

In the end it was Franklin who suggested that Edwin get in touch with Judge Bell who listened to Edwin's reasons for asking for a meeting.

Judge Bell, had long held the view that Mrs Warren was the victim of political expediency. He agreed to hold a meeting in his Chambers within one week, when he would insist that the Public Prosecutor would be present to put forward his strong reasons for withholding the date for a retrial.

At last Edwin accepted that progress was at last being made.

The following day an urgent telephone call was received from Arturo Vegas, who explained to Edwin that the arrest of the Captain and crew of the Northern Star had stirred up a hornet's nest in Mexico City with the mighty Don Pascal bringing all his legal muscle into play.

Using the guise of Federated Industries Inc., his lawyers were demanding to know why a Captain of one of the Company's sea going cruisers carrying out legitimate business around the Caribbean Islands had been detained and questioned without being allowed his choice of legal representation and then arrested. 'They used the usual technique of threatening to sue the police force involved.' What really surprised me' retorted Arturo Vegas, 'was they also claimed that a British Lawyer named Crosby was allowed to ask questions of the Captain and was permitted to use a recording device with the full authority of the police officer in charge.'

'Edwin, let me say I am both surprised and a little angry that you failed to let me know what had happened. Now can you please fill me in so that I can respond before they start proceedings to sue for compensation? Once these blood sucking lawyers get going, our costs defending the action shoot through the bloody window and my boss will have serious palpitations.'

Once Arturo heard all the facts together with Edwin's abject apologies he calmed down. 'It would appear that when the Superintendent's prisoner escaped he made contact with his boss and gave him your name. Do you realise that now makes you public enemy number one in the Don's eyes. He will now possess a detailed report of everything that happened when the yacht was impounded and will feel that the net is closing in on his Caribbean Drug Ring and that he should do something about it pronto.'

'My advice to you is to scarper back to the UK by the next available flight and keep your head down for a few months until the heat dies down. Let your friend Franklin remain as defending counsel at the retrial. He has enough ammunition to press for a mistrial and your client's discharge.'

As there was no immediate response from Edwin he carried on. 'In the meantime I will arrange a meeting with these bloody lawyers and ask them to explain why the crew were discovered to be illegally armed and in possession of drugs. That will give the Don something to think about. At the same time I will visit His Highness at his residency who will obviously deny any connection with Federated Industries Inc, the high powered cruiser Northern Star, and Captain Stanza in particular.'

'I will take the opportunity to remind Senor Pascal that the warrant for his arrest can still be renewed if I feel I have sufficient evidence to involve him in recent criminal events that have taken place in the Caribbean. I will also inform him that I now have a copy of the list he desperately needs to get his hands on, and warn him if he as much as threatens or lays a hand on Julia Warren or Edwin Crosby I and my team will make his tenure in Mexico unacceptable.'

'In the meantime I will speak to Superintendent Laneson in Jamaica and we will co-ordinate raids on Federated Industries Inc and their branch on his island to see if we can run the elusive

Captain Stanza to earth. Don't build up your hopes that we will find your star witness for the retrial of your client. In my view Senor Stanza will now be regretting the very day he joined the Northern Star, as he lies at the bottom of the Caribbean Sea with a heavy chain wrapped around his ankles.'

Before he replaced the telephone Arturo asked Edwin if he could let him have a written account of the Coastguard's arrest of the Northern Star.

The news from Arturo that Edwin's recording on the Northern Star would be null and void if his principle witness was now dead came as a bitter blow. Superintendent Oliver Laneson had assured Edwin that his small group of selected police officers could be trusted with his life was proved to be a fallacy.

Edwin was tempted in his anger to throw the useless tape away but at the last moment he regained his calm and decided that Arturo had only assumed the Captain was dead. If there was only a one percent chance that he was still alive then the tape might still be of value. With that thought in mind, he put the tape in a drawer and concentrated his mind on the meeting with the Judge.

Ch.38

The meeting in Judge Bell's chambers was scheduled for four pm to ensure the Judge and the Public Prosecutor Raymond Scott were free of court cases.

Judge Bell sat behind his large mahogany desk inlaid with dark green leather tidily set out with two telephones, a matching desk pad, surmounted with a writing pad and pen, and a computer with a small desk screen.

'Gentlemen' he said addressing the PP Scott, Detective Inspector Bishop, Edwin Crosby, and Franklin Jenson. 'This meeting has been requested by Mr Crosby who has stated that he has sufficient evidence in his possession to prove the innocence of his client Julia Warren who is currently awaiting a retrial when, as you are all aware, the original jury were unable to agree a verdict.'

'I am here to chair the meeting and if necessary to direct you all on points of law. However, if the retrial is not to take place Mr Scott will have to decide to withdraw the charges currently on record. In which case a simple hearing will take place in court to announce his decision, only then can I discharge the accused person. Before you start Mr Crosby, I have to state that I was not surprised at the juries' decision. The evidence I heard from the prosecution's witnesses at the original trial were in many cases not supported by facts. I am interested to hear what you have to say. Please begin.'

Edwin knew he had to speak briefly and positively to convince the Prosecutor he had a sound case. Never the less, he was not prepared on this occasion to put all his cards on the table.

'Your Honour, during the last few weeks my team has been active in many areas of the Caribbean after I obtained a coded list belonging to the late Walter Warren from a safe deposit box in London. My team effectively decoded the list that seems to prove that Warren was a member of a criminal group distributing narcotics purchased from a Mafia depot in Venezuela, to named persons on islands in the Caribbean. It was possession of that list that resulted in Walter Warren being accidentally murdered. I say 'accidentally' because the two men who boarded the Sunray were instructed to question Warren and even torture him until he either handed over the list or told them where it was hidden. Those two men disobeyed their Mafia boss's instructions and we are certain that one of them has since been killed for disobeying orders.'

'Certain trustworthy police officers have since interviewed persons named on that list and are willing to state on oath that the evidence they obtained clearly shows my client is innocent of any wrongdoing. In fact she is still unaware that her late husband was involved in criminal activities. Recordings of interviews with some of those persons involved in the murder of the late Mr Warren and the rape of my client are available for those sitting in your chambers to hear.'

'I appreciate the recordings are not concrete evidence but they contain sufficient details for Mr. Scott to decide whether the case should be heard before a jury. May I add that since my team started this investigation some of the men involved, appear to have been dealt with by the Mafia style of justice for those who were interviewed by the police, or myself, i.e. they are missing believed to be dead.'

'The list is now in a safe location out of the reach of anyone determined to use violence to obtain it. My team now know that person named at the trial by one of Warren's killers called 'Pascie' is in fact Senor Frederico Pascal, or Don Pascal as he is known in Mexico and throughout Central America. He has a ruthless team of enforcers, some of whom may be seeking to kidnap my client in the hope they can force me to hand over that list. The reason Don Pascal wants that list so badly is I believe that only Walter Warren knew the names and locations of his narcotic handlers. I also think large sums of monies for drugs supplied, were withheld from the Don and he is seeking retribution.'

'I have always believed my client's innocence and I think it would be a travesty of justice if she is compelled to appear once again before a jury.'

Edwin sat back to await what he hoped would be a favourable response from the Public Prosecutor.

Raymond Scott as Public Prosecutor was well aware that the murder had resulted in a great wave of interest from the general population and the local press in particular. Show trials appeared to be meat and drink to the public and the thought of their reaction if he was party to cancelling the coming retrial made him react accordingly.

'Your Honour,' he said addressing the judge. 'I have listened to my learned friend's presentation of his case in defence of his client and I admit it is plausible. However, I see no reason to waste your Honour's time listening to recordings that would never be accepted as evidence in a court of law and my learned friend must be aware of this.'

'A lot of time has been spent by his team who have collated a lot of important evidence relating to drug trafficking. That evidence will be invaluable to the police and the Drug Enforcement Administration in their ongoing attempts to stamp out this vile trade. What my learned friend has failed to do in his submission to your Honour is provide undisputed facts that his client was not involved in the murder of her husband. Everything still remains as supposition and I am therefore strongly inclined to ask your Honour to allow a retrial and let a duly appointed jury consider the evidence and hopefully on that occasion come to a unanimous decision based on facts.'

Judge Bell glanced down towards his lower frame while he contemplated his response. 'The learned defence counsel and his team have worked very hard in such a short space of time in an effort to prove his client is innocent of the charges levelled against her. There is little doubt that that they have successfully uncovered a drug syndicate that I feel sure will be fully investigated by the police on each Island working in conjunction with the DEA. That he and his team are fully convinced of his client's innocence is praiseworthy. However having listened carefully to both counsel's presentation I have to say that I agree with the Public Prosecutor. Were I to agree to the defence counsel's arguments and cancel the retrial, the public at large, and the press, would consider that justice had not been served. On this Island and indeed throughout the Commonwealth, judges are appointed to uphold the law and allow juries to reach a conclusion. If their decision is disputable under the law then both counsel's have the opportunity to appeal to the high court for a review of the case. In my view I have no alternative but to allow the retrial to take place.'

Edwin and Franklin were gobsmacked and seeing the grins on the faces of the Public Prosecutor and Detective Inspector Bishop made Edwin feel rage bubbling up inside his body. It appeared to him that a big stonewall had been built up that he was failing to climb.

Breaking the dreadful news to his client was something he was not going to enjoy.

Franklin noticing the downcast feeling on Edwin's face patted his colleague on the back and whispered 'back to the bloody drawing board friend.'

As the meeting broke up it went through Edwin's mind that he still had at least one trick up his sleeve. The question was how was he going to get his witness presently tucked away in the UK, back to the island and into court without putting the poor sod's life in jeopardy?

Ch.39

A meeting with his father was now essential so Edwin booked a flight back to the UK. He asked Franklin to pass the information that he was returning to the UK on to Cara, and for her to assure Julia that he would be back in time for the retrial. He asked specifically of Franklin that neither Cara nor Julia be informed of their meeting with the Judge, or the decision that had been made by the Judge at the end of the meeting.

Before he left he made calls to Superintendent Laneson, Private Detective Roberto Sanchez, and DEA Commissioner Levy, and asked them if they were prepared to give evidence at the forthcoming retrial.

Commissioner Levy declined on the grounds that the people in his department tended to work undercover and as such his department never sought publicity, or were prepared to answer searching questions in court particularly with the local press present. Edwin replied that he fully understood. Oliver and Roberto both accepted.

The long flight back to Gatwick was much better than Edwin anticipated when the stewardess whispered to him as he entered the aircraft that he had been upgraded and should make his way to the upper deck of the aircraft. As he settled down in the super seat it went through his mind that he should spend the extra on future flights and damn the expense.

It was lunch time on the following day before his father was free to see him. Edwin explained the problem he had faced and the negative reaction from the Public Prosecutor.

'I appear to have no alternative but to produce my Genii out of the bottle but am worried that I will put Emille Segura in great danger if I take him back to St Lucia to be a witness. Do you think I could get him to make and sign a statement in front of an independent Notary and present that as evidence at the retrial?'

His father shook his head from side to side. 'You know the law son, the Judge may accept it as evidence to be presented to the jury, but the Public Prosecutor is bound to lodge an objection on the grounds he is unable to cross exam your witness. If Emille Segura is the vital witness to clear your client of the charges against her, then Senor Segura will have to take his chance with the Mafia enforcers and give evidence at the retrial.'

Father Crosby looked for his son's reaction. 'I see from the expression on your face that you are not in favour of my suggestion. Bear in mind that this young hoodlum has committed a murder and is currently living safely in this country at our expense, when he should be facing a Judge and Jury to pay for his dastardly crime.'

'Come to think of it, only his partner in crime has paid for disobeying the Mafia Don's instructions. It is unlikely Segura will be punished by the Don, providing he sticks to your instructions to only respond that he and his partner had never met Julia Warren, or been paid by her to commit a murder.'

Edwin appeared to accept his father's judgement but he still felt uncomfortable taking his witness back to St Lucia. 'The one thing that bothers me dad is the possibility that Emille may be silenced by the Mafia before he gets the chance to make any statement at the retrial. If that happens I am back to square one again, and the Public Prosecutor and Detective Inspector Bishop will both be gloating at my embarrassment.'

Father nodded his acceptance of the possibility. 'Perhaps you are right to be cautious. After all, you have experienced the Mafia's sample of justice. There has to be a solution to your disquiet so leave me to think about it for a couple of days. In the meantime your in tray must have reached the ceiling during your absence, so take your mind off the trial and do a little bit of uninteresting case work while you are here.'

‒ ‒ ‒

The next day Edwin ignored his father's instructions and took time off to visit Julia's home. He spent some time with the two remaining staff, to reassure them that their services were still required until Julia was released and could confirm their appointments. He was assured by both that they were being paid regularly and that the house and garden were in good order. When they asked how long it would be before the mistress returned home he told them that it would not be too long. They failed to see his fingers crossed behind his back.

Edwin would have like to visit Emille in his safe house, but realised he would soon have to inform the worried young man that he had to return to the Caribbean with the distinct possibility of having to face his own murder trial and many years in prison.

— — —

It was three days before his father came up with a most unexpected solution that left Edwin feeling incredulously surprised and specifically nervous about it working. In the end, after a night's pondering over the proposal, Edwin came to the conclusion that there was no other alternative that had the remotest chance of succeeding. To ensure the possibility of success he asked his father if he could take his secretary along to offer moral support.

When that was agreed Edwin set about making his father's plans come to fruition.

First he contacted the Flight Manager of Liverpool airport to see if he could book a small private jet capable of flying to St Lucia without having to refuel en route. When that was confirmed, he set about finalising his plans that included the help of Roberto Sanchez and Franklin Jenson, who both acquiesced when they realised how audacious the whole idea was.

Ch.40

Edwin applied himself diligently to the outstanding work load. His secretary had already explained to him that the Chambers were losing clients who were becoming exasperated when their case was effectively put on hold awaiting the return of the prodigal son, as the secretary put it, by expressing her own irritation.

As the pressure began to build up Edwin at last realised why his father was becoming irritated by his long absence from the business he had built up so successfully for many years.

There were however, moments when Edwin wished he was back in the Caribbean. As he sat over a cup of welcome coffee his thoughts turned to Julia. He understood and respected his father's concern about being involved in a personal way with clients, but she still crept into his inner thoughts, not because of her beauty because that was an indisputable fact. Somehow the way she conducted herself whilst under extreme pressure got under his skin. She seemed to possess that regal charm that made her stand out against the crowd, someone to be admired and appreciated; someone very special in his eyes.

What was bugging Edwin was the fact that there had been no reciprocation from Julia. It appeared that she only regarded Edwin as her lawyer looking after her affairs in the UK. Every meeting or discussion he had held with her had never been met with a friendly or intimate response that Edwin so earnestly desired. He accepted that she had only recently lost her husband and may still consider she was expected to be in mourning, but he knew from the information gleaned from her first interview with the local police that she was beginning to realise her marriage to Walter Warren was a sham.

The urge within him to get back to St Lucia to see Julia, was causing him to neglect the concentration required from a diligent lawyer doing his utmost on behalf of his long list of clients.

Edwin put down his coffee, picked up the next file on his desk, and gave a deep sigh as he started to read his client's complaint against her better half's reported infidelity.

– – –

He heaved a sigh of relief when the week end arrived. At last he had a brief respite from the hum drum repetition of defending stupid rich motorists who were about to be banned from driving for drinking and taking to the road. Their appreciation when he successfully had a driving ban reduced from twelve months to six months sickened him. But as father pointed out this was the bread and butter of their business and was not to be sneezed at if it paid the mortgage on the new country cottage and meant they could both have exotic holidays instead of going to Brighton or the Lake District.

It was that weekend when Edwin thought it the right time to discuss the impending retrial with Emille.

He made the short journey to the safe house on the outskirts of Bootle some three miles from Liverpool. The address he had been given was part of a three story block of flats overlooking a business park that had seen better days when the area was more affluent. He was met at the door by the day shift security guard who carefully examined his credentials before asking Emille if he could vouch for the visitor.

Emille, bored to death with his enforced restrictions was delighted to see someone from the Caribbean that he recognised as the possible saviour from certain death at the hands of the Mafia. 'Mr Crosby, I hope you have brought some good news because this is an awful place where I am being confined. Please can I go back to the Caribbean where it's nice and warm and not as dismal and unfriendly as miserable hole is?'

Edwin walked into the small living room and suggested Emille sat down while he put a proposal to him that could mean his return to blue seas and the smell of gardenias and mimosa.

'I need your help on the Island of St Lucia, but it would be totally impossible for you to return as Emille Segura. The Mafia have many spotters watching all the airports and harbours checking to see if persons on their wanted list are trying to get back into the area of the Caribbean to re-establish themselves. You would be picked up by their enforcers, many of whom are police officers in their pay and your life would be forfeit within hours of your arrival.

My father and I have decided that the only hope I have of getting you to give evidence at Mrs Warren's trial is for you to enter the Island completely changed in character, accompanied by my female secretary who will act as your daughter. I have reserved seats for us on a private jet that will drop us at a small airfield outside Castries that currently is the home of a private flying school. You will be taken to a safe house outside Castries until you are required at the trial. As soon as your attendance in the witness box is over, my friends will spirit you out of the country before the police have a chance to obtain an arrest warrant.'

The look of horror on Emille's face was something to behold. 'Are you suggesting that I dress up as an old man? The immigration officers, or police, will recognise my disguise as soon as they see me walk or hear me talk.'

Edwin smiled. 'That is why my secretary will always be at your side to fend off questions and help you act the role. You can of course refuse, in which case you can no longer help my client and I will pay your fare back to Jamaica and wish you the best of luck for the future. Please remember you were party to the murder of Walter Warren and as a result my client Mrs Warren is awaiting trial for the murder of her husband. I want to put you on the stand at her trail and hear you tell the jury that Mrs Warren did not pay you to murder her husband. You were taken to the Sunray yacht by the captain of the Northern Star with your mate Enriqué Costello with instructions from your Mafia Boss to obtain an important list from Walter Warren by any means. It was Costello who went too far and has since paid the ultimate penalty for disobeying orders.'

I am a lawyer Emille who is prepared to go to any lengths to prove my client's innocence. If you refuse to go voluntarily I will not hesitate to hand you over to the British Police and arrange an extradition order to have you delivered to the St Lucian police in handcuffs. What happens to you afterwards is your problem, but I estimate you will spend at least thirty years in prison if the Mafia doesn't get to you sooner. The choice is yours.'

Emille suddenly became indignant. 'You said earlier that if I refused to help you, you would put me on a plane home and wish me the best of luck.'

Edwin nodded that he acknowledged the offer made. 'I could see on your face that you would never agree to appear in court on behalf of my client. You are a ruthless little toe rag working for the Mafia and I have little sympathy for you or your departed friend. I am prepared to keep you out of prison to the best of my ability, but in return I demand your co-operation. So from your point of view it is co-operate and stay out of prison, or refuse and God help your soul. Which is it to be?'

The answer was inevitable.

'Now that you understand that my first priority is to protect my client, let me explain how the disguise will work. I know a person who works at one of the local theatres and she is an expert at changing the characters of actors to meet the part they have to play. She is prepared to make you look like an old frail man who needs a wheel chair and a companion. When we arrive on St Lucia and land at the private airfield the crew of the aircraft will assist in getting you off the plane while your 'daughter talks to the immigration officer. I am sure he will not want to bother you with formalities and will wave you and your chair through to the departure area where we will be collected by one of my friends who will be waiting at the airport.'

'You will have to act the old man for a couple of days but just before you go into court you will abandon the wheel chair while you go into the witness box. Even old men can have a clear voice so the change will not be recognised. After giving evidence you will ask the court usher to allow you to leave the court room to visit the toilet. As soon as you are out of the courtroom one of my colleagues will show you the way to the toilet. Once inside your daughter will help you remake your makeup until you look your old self. Use the wheel chair to get out of the building with my colleague, who will take you to a safe house where I will collect you and take you to the airport where you will be immediately flown back to the UK and safety.'

Once you are safely off the Island and back in the UK we can decide where your future lies. The fact that you murdered Walter Warren does not rest heavily on my conscience as he was an unscrupulous rogue and the world is better off without him, so I am not interested in seeing *you* spend time in prison for his demise.

Edwin watched as Emille let out a sigh of relief. 'What happens if someone in court sees through my disguise?'

'They can do nothing until you have left the witness box and by the time they have got someone to check, the old man will have disappeared into thin air.'

Edwin paused for a moment before continuing. 'There will always be an element of risk in what we are doing, but the alternative you are likely to face is not worth contemplating is it?'

Emille also thought about it for a moment before agreeing that the alternative of years in prison, or a heavy chain round ones ankles, was worth the risk of becoming an old man for a few hours.

– – –

The first visit to the makeup artist by Emille and Edwin was hilarious from Edwin's point of view, but not Emille's who was as nervous as a kitten.

The artist Helen was young and bubbly and enjoyed her special skills as she applied make up to Emille's face and slowly coloured his hair before she applied the finishing touches by adding blue blotches to the back of his hands. 'No use me making your face look old' she said, 'while your hands look ready to tickle a young girl's fancy.' She gave a hoot of laughter as she applied a touch of grey to the hairs coming out of his nostrils.

Edwin looked quite impressed with the makeup artist's skills, but Helen critically examined at her handiwork looking for flaws. 'An old man would not be seen dead in the clothes you are wearing,' she told Emille. 'I'll fit you out in an old man's suit that he would have bought at least thirty years ago. Wide lapels on the jacket, single breasted, 24 inch bottoms on the trousers, a tie complete with food stains, and black down at heel shoes.'

When Emille was eventually fitted out Helen gave her sign of approval. Turning to Edwin she said. 'Let him try them out for twenty four hours so that he can practice being an old man. It will also allow you to see if there are any flaws that may be picked up by an observant official'

As they left the theatre Edwin was quick to remind Emille of his new image. 'You're walking along the pavement like a twenty seven year old instead of a seventy year old. Stoop a little and walk very slowly. Remind me to get you a walking stick,' he added.

After a few intensive hours of coaching Edwin was reasonably satisfied that Emille could play the part. If it all went pear shaped on the day, Emille was the one who would suffer the pain of being arrested and punished. All Edwin would suffer, would be embarrassment in front of his peers that his subterfuge had failed at the critical moment; plus a strong reprimand from the judge.

He returned the props to the theatre the following day and asked Helen if she could make herself readily available at short notice. Helen told him she would love to participate in whatever charade Edwin had in mind. 'When I am behind the scenes at the theatre I can quickly touch up the artist's makeup between scenes if it is showing defects under the hot lights.'

Her suggestion gave Edwin a sudden inspirational idea. 'Can you get a few days leave from the theatre to accompany me on this charade as you call it. I will pay you a handsome fee and all expenses that will include a short stay on the Island of St Lucia. If you agree, I must warn you that there is an element of risk, but nothing criminal is intended. I am involved in defending a client on the Island and need to get my witness into court without being recognised. If he is discovered, the fact that you are being paid to change his character could bring a rebuke from the Judge.

Helen burst out laughing as she nodded her head to show she accepted the offer. 'At long last I get to be part of the cast and at the same time am being paid to get a free sun tan. My colleagues will be both jealous and intrigued.'

Edwin quickly reminded her that she could not discuss any of this with her colleagues 'until after the event,' he added with a smile.

Ch.41

The days flew by quickly as Edwin became more and more impatient at the delay to set the date for the retrial. When it arrived on his desk he was surprised to find he had only two weeks to organise everything he had in mind for his defence.

Franklin telephoned the following day to inform Edwin that he had been pressing the court administration for an early date and had only two days ago been informed that a lengthy case had been cancelled and he had been allocated the slot.

Following a brief discussion with his father he set up the flight time in the private jet from Liverpool airport, arranged with Helen to obtain some holiday leave, and advised a very worried Emille that he was about to become an actor on the world stage.

He arranged to meet Franklin and Roberto as soon as possible after he landed on St Lucia. Finally, informing his secretary to her dismay, that he no longer needed her services as there had been a dramatic change of plan.

— — —

On the morning of the planned flight he picked up Helen with her sophisticated make up kit from her home in Crosby and Emille from his flat in Bootle and made his way to Liverpool airport where the jet was waiting with the pilot, co-pilot and stewardess ready to take off for St Lucia.

A young Jamaican was quickly cleared through immigration and a seventy year old cripple needing a wheel chair descended from the plane at the private airfield on St Lucia, but not before an excited young makeup artist had worked magic during the flight over the Atlantic.

Helen found it difficult to accept that they had left Liverpool at ten am UK time, had taken eight hours to cross the Atlantic, and yet had landed on St Lucia at lunch time, Caribbean time.

Acting as the invalid's helpful nurse they were quickly cleared by the Immigration Officer who never looked at any passports. In his view, rich people who could afford private jets did not like being hassled by airport controls, so he waved them towards the departure area where a car was already waiting to pick up the old man and his retinue.

When they arrived at Cara's hotel the new arrivals were placed in adjoining rooms. Edwin's had an internal connecting door with Emille's bedroom that was normally kept locked, but because of the need to keep constantly in touch without Emille having to go into the corridor on this occasion it was left ajar. Just how Edwin would be able to protect Emille if the Mafia's hit men paid a social visit, he had not even contemplated. One thing was certain, he could not involve the police, or pay security guards, for this act would bring Emille's presence in the hotel immediately under scrutiny even though he was acting the old man role as if he was a consummate professional actor.

The meeting between Franklin, Roberto, Helen and Edwin was planned to cover every contingency, but even at this late stage in the planning the three men were still dubious that they would get away with their plan to put Emille on the stand, then spirit him out of the country before the police could arrest their number one witness.

The meeting had broken up and Franklin and Roberto were on their way back to his office when Roberto received a call on his mobile from the security man on duty in Julia's flat. He reported that a black female who lived on the ground floor with her husband, who between them managed the building looking after cleaning and general servicing, had been accosted by two men who professed to be plain clothes police officers. They asked if a Mrs Warren was renting one of the flats in the building. The black lady, having been made aware that one of the flats was regarded as a safe house, for which they were suitably rewarded by Roberto, they denied that any one of that name was registered with them.

When the two police officers asked if they could see the register of tenants, her husband told them he would only produce the list if they showed him their warrant cards and gave him a telephone number he could ring at police headquarters to check their identity.

They threatened him with arrest but he still persisted, until they said they would be back with a search warrant next day. Actually he was responding to what Roberto told him might happen as the local Mafia continued with their search of the Island's properties in an effort to locate Julia Warren. When the men departed the husband turned to his wife and said 'I told them the truth and they still did not believe me.' Someone matching the description they had given *was* living in one of the flats, but her name was Jennifer Lang. The fact that Miss Lang had twenty four hour security cover by professional ex police officers was something he thought was not worth mentioning.

Roberto called at the ground floor flat to thank the two occupant's for their diligence and told them he would recommend them for a bonus from the Lawyer who had given them the task of protecting their tenant from nosey parkers.

It was obvious to all and sundry that the Mafia were never going to give up. Their permanent objective was to protect each zone by eliminating any opposition to their grand scheme to ensure total control over narcotics, prostitution, and gambling that bring untold wealth to the hierarchy in the Mafia organisation. i.e. Dons like Frederico Pascal.

Ch.42

The morning of the retrial was a testing time for all concerned. The reputation of the Public Prosecutor was at stake if his continuous pressure to prove that he was right to put Julia Warren on trial for murder proved to be a serious waste of public finances. He could expect a hard time from his superiors in the department who were more concerned with the political aspects of their work.

Detective Inspector Bishop had not slept well the previous night. Although confident that his investigative professionalism would prove to his superiors that hard work and dedication to detail always brought positive results, he still had a nervous underlying feeling that the defending team had something up their sleeves that he had failed to uncover; hence the lack of sleep.

Franklin Jenson had also not slept well. As a lawyer he liked every twist and turn in the courtroom to be under his control. Crossing the t's and dotting the i's before facing a discerning Judge were bread and butter to him. The scheme proposed by Edwin Crosby bore all the hallmarks of an impending disaster, putting Franklin's reputation as one of the best lawyers on the island under severe test.

Edwin, on the other hand had slept well before the court case commenced. Julia Warren had behaved impeccably by remaining under cover until she was required to face the charges levelled against her. Superintendent Oliver Laneson had arrived on the Island and was geared up to give evidence that would support Julia's claim that she was innocent. And finally his master stroke, although a quivering mass of nerves was being prepared by his team to give the vital evidence that would finally convince the jury that Julia Warren had been the victim of circumstances beyond her control.

Edwin had learned earlier that night that the presiding Judge was His Honour Sir Gavin Wainthrop who had a long standing reputation of becoming extremely impatient with long winded counsellors who took an inordinate time to get their salient facts across to the jury. It was not unknown for his Honour to call the prosecuting and defence counsels before his bench, or even into his chambers and warn them to cut out the clap trap and get down to the nitty gritty. 'I am required by law' he would explain to the offending counsel, 'to write down all the salient facts of each case I hear, and when my time is wasted writing down irrelevant rubbish I feel inclined to issue a verbal warning to counsel on both sides that confusing the jury with legal jargon and extraneous claptrap will not be allowed in my court.'

Edwin duly noted his Honours reported temperament and was prepared to drive a straight line, avoiding hairpin bends, when he presented his defence on the morrow.

— — —

The court was convened promptly at ten o clock with his Honour Justice Sir Gavin Wainthrop dressed in his robes of office, sitting on his raised dais ready to commence the retrial of Julia Warren who was sitting between her two counsellors.

There being no objections from either Counsel the Jury were duly sworn in by the Court Clerk.

A silence descended on the assembled public and press as the Judge addressed the Public Prosecutor. 'Mr Scott before you proceed, may I point out to the Jury and all other persons associated with this case, that everyone will have read the press reports of the earlier trial and formed opinions as to the guilt or innocence of the accused. Put that prior knowledge out of your heads and concentrate on the evidence now being presented by both Counsels at this retrial. Nothing outside this court in the past has any relevance, or should be taken into account by members of the Jury in reaching their deliberations at the end of this retrial.'

Having said his piece, his Honour turned to the Public Prosecutor. 'Mr Scott you may now proceed.'

It became obvious to both Franklin and Edwin that the Prosecuting Counsellor had not done very much additional preparation for the retrial. In the Prosecuting Counsel's opinion the evidence although partially circumstantial was beyond challenge and no further work was necessary.

The same old faces were called to the witness box to give a broadly similar testimony of the events following immediately after Walter Warren's murder.

Captain Fisher the owner of the yacht Lion King told how he answered the call for help from Mrs Warren and called the Harbour Master on the radio to call the police.

The Harbour Master went to some lengths to say how he recorded the call for help and how he summoned the Coast Guard and police to go out to the Sunray.

Detective Inspector Bishop reported how accompanied by Sergeat Totti he boarded the yacht and was immediately suspicious about how the murder was committed. He went to great lengths to report how Julia Warren was charged and ultimately remanded to prison.

He made a great play on Julia Warren's statement, that one of the two persons who had raped her, mentioned someone called Pascie and although the police had made a detailed search through the computer records no such person existed.

By day five even His Honour the Judge looked frustrated. Time and time again he had to reprimand the Prosecuting Counsellor for presenting opinion rather than fact to the jury. 'Supposition' he reminded the Public Prosecutor 'is all very well for the reporters in the court to provide headlines for their newspaper, but it is unacceptable in a court of law and especially in my courtroom.'

Telling the jury to disregard much of the evidence presented, he eventually came to the same conclusion as Franklin that the Prosecutor had little new to offer from the transcript of the previous trial that the judge had been compelled to read before he was allocated the retrial.

Adjourning the hearing for the week end His Honour looked forward to a quiet game of golf on Saturday, followed by a family get together including his grandchildren, where his son had agreed to do a barbecue with all the trimmings that young children adore. Sausages, chicken drum sticks, beef burgers, and chips followed by ice cream; while the adults would be served with kebabs and beef steaks, accompanied by copious amounts of wine.

– – –

Sir Gavin Wainthrop was not looking forward to the next few days of the retrial and had come to the sad conclusion that if there was any further attempt by either counsel to try and convert supposition into fact he would have no alternative but to come down hard on the perpetrators.

All of the following two weeks were taken up by the Prosecutor, outlining the discovery and recovery of the body of the late Walter Warren and the presentation of complex reports by the Coroner and the Forensic Scientist.

Each time the Prosecutor sat down the Judge asked Mr. Jessop if he wished to cross examine the witness.

Franklin out of kindness to his opposite number the Prosecutor, asked the witness to elaborate on some particular point that had been presented, but on the whole kept his questions to the minimum. It seemed to please the Judge, who like his predecessor at the original trial had to make a written record of all the salient points raised in order to direct the jury at the end of the retrial.

The retrial had been scheduled by the Judge's office to take about six weeks but the way the prosecutor had dragged out his case the Judge had a horrible feeling that this case was going to last months. In his considered view the counsel for the defence had not yet come to the crease (His Honour loved watching cricket) and came to the sad conclusion that Defence Counsel had to do something spectacular to convince the jury that his client was innocent. All the evidence he had heard so far had pointed to the fact that Mrs Warren had sufficient grounds for arranging the murder of her husband and glancing in the direction of the jury he had a feeling they were of the same opinion.

— — —

At long last it became the turn of the defending counsel to present his witnesses. Before doing so Franklin Jenson drew the Judge's attention to a degree of incompetence by the police in their failure to recover the body. He outlined how his team had contacted each of the yachtsmen anchored in Rodney Bay and from their observations of the position of the Sunray when Walter Warren was murdered had decided to notify the police of his findings and request their cooperation in conducting a search for the body. In the meantime, two local divers, trawling for shellfish on the sea bed, accidentally discovered the body and notified the coastguard who arranged with the police to send down divers to bring the body to the surface. It was later identified as that of the late Walter Warren. He handed a copy of the map his team had drawn to the Judge as evidence.

He then went on to explain how his team had tried to find an explanation for Mrs Warren's statement that one of the two suspected murderers had indicated that they were looking for a list and if they failed 'Pascie would be angry' or words somewhat similar.

'My colleague from England and fellow counsellor Mr Edwin Crosby sitting beside me, requested written permission from Mrs Warren to search her house in England to see if he could find any clues relating to a list. He discovered a key to a safe deposit box and was given permission to check the contents. Inside he found a range of contents including a coded list including the names of certain persons currently residing on various islands in the

Caribbean.' Franklin failed to mention that the list had been obtained illegally by his colleague using subterfuge techniques.

The Public Prosecutor immediately bounded to his feet and complained to the Judge that he had not received a copy of this list from the defendants lawyer and demanded a copy so that he could consider whether it was relevant to the case.

Franklin Jenson shook his head from side to side indicating he had no intention of handing the list over.

Judge Wainthrop put down his pen and looked accusingly at Franklin. 'Mr Jenson if you have a copy of this list why is it not included in the documents handed to me earlier?'

'Your Honour, some of the names mentioned on that list would be put at great risk if it fell into the wrong hands.'

The judge adjourned the hearing for one hour and asked both counsellors to join him in his chambers at the rear of the courthouse.

Sitting in the Judges room the Judge turned to Franklin and asked him to explain the reason for withholding an essential document from the court.

'Our team worked on the code until they were confident they had found the answer. The list contains names involved in a Mafia drug chain and if this list was made public some of those people's lives would be seriously at risk. Under the circumstances I am not prepared to make it public.'

'The Judge huffed and puffed in annoyance. 'You must give the Prosecutor and me a copy that will remain as a confidential document not available to the jury.'

Franklin shook his head again from side to side. 'I'm sorry Your Honour but I do not trust anyone to have possession of this document and that includes your Honour and the Prosecuting Counsel. I ask your Honour to bear with me, until you have heard all the defence evidence when it will become clear why I refuse your order. In case you think I have it in my possession I can assure you that a copy is not anywhere in the Caribbean.'

Judge Wainthrop scowled. 'I will allow you to continue with your defence, but rest assured if you have attempted to mislead me I will not hesitate to fine you heavily for contempt of court. Now let us return to the court. The day is drawing to a close so I will adjourn the court until tomorrow.

Raymond Scott's face showed he was not best pleased with the decision. He detested groping in the dark, knowing that documents held by the defence were being withheld unfairly from his clutches. He decided he would prise the information out of a witness once he was given the opportunity to cross examine.

Ch.43

At ten am the following day Franklin Jenson called Superintendent Oliver Laneson to the stand. After being sworn in and giving his name he refused to give his address on the grounds that his position in the police could put his family at risk with criminal elements.

Franklin asked the Superintendent to explain to the court how and why he was contacted by Edwin Crosby. Oliver explained how a young criminal had stabbed another person in a separate incident not related to this case. He told how after the stabbed victim died he had charged the young perpetrator with murder and had been given information about two persons who had committed a murder on the island of St Lucia. He had passed that information on to Edwin Crosby as it was relevant to his defence of his client.

Interrupted by His Honour the Judge he was asked why he had not given that information to the local police.

'I left that to Mr Crosby and his colleague,' he replied. 'Maybe I was wrong not to do so, but that was the decision I made at the time.'

The Judge nodded to Mr Jessop to continue.

'What happened after you passed on the information to Mr Crosby?'

'Further inquires took place and from those inquiries we discovered that the crew of a cruiser called the Northern Star could be implicated in murder. My team of officers in cooperation with the local coastguard tracked the Northern Star en route to Cuba and stopped the cruiser before it entered Cuban waters. My officers boarded the Northern Star and after a detailed search of the boat found it necessary to arrest the Captain and crew for possession of arms and drugs.'

One could have heard a pin drop in the court room.

He went on to explain his embarrassment when the Captain of the Northern Star escaped from the place where he was under police guard and has not been seen since. 'I presume that he reported to his Mafia masters and has been dealt in the customary way as they would not wish to have their Captain interviewed under caution by my officers,' he added. His statement took up most of the day until the court was adjourned.

– – –

The following day counsel for the prosecution cross examined. He asked the Superintendent where he was based.

'I'm not prepared to answer that due to the risks previously explained.'

The Judge accepted the point.

'Where did you apprehend the Northern Star and its crew?'

'A Coastguard Cutter with me on board stopped the cruiser en route to Cuba.'

'From where?'

'I'm not prepared to answer due to the risk factor.'

'How do you know the Captain and crew were in the pay of the Mafia?'

Franklin Jenson jumped to his feet. 'Your honour the Prosecutor is trying by a devious route to undermine the decision you made yesterday.'

Judge Wainthrop reprimanded Prosecuting Counsel and told him to restrict his questions to those affecting the case before the court.

Mr Scott obviously frustrated, ended his questioning and resumed his seat.

– – –

The next morning Franklin caused consternation by announcing he was calling Ex Detective Roberto Sanchez to the stand. The Prosecutor and the press were well aware that Roberto was a Private Detective with his office situated on the Island. It was his involvement in the murder that resulted in the expression of surprise

Franklin went straight into the attack. 'Senor Sanchez, can you explain why you were engaged by the defence counsel?'

'I was asked to check the polling lists on each Island in the Caribbean to see if I could find anyone with the name of Pascie or something similar.'

'And what did you discover?'

'No one by the name of Pascie, but I found names like Pascalino, Pascarli, Pascento, and even a Pasternac. I checked each person's background and none had any link with criminal activity.'

'What did you do then?'

'I widened the search area to other countries in Central America and came up with a Senor Pascal based in Mexico who possessed a criminal record and had direct links with the Mafioso. I reported the fact to Mr Franklin who paid me for my efforts. What happened after that was his concern.' (A blatant lie while under oath, but Roberto was not prepared to invite any other questions that were not his concern).

Ch.44

Edwin had already pre agreed with Franklin that he should be placed in the witness box prepared to deal with the Pascal incident, so on the following day when Franklin was asked by the Judge to produce his next witness he asked if it was permissible to call is colleague to the box.

When his Honour the Judge agreed, up popped the Public Prosecutor to complain that witnesses were not normally allowed in the courtroom until after they had given evidence; reminding the Judge that Mr Crosby had remained beside the defending counsel since the start of this case.

When the Judge frowned it was obvious that he was not best pleased to be reminded of court procedure. 'Overruled' he said testily. Turning to Franklin he told him call his next witness.

When Edwin was seated, Franklin approached the witness box. 'Please tell the jury what you did after Roberto Sanchez reported that he had found the mysterious Pascie.

'I contacted the Central Police Department in Mexico City and was put in contact with a Captain Arturo Vegas who arranged for me to meet a Senor Frederico Pascal at his hacienda. Senor Pascal is well known in Mexico as the region's Mafia Don.

Edwin then went on to outline what happened when he agreed to exchange some information in his possession in exchange for the names of the two men who had murdered Walter Warren.

The Judge asked what would have happened if Senor Pascal agreed to the exchange.

'I was instructed by Captain Vegas to agree to a meeting away from the hacienda and when the Don sent his delegate to collect the information I would give a signal to concealed police officers as soon as I was in possession of the two names I required. The Mafia delegate would have been immediately arrested and the written information recovered before anyone had a chance to read it.'

'The fact that I was unsuccessful was not a surprise to the Police Captain, who warned me that having informed the Don that I held information he required, the life of my client and myself were at risk. Having received the warning, I immediately moved my client from where she lived on the Island to a safe house and placed her under constant guard. For myself from then until now I have never gone out alone in Castries.'

The Public Prosecutor jumped to his feet as soon as Franklin sat down. 'Mr. Crosby, as soon as you discovered the name Pascal, and his location, and the fact that he was head of the Mafia surely you had a responsibility to bring it to the attention of Detective Inspector Bishop who is heading the investigation into the murder?'

Edwin looked at the Prosecutor as if the man had not got the gist of his confrontation with the Mafia Don. 'My team discovered a complex network of agents throughout the Caribbean and I decided to keep the information secure for there was no one I could trust other than my team. It was just as well I came to that decision because one of those agents is currently sitting in the corridor outside this courtroom.'

The Prosecutor was agog with curiosity. 'Can you name that man?'

'I can, it is Detective Sergeant Totti.'

The Judge looked astonished. 'Mr Crosby have you got evidence to substantiate your accusation?'

'Yes your Honour. Commissioner Levy of the Drug Enforcement Administration will have already contacted the Police Commissioner of St Lucia to affect an arrest. He possesses written evidence under oath that Sergeant Totti is the most important Mafia contact on the Island.'

His Honour Sir Gavin Wainthrop suddenly realised that this mundane retrial that appeared to be boring to the extreme was suddenly turning into an interesting scenario. Turning to the witness Edwin Crosby he leaned forward and asked if there was any connection between this startling announcement and the murder charge hanging like the Sword of Damocles over his client.

'Your Honour, I hope to prove conclusively that the late Walter Warren was a Jeckyll and Hyde character as far as his wife was concerned. She, in her innocence, regarded her husband as a successful business man and entrepreneur, who made a fortune out of his import Export Business, when in fact he was a leading figure in the despicable narcotic trade. I have proof that he was running a team of agents across Central America and perhaps Europe as a top enforcer for the Mafioso. His visit to the Caribbean wasn't for the holiday she expected. It must have been ordered by the hierarchy of the Mafia to resolve the reduction of certain funds due to be paid into their coffers. The very young Mrs Warren was totally unaware of her husband's nefarious activities and as such is completely innocent of the serious charges levelled against her.'

When the Judge asked the Public Prosecutor if he had any questions he looked at his associates sitting at the table who nodded their heads from side to side completely baffled by the sudden turn of events.

'I have no questions at this stage for the witness,' he said.

The Judge looked in the direction of Detective Inspector Bishop, who with his right hand clasping his chin, appeared dumb struck by the unexpected turn of events. For a considerable time he had suspicions that his sergeant was protecting certain individuals from investigations into their suspected drug distribution activities. But without concrete proof, he had put the reluctance of his sergeant down to overwork in other areas of crime on the Island. Looking a bit like a burst balloon, his interest in this murder case was suddenly less important than the effect on his career.

Another long day sitting in court was about to come to a close when the Judge called a halt to the proceedings.

Franklin Jenson was exhausted; certain members of the jury were confused by the unexpected change of direction; and the reporters' in the press box were aware that their Editors would be screaming for copy to catch the following day's early edition.

In all this frenzied activity Edwin remained worried about his final witness, hoping he would not panic and refuse to testify at the last possible moment.

It even went through his mind that sufficient evidence had been produced to convince the jury that the late Walter Warren was not the loving and devoted husband portrayed earlier by the press. The question remaining unanswered, was whether the jury had been convinced that Walter Warren had been 'accidentally' murdered by two novice enforcers of the Mafia and not by Julia Warren as indicated by the Public Prosecutor.

Edwin decided it was a risk keeping his final witness off the stand and decided that Emille must be produced on the morrow to finally nail the lid on the coffin.

Ch.45

The news of Totti's suspension and the impending arrest of his accomplice Rafael Bonico, Head Chef of the Lido Star Hotel was headline news in the Morning Post and other national newspapers. At breakfast Edwin had an underlying feeling that Detective Inspector Bishop would be very angry with him for using the witness box to announce his deputy's criminal activities. It could make the detective even more determined to see Edwin's client sent to jail.

However, there were more important issues to be resolved that day some of which, or all, could rebound on his client depending on the reaction of the Public Prosecutor and members of jury.

Edwin checked with Helen to ensure that Emille was still in the mood to act sensibly at the trial and that the plan of action was in full operational state.

Assured that everyone involved, including his star witness, were all geared up and awaiting his call when he told her a car would be outside the apartment at 9.30 to pick them up.

— — —

Early next morning Helen made sure that Emille had no signs of the grey tints in his hair as she touch it up with a black dust powder that could be quickly removed by a hair brush. She made Emille dress in the old suit trousers but told him to wear a clean white shirt with a tie. When she had finished Emille looked his right age of twenty seven and ready to be presented in court.

'When you ask to go to the toilet don't forget to use the disabled toilet. You'll find it easy enough, because one of your private security guards who you will recognise, will be standing next to the toilet door holding a disabled chair.'

Satisfied that she had everything under control, they waited for the car that would take them to the Central Criminal Court where they would meet up with Franklin Jenson and Edwin Crosby. She had no fears of anyone from the Mafia intercepting them because she and Emille were to be accompanied by Roberto Sanchez who she knew was armed.

Helen gathered together her magic make-up box and checked that Emille was dressed in the trousers of the suit he would ultimately wear, including a clean white shirt and appropriate tie.

'Remember' she warned him, 'in the witness box you are the twenty seven year old being questioned about a crime. Once you are told by the judge to sit in the well of the court, ask his permission to go to the loo, emphasizing you are desperate. Make sure you go into the men's disabled loo where I will be waiting to convert you into an old man. I will only have a few minutes to carry out the change so don't muck me about by asking questions. Just do as you are instructed and all will be well.'

Helen heard the car tooting outside the flats and grabbed her kit while pushing Emille towards the door.

— — —

When they arrived outside the courthouse Roberto handed his automatic to the driver.....one of his colleagues, because there was no way he would get past the entrance hall in the court without being checked for weapons.

Emille was given a golf hat complete with the sun visor to wear, pulled well down over his face to avoid being recognised, even though it was unlikely that anyone from the Mafia or Jamaica would be present.

In the court corridor Franklin and Edwin waited in wig and gown ready to take their place on the defence counsel's table. Emille was instructed by Franklin Jessop to remain with Roberto and sit on a wooden seat waiting to be called.

Roberto could feel the tension mounting in Emille as the young man clenched his hands together and nervously kept licking his dry lips. 'Try not to look so tense,' Roberto chided him.

Edwin and Franklin will look after you while you are in court and I will be waiting by this door to lead you towards the toilet. Once you are inside the toilet, follow Helen's instructions without question and we'll soon have you back on the plane.

— — —

Not surprisingly, no one recognised Emille as he was escorted into courthouse by Roberto Sanchez who took the opportunity to point out the location of the disabled loos, before they occupied seats outside the courtroom entrance door.

Inside Franklin and Edwin awaited the arrival of the trial judge hoping his Honour would be in a better mood than yesterday.

Promptly at ten o clock His Honour took his seat and the day's proceedings commenced.

Franklin recalled Edwin to the stand where the Judge reminded Edwin he was still under oath. Renewing his questioning he asked Edwin Crosby if his team of investigators had ever managed to discover the names of the two perpetrators who were reported to have boarded the Sunray and killed Walter Warren.

When Edwin turned to the Judge and replied 'yes your Honour we were told the names of the two men by accident having been rebuffed by the Mafia Don. He explained how another person on one of the Islands had committed a serious offence that would have resulted in a long term of imprisonment.

'The man was being interviewed in a cell by police officers offered to provide the name of one of the men who committed the murder on board the Sunray. In return he asked for a reduction in his sentence. The name he gave was a local called Emille Segura who had recently been admitted to hospital with injuries sustained by Mafia enforcers as a warning that he should keep his mouth shut about the murder. I interviewed Segura who told me that because his accomplice had failed to carry out the Don's instructions he saw his friend tied up and transferred to another cruiser.'

'I asked if he knew what had happened to his friend? He replied that he was not sure, but expected he had been weighted down with a heavy chain before being pushed alive over the side of the other cruiser into deep water in the Caribbean.'

'Naturally Segura didn't want to respond to my questions until I offered to protect him for life by spiriting away from the Caribbean.'

Franklin looked directly at the judge before addressing his next question to Edwin. 'And do you know where this Mr Segura is at present?'

Edwin nodded. 'He's just outside the courtroom door waiting to give evidence.'

Members of the press immediately rose from their seats rushing to obtain photographs of Segura and get them to their news editor a.s.a.p.

The Judge would have none of it. 'Sit down' he ordered in a strong voice. 'And bailiff, check each person to make sure their mobile phones come cameras are switched off. If not confiscate them until the end of the day. He then told the journalists that they were confined to court until he allowed them to leave.

The Prosecuting Attorney was once again feeling he had been outmanoeuvred by defence counsel so he declined from asking Edwin any questions.

When Edwin left the witness box a buzz ran round the courtroom. One could sense the tension as a Mr Segura was called to the witness box.

After giving his name and refusing to give is address, the oath was taken, allowing Franklin to begin his questions.

'Mr Segura were you a member of the crew of the cruiser named the Northern Star?'

'Yes.'

'Did you sail with the Northern Star to the Island of St Lucia?'

'Yes.'

Did you know the purpose of your visit to that Island?'

'Yes. I and my friend Carlos Jocelin were instructed to board a yacht called the Sunray and ask the Captain a question about whereabouts of a list he was supposed to have in his possession.'

'What time at night did you board the Sunray?'

'It was dark roughly about 11.30pm.'

'What happened when you boarded the Sunray?'

'The captain suddenly appeared on deck so Carlos hit him with a lead weighted cosh.'

'Did your friend Carlos ask the Captain where he kept a list you wanted?'

'Yes.'

'Then what happened?'

'The Captain denied any knowledge of a list so Carlos hit him again on both knees while I was told to tie the captain's hand and feet.'

The silence in the court was overpowering.

'What happened when he refused to talk?'

'We went down to the cabin to see if we could make his wife give us the combination to the ship's safe.'

'What happened next?'

'We found her lying naked on the bed. Carlos made a comment that she was a bonus and immediately mounted her and told me to do the same after he had finished.'

'And did you rape her?'

'No. I went through the motions to keep Carlos from hitting me, but I never raped her she was begging us to leave her alone.'

Franklin paused for a moment. 'Is all this point about rape a fantasy? Did Mrs Warren pay you to kill her husband and the idea of including rape was to convince the police that she had been attacked by intruders?'

'We knew the captain's wife was aboard, but our instructions to find a list came via the Captain of the cruiser Northern Star. I expect his instructions came from his boss who controlled the operations of the Mafioso in the Caribbean area.'

'You are certain that Mrs Warren was not involved in the death of her husband?'

'Absolutely certain.'

'Thank you Mr Segura. No more questions.'

Counsel for the prosecution got up from his chair and strolled slowly towards the witness box. 'Mr Segura is the jury to believe that you admit to committing a murder, raping the wife of the man you murdered, and yet you volunteered to appear before this court knowing you would be arrested and eventually be condemned to life in prison?'

'I did not rape the lady on the yacht and I was ordered to help Carlos. I did not expect him to throw the Captain overboard.'

'Not one single person in the other yachts anchored in the bay saw another boat in the vicinity of the Sunray that night. Did you use a small boat and row from the shore of Rodney Bay on Mrs Warren's instructions in order to murder her husband?'

'I've never heard of Rodney Bay, where is it?'

'Mr Segura you are a criminal and a liar. Why should this jury believe you?'

'I have taken an oath to tell the truth, regardless of the consequences.'

'Do you understand the meaning of telling the truth?'

'Yes'

'No one in this courtroom believes a word you have said.'

'My mate Carlos was ordered to obtain a list from the captain of the Sunray. The fact that he decided to kill the captain against the orders of our Mafia boss, resulted in Carlos being killed as a warning to anyone who disobeys an order. Why should Mrs Warren kill him and not me in order to cover up her tracks?'

The Prosecutor had no answer to that question so he rested his case.

Ch.46

The Judge told the witness he could stand down reminding him that he must remain in the courtroom.

'I desperately need to go to the toilet,' he told the Judge, holding his crotch.

'Bailiff, escort Mr Secura to the toilet and see that he returns to the court room immediately afterwards.'

The Bailiff took hold of Segura's arm and led him out of the courtroom to the nearest toilet that happened to be the disabled toilet. 'I need a crap' Emille told the Bailiff so I will be a little longer than usual.'

Emille went into the toilet and locked the door as soon as he saw Helen hiding in the corner.

She quickly brushed the blackening dust out of his hair; gave him the jacket matching the suit to put on; fitted a large bushy moustache to his upper lip; pulled a soft sun hat over his head and gave him a walking stick. It only took five minutes to make the change.

The Bailiff accepting that his charge was having a dump after the gruelling he had just received, walked over to the large window overlooking the main road and watched the collection of camera men waiting for the court to finish so they could get pictures for their respective newspapers.

He heard a disabled toilet door open and saw an old man being helped out of the toilet into a wheel chair that was being pushed by a bloke who was in conversation with the lady helping the old man who must have been having a pee. The Bailiff thought his charge had gone into the male toilet, but it was an old man who emerged, so he thought he had been mistaken and his charge must have gone into the ladies loo by mistake.

He waited another ten minutes before he knocked on the door of the ladies loo and asked his charge if he was finished.

When he got no reply he found an attendant and asked him to use his master key and open the door. The shock on his face when he found the toilet empty registered the fact that he knew he had been duped. With no windows in the toilet he was completely puzzled how the young man had managed to escape without his knowledge. How the Judge would react to the news that an important witness had disappeared was unthinkable. How the hell the young man had disappeared into thin air was to say the least unbelievable. A quick search of the corridors and asking questions of various officers on duty resulted in a blank. As far as they were concerned one or two people had departed from the court but none fitted the description the bailiff gave them.

– – –

In the meantime Emille was helped out of the wheel chair and into a car by Roberto before being whisked away to the private airport where a jet was waiting to take him and Helen back to the UK. As soon as they arrived at the airport the immigration officer, taking pity on the old man, helped Helen lift her disabled companion up the steps to the aircraft which shortly afterwards took off for the UK.

As soon as the aircraft was over the Atlantic, Helen removed Emille's makeup and gave him a hug. 'We won't know whether your performance in the witness box will save Mrs Warren, but I watched your performance and have to admit that you were bloody good. I heard you make a statement in court that you never raped Mrs Warren. Is it true or false?'

When Emille told her it was true, she told him that Mrs Warren might be prepared to forgive him if she accepted that he had been dominated by the older man into committing the murder and the rape. 'Your agreement to appear in court while putting yourself at considerable risk in an attempt to save her from prison, must make her feel that you have made a serious effort to atone for the punishment she has suffered over the last few months.'

Emille was not convinced he would ever be forgiven, and assumed that as soon as Mrs Warren was found to be not guilty of the charges against her, her Lawyer would put him back on a plane to Jamaica where the Mafia would make sure he was silenced forever.

In the meantime, the bailiff duly reported to the Judge that his charge had mysteriously disappeared after escaping from a toilet that had no windows. His Honour Sir Gavin Wainthrop, mindful that court bailiffs were not the brightest of persons, gave the man a severe dressing down in front of the crowded court and felt it was sufficient punishment bearing in mind he admired the young man's strength of character in agreeing to appear in court to admit he had been complicit to a murder.

– – –

As there were no more witnesses he asked the opposing attorneys to prepare their closing addresses to the jury and adjourned the court until the following day.

A meeting was held later that evening when Franklin, Edwin, Roberto, Julia, and Cara sat round the table discussing the events over the last few days. Edwin asked Roberto to report on Emille's escape from justice.

Roberto sang the praises of Helen and her amazing transformation of Emille, from young man, to an elderly infirm gentleman, in the space of less than ten minutes. 'I had no problem getting him out of the court in a wheel chair. In fact one of the police officers guarding the entrance helped me lift the old man into the car. Even the pilot had the engines warmed up ready for takeoff and Emille and Helen were on their way to the UK less than two hours after we spirited him out of the court.'

Directing a question at Franklin, Edwin asked him what he thought were the chances of getting an acquittal?

'About 50/50' came the reply that rather surprised Edwin who would have rated it more 80/20in their favour.

Franklin's lack of optimism surprised both Julia and Cara who both thought the defence evidence was very much in Julia's favour.

They all wondered how the jury would interpret the evidence and how the jury would be directed by the Judge whom Julia thought was a pompous old prick. In her view he seemed over keen to show both the Prosecuting and Defence Counsels that His Honour was more au-fait with the law than the two counsels put together.

However it was agreed that only after the jury had deliberated and given their decision would they know whether the scales of justice would at last put Julia out of her unfair period of confinement to the Island.

Ch.47

There was a feeling of tension in the court. The press were there in larger numbers hoping the jury would reach a decision before the the dreaded deadline for printing the evening newspaper. The jury already in their seats looked uncomfortable knowing their decision would either make the accused a very happy person, or the police would place handcuffs on her wrists as she was led off to prison.

The ghouls in the upper gallery where wetting their lips in anticipation of mayhem in the court below. While both counsels had their heads buried in notes and scribbling frantically as they made amendments to their final draft prior to the arrival of the Judge.

Just to add to the feeling of gloom, it was pouring with rain across the Island with deep rumbles of thunder and periodic flashes of forked lightning to increase the tense atmosphere.

The Honourable Sir Gavin Wainthrop clad in his judicial robe and grey wig mounted the dais promptly at ten am. Bowing to the two counsellors he took his seat and asked Mr Scott if he was ready to address the jury.

Raymond Scott stood up, picked up his 'memory' script and commenced to address the jury using broadly similar words to those used when he addressed the jury at the previous trial. He drolled on for nearly an hour, emphasizing the jury's need to note various points he had made about flaws in defence counsels arguments.

Edwin felt his eyes closing as his interest in the arguments waned until he suddenly realised the Prosecuting Council had at long last got round to the evidence given during the preceding days

'Members of the jury, learned counsel for the defence has endeavoured to prove with his last witness that the accused Mrs Julia Warren did not commit the murder of her husband, or pay two well known criminals to commit the act on her behalf. No one can ever believe a criminal's evidence even when given under oath. They are well known for their skills at lying in an attempt to save their own skins from prosecution, or get a reduction on their sentence when they eventually appear before a judge. Mr Segura is no exception. He had obviously been primed by the defence counsel to utter the appropriate words that would save counsel's client from the charges against her. Whether Counsel has offered to get Segura a reduce sentence, or offered a substantial sum of money will never be known. But I ask you members of the jury to discount his evidence as seriously flawed as he lied through his teeth.'

'Counsel for the defence has not provided one shred of conclusive evidence that Mrs Warren is innocent. There is not one single statement from the Defence Counsel's witnesses countersigned by the police that have been place before His Honour the Judge because those witnesses are themselves unreliable. I ask you to find the accused guilty on all counts.'

Raymond Scott bowed to the jury and resumed his seat.

It was at that moment that the court was interrupted by a bailiff accompanied by a uniformed police officer entering the room and walking to the Prosecuting Attorney's table allowing the officer to hand a note to Detective Inspector Harry Bishop. Having read the note the Inspector handed it to the Prosecuting Attorney before rising from his seat and accompanying the officer from the courtroom.

His Honour the Judge watched the proceedings with a deep frown on his face. There were lots of things he took exception to, and one of those was anyone interrupting court proceedings without a 'by your leave' before requesting permission from the Judge.

Raymond Scott rose to his feet and requested permission to approach the Judge. When he was granted permission with a nod from his Honour he handed the note he had just read and watched the Judge's face as he read the contents.

Turning to the defence counsel's table he asked Mr. Jenson and Mr. Crosby to join Mr. Scott in his chambers immediately. Naturally the courtroom was abuzz with chatter wondering what was so important that defence counsel's closing address could be interrupted.

As soon as the completely bemused defence counsellors were seated in the Judges room the announcement from the Judge came out like a bombshell. 'The police were called to the Adelphi hotel less than two hours ago by a member of the hotel staff, who told them that the owner Cara Phillipé and a room maid had been abducted by three men and been taken away in the back of a van. Although a series of road blocks was mounted within a short time there has been no sign of the two women.'

The audible gasp and grimace from Edwin was noted by the Judge. 'I noted from the court records that you are residing at the Adelphi. If you wish to go to the hotel before it is closed by the police you may leave the courtroom. Turning to Mr. Jenson he said he understood the relationship that had developed between the two. 'You are about to give your final address to the jury and there is nothing you can do about the abduction which is now in the hands of the police, so I expect you to remain so that the jury can arrive at their deliberations a.s.a.p.'

Edwin excused himself and immediately left the room determined to do two things virtually simultaneously. One, to check that Julia was adequately guarded, and two, to do everything he could to find out why Cara had been abducted although he had a suspicion he would soon find out.

Ch.48

The shock left even Franklin stunned. Never the less he had to agree with the Judge that there was nothing he could do in the interim and his first responsibility as the defence lawyer was to look after his client. He came to the immediate decision not to inform Julia of Cara's abduction. He had to present his closing address to the jury and the last thing he wanted was to have a hysterical client on his hands during that critical period.

When the court was reassembled the Judge looking his usual calm and collected self, apologised for the temporary delay. Turning to the Defence Counsel he said 'Mr Jenson are you ready to present your closing address?'

It was now Franklin's turn.

'Members of the jury, Counsel for the Prosecution has presented a strong case and I have to admit I find it difficult to challenge his reasoning. However, you are not being asked to judge whether there are flaws in defence counsels presentation, but whether in your joint opinion it has been conclusively proved by the prosecution that Mrs Julia Warren murdered her husband, or paid two criminals to do it on her behalf.'

Counsel for the Prosecution argues that criminals cannot be trusted and lie to save their skins. My witness Mr Segura has openly admitted in this court that he was a party to the murder of Mr Warren. No Counsel that I know of could offer a reduction in sentence to someone who admits their guilt to one of the most heinous offences throughout the world. By his own admission he can now be arrested and spend the rest of his days in prison, yet he offered to state under oath that it was the Head of the Mafia who employed him and arranged for him to make contact with Walter Warren. He has stated on oath that it was the unexpected change of his partner's attitude that resulted in Mr Warren's untimely death.'

'You may or may not believe Mr Segura, but the evidence given by Police Superintendent Oliver Laneson under oath cannot be challenged. I will remind you he boarded the Northern Star and found both drugs and illegal weapons aboard. He questioned the Captain who voluntarily refused legal help from his employer before making a statement to the affect that two of his crew were placed aboard the Sunray to demand a list from Walter Warren on the orders of his boss the regional head of the Mafia. Superintendent Laneson stated under oath that the Captain of the Northern Star emphatically denied that Mrs Warren had paid any of his crew to murder her husband.'

Bearing in mind that several members of the crew have not been seen since they fell foul of their Mafia Boss and are most likely residing at the bottom of the Caribbean in Neptune's Parlour, as it is commonly called by local fishermen.'

'I ask you to consider whether a respected Police Superintendent's word under oath, is more valuable than a statement signed by a criminal who the Prosecuting Counsel has stated is liable to lie even when under oath. I trust that your deliberations will bring about the acquittal of my client who has protested her innocence from day one of this tragic death. I and my team are convinced she is not guilty; I hope you will all agree with our honest endeavours to prove her innocence. I rest my case.'

It was now up to His Honour the Judge to sum up before requesting the jury to retire.

Judge Wainthrop lowered his busy pen to the desk top before addressing the jury. 'Members of the jury you have been extremely patient during this long retrial and I suspect some elements of the laws of this Island have gone over your head. However, you are charged with determining whether Julia Warren is guilty of murder, or as indicated by the defence Lawyer she is entirely innocent. Try to disregard all the circumstantial evidence and concentrate your minds on the facts. You have to decide whether Julia Warren seriously wanted rid of her husband, or whether her husband's possible links with the Mafia brought about his demise. I await your response.'

The jury rose from their seats and retired to the jury room to consider their verdict.

Franklin Jenson glanced at the empty jury box and wondered how many whiskies he would have to down to stay the tremble affecting his whole body. The jury were not aware of the crisis that was unfolding behind the scenes but would it have affected their judgment had they known. It was a debatable point.

That there would not be another retrial was fairly obvious, but if the verdict went against his client he would forever feel he had not done enough work to ensure she was found not guilty. How he would live knowing an innocent woman was behind bars was something that would rest with his conscience for the rest of his life, knowing his services would most likely not be used during her appeal against the sentence.

Recognising that even one whisky might impair his thinking powers, he continually used the coffee machine in the lobby as everyone waited a call from the clerk of the court to resume their seats to hear the jury's decision.

– – –

On this occasion the jury accepted without equivocation that the foreman was chairman and in charge.

'Before we begin our deliberations can I have a show of hands of those in favour of a guilty verdict' He looked around the jury members before asking for those in favour of a not guilty verdict.' Having ascertained their response he suggested that it would be inappropriate if they returned to the court after such a short adjournment. 'Let us have a quiet discussion about why each of us has come to a similar conclusion to fill in the next two hours before I inform the judge that we have reached a decision. All in favour?' A show of hands was unanimous.

Surprisingly to both counsels, the reporters in the press box, and those members of the public who had decided to delay their departure in order to enjoy the final moments of this case that had rocked the local population to the very core. Murder cases where few and far between on this idyllic holiday island and the gory details had to be enjoyed to the full.

The Clerk of the Court shortly after two hours had elapsed announced that the jury were returning to announce their verdict.

As the jury resumed their seats the elected foreman remained standing.

His Honour Sir Gavin Wainthrop asked the Clerk of the Court to collect the jury's decision. When it was handed up to him he glanced at the written decision before asking the foreman to announce the jury's decision.

In a loud voice, the foreman said that the unanimous decision of the jury was to find the accused not guilty on all charges.

A hubbub broke out throughout the court room with everyone totally ignoring the judge as he angrily rapped his gavel calling for order.

When order was finally restored by the court bailiffs, the judge turned to Mrs Warren who was standing next to Franklin looking totally bemused at the absence of Edwin Crosby and wondering how he could miss such an important moment affecting her future. 'Mrs Warren the jury have found you not guilty and I totally concur with their decision. Your passport will be returned to you within the hour and I will issue an order to release those of your husband's assets that have been frozen during this trial. No doubt you legal advisors will now take the appropriate steps to apply for your late husband's assets to be distributed in accordance with his wishes. You are now formally released from this court.'

Standing up he bowed to both Counsels in turn before retiring gracefully to his chambers to await the next case on the court list.

Franklin gave Julia a hug as tears of joy rolled down her face. The long ordeal was finally over, or so she thought.

– – –

It was time for Franklin to bring Julia up to date and he was dreading her reaction when she heard the awful news about her dear friend. Leaving the court he took her outside and sat her on a public bench where he explained the reason for Edwin's absence, before adding that was as much as he knew and it was his intention to go immediately to the Adelphi Hotel to see Edwin and get an update as to what was going on. He warned Julia that her life was still at serious risk from the Mafia and it was in her best interest to return to the safe house where he would contact her as soon as he had news.

A tearful Julia reluctantly agreed on condition she was kept informed.

Franklin after seeing that she was being escorted back to the safe house by one of Roberto's security guards, made his way with trepidation to the Adelphi Hotel to link up with Edwin. As expected there was a line of police vehicles parked outside and two officers were on duty at the entrance barring anyone, and particularly reporters looking for a scoop.

Ch.49

When Edwin informed the officers he was a resident and showed his key to his room as evidence, they let him in and told him to register with the officer on duty at the reception desk. That proved unnecessary as he was met by Detective Inspector Bishop in the foyer.

'Please update me of any news' requested Edwin.

The Inspector was pleased to see the lawyer but didn't say so. Instead he told Edwin that the abductors had left a message to say they would be in contact within the next twenty four hours, but that no contact had been made up to the time of Edwin's arrival.

'Do you think they are after a ransom?' He asked naively and prematurely having not thought through the reason for the abduction.

Inspector Bishop raised his eyebrows to express his surprise at the question. 'The Mafia have failed to track down the location of Julia Warren and appear to have decided to take Cara Phillipé to exert some pressure on you,' he replied. 'Somehow they have found that Cara and Julia were friends and they have taken her hostage until they are supplied with something they urgently need. 'Have you any idea what that would be Mr Crosby?' he asked.

Without waiting for a reply as he was well aware about the crucial list, having been informed by the Public Prosecutor of its importance to the Mafia, he went on to inform Edwin what arrangements had been put in hand for the expected call.

'We may not be as sophisticated as the London Met., but the police force on the Island do have some important equipment to help us in our search for Mrs Phillipé. I have installed a telephone connection with the phone on the reception desk that records the message of the person calling, while another piece of equipment, a voice synthesiser, records the voice pitch to help us define who is calling. I am pleased you are here,' he told Edwin. 'Because I would like you to answer the telephone and try to find out what it is they want. They will expect the police to be in attendance, but I want them to think we are so inexperienced that we will have to call in experts to solve the reason for the abduction.'

There was a long and tedious wait for the phone to ring and the Inspector was inclined to call it off when nothing had happened by ten o clock in the evening. They were all ready to call it a day when the phone trilled loudly giving them all a start.

The police officers on duty switched on the equipment and indicated to Edwin he should pick up the receiver. A voice at the other end asked who was speaking and when Edwin told them his name there was a brief pause while the caller consulted someone in the room with him.

'Mr. Crosby you have been meddling in affairs that are not your concern. You are only in St Lucia to defend a Mrs Warren.' There was another long pause. 'We have been trying to find Mrs Warren without success in order to obtain information she holds, and to remind her lawyer that deviating in matters that are not his concern brings about harsh penalties. You will receive our warning within the next few hours. Please hand over the list and return to the UK on the next available plane.

The telephone went dead.

Inspector Bishop who was listening on another line turned to Edwin. 'I think you and your colleagues have stirred up a hornet's nest and the bastards on the other end of the line are objecting to being stung. Have you any idea what they meant by a warning? There was no mention of releasing the hostages if you handed over the list they want before buggering of to the UK on the next plane?'

Edwin had listened intently to the voice and was fairly confident that the person on the other end of the line was the Jap who was Don Pascal's protector and strong arm the last time they had met at the hacienda. He told Inspector Bishop, who turned to the synthesiser operator and asked him if he could define from the information on the screen the nationality of the person who was making the call.

Edwin listened to the sounds from the machine that came over as double Dutch to him, while the operator listened intently using a set of headphones to magnify the sound. He turned to his boss and told him that he would need more time to be specific, but from the first run of the sound patterns he was reasonably confident that the person on the other end of the line was Occidental and from Japan, China or Korea.

Edwin was heard to mutter 'bingo'.

Shortly afterwards Franklin Jenson was admitted to the hotel after being cleared by the Inspector. He informed Edwin of the good news that was now heavily overshadowed by the current situation. He assured Edwin that Julia was being heavily protected by Roberto's armed guards and arrangements were already underway to get Julia off the Island now she was in possession of her passport.

As there was nothing that Franklin could do to help in the current crisis, he was asked to leave by the Inspector.

– – –

The news arrived unexpectedly that rocked everyone back on their heels. It was two o clock in the morning when everyone at the Adelphi was either asleep, or dozing at their stations, in case further calls were made from the abductors.

The call came from a mobile police unit who had been called out by a vagrant who found the body of a woman on the road side who appeared to have been shot. An open purse was lying beside the body and the vagrant was found by the police driver to have fifty Caribbean dollars and a credit card in the name of Rula Mooney in his possession. The officer said he had arrested the vagrant and required further assistance at the scene of the crime.

Without needing to look at his notes the Inspector knew immediately the Rula Mooney was the chamber maid abducted with Cara Phillipé. Instructing the officer to avoid touching the body, or disturbing the area, he told him that forensic officers from his HQ were on their way to examine the body and search the area for clues.

Turning to Edwin who was still half asleep he explained what had happened and the steps he had taken to have the victim identified and tested for evidence. 'I have a strong feeling that the abductors discovered they had abducted the wrong person and took steps to see she was unable to identify them by killing her. I wonder who they were after, rather than the maid?' he asked, knowing he would not receive an answer from the shocked quartet gathered round the reception desk.

'God help Cara,' came the cry from another of the hotel staff, who unable to sleep had wandered unnoticed into the reception area and overheard the discussion.

Edwin stepped forward to offer his support to the assistant cook who was part of a small dedicated team determined to ensure that the Adelphi won high praise for the quality of its food and excellent service to its customers.

'The police will soon run these murderers' to justice,' he told her, while thinking to himself that the Mafia were too clever by half to allow their enforcers to get caught.

Ch.50

It was daylight before the Inspector received the first report from the crime scene. Apparently Rula Mooney had been shot in the back of the head before being dumped from the van at the roadside to be discovered by the vagrant in an area between Marigot Bay and Castries.

A burnt out van was also reported to have been found on a deserted beach in a small bay north of Marigot Bay.

Inspector Bishop thought it now possible that the abduction party were headed for this bay to put their prisoners on board one of the high speed cruising yachts owned by the Mafia. 'I'm very much afraid Cara Phillipé could be anywhere in the Caribbean by now,' he said. 'However, I have warned the coastguard to be on the lookout for any yachts or cruisers at sea and to check them out.'

He reminded Edwin that the Mafia would be checking the airport at Castries to make sure he had left the Island as ordered. To which Edwin replied that he had been too shocked by the death of the hotel employee to make the necessary arrangements to fly back to the UK.

When the Inspector authorised Edwin to use the telephone they now controlled, Edwin immediately contacted the airport and asked for the first available seat on an aircraft to the UK. 'Any class of seat will do,' he told the booking clerk who informed him that a seat in the Business Class had been reserved for him on an aircraft departing at eight pm that evening. 'The flight number was A4521' she told him.

As he put down the telephone it rang again making everyone's heart take a quicker pace, such was the tension within the hotel foyer.

When Edwin picked up the phone it was Franklin who caused Edwin to utter a savage oath and bawled at his counsellor friend that he should know better than to ring the hotel when the phones were being controlled by the police.

Franklin apologised profusely, but explained that he had decided to make the call to put Edwin in the picture. 'Julia was escorted to a plane flying to Florida in the USA where she will be transferred to another flight bound for the UK,' he said. 'It was the only seat available out of Castries. After I explained the need to ensure her safety the airline agreed to ensure she got a seat next to the Air Marshall. She's on her way to England by now Edwin so I am happy to say she is safely out of the hands of the vengeful Mafia.'

Edwin apologised for his blasphemous outburst and thanked Franklin not only for his fine presentation in freeing his client, but for his friendship and his participation in getting Julia back to her home and friends in the UK.

When one of the Inspector's staff indicated he had spent too long on the telephone he said goodbye to Franklin and replaced the receiver.

– – –

One of the resident police officers approached Edwin and explained that the Inspector had arranged to guide the remaining staff through a series of rogue pictures of known criminals with Mafia connections. One of the chamber maids had professed to recognise a picture of one of the three men who had abducted Cara and Rula. The officer told Edwin, 'that he is called Gregori Mathis and is well known to us as a supplier of drugs and is also a Mafia tough guy. He has a prison record as long as your arm but is known to be free at the moment. I have put out a general order to arrest him on sight on suspicion of kidnap and murder, but so far he appears to have gone underground. We know who his friends are, but the chamber maid does not recognise their pictures as either of the other two men.'

Edwin thanked the officer and began to understand that his belligerent attitude to Inspector Bishop may have been seriously misplaced. The Inspector was doing what he was best at; that is investigating serious incidents of crime.

The telephone rang again with even more bad news. A woman's body had been washed up on the beach north of Marigot Bay. The local police reported that she did not appear to have been in the sea for very long and had been found wearing a lifejacket. It was assumed by the officers that she had fallen overboard from a yacht and had drowned before her body had been carried ashore by the incoming tide. However, on further inspection it was discovered she had been shot in the back of the head.

Edwin felt an ice cold feeling envelope his entire body. He knew who it was, even though the body had not been identified.

The body was later identified as that of Cara Phillipé, aged forty one, the owner of the Adelphi Hotel in Castries.

Everyone associated with the lovely Cara was devastated with the sad news. The staff was in tears, while partly wondering what would happen to them, now that their employer was dead.

Inspector Bishop was extremely angry and lashing out in all directions with his tongue. Every police officer on duty both at the hotel and in the headquarters tried to give him a wide berth until he calmed down, but he was not in the mood to be appeased. Those out on patrol in cars felt his wrath, as did those on duty at checkpoints, for failing to apprehend the abductors. Even those searching in vain for Gregori Mathis did not escape. He was one very angry and upset police inspector. But there was a growing determination on his face that the perpetrators would be brought to justice and God help them when he eventually got them into his cells.

It was growing dark outside when the telephone once again brought the officers manning the desk to a state of readiness. Edwin, with his bags packed was sitting in the foyer waiting for the taxi to take him to the airport, while attempting to read a book in an endeavour to keep his over active mind occupied. The officer called him over to the desk to answer the phone while the officer concentrated on the other equipment used to decode voices.

It was the same voice on the line. 'Mr Crosby, you are still at the hotel and ignored our warning that you must leave the Island on the first available aircraft and keep your nose permanently out of our business or face the consequences. Perhaps you now understand what happens when you ignore a warning.'

Edwin could not contain his anger. 'I know who you are you miserable piece of shit and I will hunt you down as long as I live. The poor chamber maid and Cara who your cold blooded hoods murdered, were innocent people who never did anyone any harm. Every one of you, and that cold fish who will be sitting listening to this conversation, can rest assured that I will never give up until you are all dead. The police will want you behind bars for the rest of your days.....me, I want you dead.' And having got the angry words off his chest he slammed the phone back on its receiver.

The officer listening to his rant, understood Edwin's anger, but pointed out quietly that he should have controlled his temper and stretched out the conversation to give him and his team time to try and trace the call back to its base.

But on this occasion Edwin was not in the mood to be co-operative as he angrily responded. 'I know exactly where the bloody call came from, and I know who is bloody well responsible for the deaths of my friend and her employee. *I've* been worried for months about my client, now it's *their* turn to bloody worry. I will not rest until I hunt the bastards down like the vermin they are and spit on their coffins and feel justice has been served as they are rolled into the crematorium ovens.'

Turning to the officer who was not surprised at the outburst he asked him to ring the bloody airport and cancel his seat that had been reserved on flight A4521.

Ch.51

Arturo Vegas, sitting in his air conditioned office in steamy Mexico City was bringing himself up to date by digesting the latest news in the morning newspaper he had collected from the local newsagent on his way to the office, caught a late news item headed

English Beauty Cleared of Murder on St Lucia.
Local drug ring exposed.

He had not forgotten the visit from Edwin Crosby, or the controversial visit to Don Pascal's fortified hacienda. In his view the mad English took an enormous risk treading on the Don's toes. Not many unwelcome visitors to the Don's hacienda left the premises alive. Reading on, he discovered that Edwin had provided sufficient evidence to result in the jury finding his client not guilty. At the same time local reporters claimed that the Englishman's diligent enquiries had unearthed a major drug syndicate in the Caribbean islands resulting in the shocked arrest of a local senior police officer.

Arturo immediately sat down and penned a letter of congratulations to Edwin addressing it to the Adelphi Hotel. Castries, St Lucia.

Hello once again Edwin,

This morning I read the news of successful court case resulting in the jury deciding your client was innocent of the murder of her husband. The report gives graphic details of the length and complexity of your investigations resulting in the exposure of a major drug syndicate in the Caribbean.

It reminded me that my bête noir, Don Pascal, still sits comfortably in his hacienda knowing that there is not a shred of evidence pointing the figure in his direction.

The daily newspaper gives the impression that the Don claims he issued the orders to the Captain of the Northern Star to recover a document from Walter Warren, but claims that it had nothing to do with illegal drugs and denies that he has ever been involved in anything illegal. Then the old rascal would, wouldn't he. He is also reported to have said that no instructions were given to assault Warren or harm his wife. It appears from what I have read about the trial that one witness stated that his accomplice one Carlos Jacelin acted without authority in killing Warren and raping his wife.

I do feel that I should put the record straight.

Don Frederico Pascal should never be underestimated. He is highly intelligent and devious enough to escape the law even though all those who have tried to bring him to justice have failed, including yours truly.

In my view for what it is worth, Don Pascal carefully selected the two men who were sent to the yacht to 'interview' Walter Warren. The Don would be well aware that Carlos Jacelin was a tough ruthless enforcer who was known to have disposed of many of the Don's enemies without ever being caught; and that Emille Segura was only a paid helper.

The Don, although never giving the order, would also realise that Jacelin would lose his temper when Warren refused to hand over the document he was seeking, and was likely to kill Warren as a result. It is fairly obvious to me that the Don wanted Warren disposed of, possibly because he was the main person holding the copy of the list you showed me and was suspected of taking an extra cut from the payments due to be paid into the Don's coffers and therefore had to be disposed of.

The rape of Warren's wife by Carlos Jacelin became an added bonus when Warren's wife became a suspect. It is possible that the St Lucia police officer, who has since been arrested for drug dealing, put the idea that Warren's wife could have committed the murder to his own boss who was grasping at straws in an attempt to solve the crime.

I will never give up trying to put the Don behind bars, but I decided to write to you my friend so that you understand my feelings following this long trial of your client.

Sincerely,

Arturo

ps. I think your missing captain may also be at the bottom of Caribbean.

Ch.52

Following the two deaths, the police had no option but to close the hotel and order all residents to move out and find other accommodation. Edwin asked Franklin Jenson to recommend a small quiet hotel for him for a few days until he decided how to deal with his future commitments. Franklin quickly came up with a small Guest House only two streets away from the Adelphi where the owner had a vacancy and had agreed to reserve a room for him.

As soon as he was in the new accommodation he telephoned his father and told him the whole sad story.

James Crosby was sympathetic and recognised his son's dilemma, while advising Edwin that now that the case against his client was satisfactorily concluded there was no reason for him to remain in the Caribbean. 'Julia Warren is safely back in the UK and the drugs issues you have raised will be handled by the local police. You have done an excellent job for your client, but your place is back in these chambers where the work load is piling up in your absence.'

There was a silence for a few moments until James asked if Edwin was still on the line.

'I'm still here' replied Edwin with a deep frown on his face. 'I understand why you want me back a.s.a.p. However, I have promised myself that the murders of two innocent people must be avenged, because they were killed as a result of my accidental involvement in the activities of a drug cartel. I hold myself responsible for their deaths, so I have decided not to return to the UK until I see justice done to the killers and their bosses. I know you need my services, but there are other lawyers available in the UK who would be delighted to join your chambers; I am therefore tendering my resignation with immediate effect.' Without waiting to hear his father's views he put down the phone knowing full well that as he had changed his hotel his father could not call him back.

The letter from Arturo Vegas arrived at the Adelphi Hotel the next morning and was delivered by hand by a police officer who was aware of Edwin's new address. Edwin read the letter and crumpled it up in anger and threw it in the waste paper basket in disgust.

– – –

The coroner's summing up at the inquest was as expected. The two females were killed by persons unknown and the crime was being investigated by the police. When Edwin asked Inspector Bishop why Cara had been put in a lifejacket, he replied that the killers wanted her to be washed ashore, so that her execution would serve as a final warning to those persons interfering with the operations of the Drug Cartel.

When Edwin told the Inspector he could not understand why the chamber maid had been abducted, Inspector Bishop replied that he had felt the same way until one of his officers questioned the other staff in the hotel. 'They told the officer that Rula was at the reception desk when the killers entered the hotel and they may have heard her name mentioned, misinterpreting Rula as Julia. It is possible, but a little farfetched, but it is the only reason I can think of why they would take her,' replied the Inspector.

The funerals of Rula Mooney and Cara Phillipé took place on the following Monday in a packed Catholic Church with a large number of mourners spilling onto the surrounding graveyard and even blocking the road that ran past the church. The Island's population were up in arms about the brutal murders and strong representations had been made to the Island's Governor and the elected Council to bring the perpetrators to justice as quickly as possible.

The Chief of Police in particular came under intense pressure to find the culprits and there were mass mutterings that the law should be changed to allow hanging to be returned to the Island.

Rula Mooney was well known in the community and her death at fifty one years had left a bereaved husband and two girls aged twenty and twenty two who were still single. They lived in a three bed flat on the outskirts of Castries and their mother had worked in Cara's hotel for ten years.

Cara Phillipé had also been married but no children had resulted from the marriage. Although one should never speak ill of the dead, it was rumoured that her husband was a ne'er do well and known drug addict, who walked out of a bar opposite the harbour coked up to the eyeballs and fell into the harbour, where his body was recovered the following day. It was also whispered that Cara mourned the loss of her husband, but showed a sense of relief once he was buried.

She sold their house in Castries and invested the money in the run down Adelphi Hotel that she decorated by herself, and built up its reputation over a number of years by shrewd management and excellent customer relations. Everyone was surprised to find she had left a Will, and even more surprised that she had left the hotel to the staff she employed irrespective of service. The chef, assistant cook and three chamber maids were listed by name in the Will. One of the three being Rula Mooney, that meant her husband was now a part owner of the hotel.

Cara being ever thoughtful before her death, suggested that the new owners employ a hotel manager to run the hotel and that they continue to operate the hotel in their normal jobs making due allowance for their ultimate retirement.

After a brief meeting held by the new owners, they asked Rula's husband if he would accept the role on manager while attending courses to improve his knowledge of how a small hotel should be run efficiently. Rula's husband initially shied away from the offer, but after further pressure from Rula's friends at the hotel decided to give it a go. To his relief on accepting the offer, the new joint owners also invited his two girls to join the staff. The younger to be trained as a waitress with responsibility for cleaning the dining room and her elder sister as the bar manager, come book keeper, to aid her father in his management responsibilities.

The hotel reopened after two weeks of frantic activity to be renamed the 'Cara Adelphi Hotel'.

– – –

Away from all the tragedy and frustrated anger of the local population on the Island, Julia Warren now residing back in her home in the UK was receiving a visit from James Crosby, who quietly informed her of the double tragedies that had occurred on the Island.

Julia's initial reaction was one of shock with a flood of tears, followed by stating her intention of flying back to St Lucia on the first available aeroplane to offer her condolences and attend the funerals.

James explained that the news of the deaths had been withheld from her to give her time to recover from the traumas of her double trial; that the funerals had already been held; and that there was no reason for her to return to the Island where her life could still be at risk.

It went through Julia's mind that a lifelong and trusted friendship with Cara had not meant to last, and she was saddened that it was not to be. Friendships that are 'forever' can only last until one of the friendships is severed by death.

When Julia asked how Edwin had taken the news of the deaths, James remained tight lipped about his son's resignation from the firm and told her that Edwin had been shocked, but was getting over the loss.

Ch.53

In a surprising turn of events, Superintendent Oliver Laneson was sitting at his desk in the Police Headquarters in Kingston, Jamaica, when he received a long distance call from the Royal Mounted Police in Ottawa in Canada.

Oliver was informed by the switchboard operator that Chief Superintendent Hawk of the RCMP was on the line. 'A pleasant surprise Chief Superintendent; I have never received a call from colleagues in the far north although I have met some of your officers who have holidayed on Jamaica. I can hazard a guess at the reason for you call, but please put me in the picture.'

Chief Superintendent Hawk said he was pleased to make the Superintnedent's, acquaintance and the reason for the call concerned a Captain Hulio Stanza of the yacht Northern Star.

Surprise, surprise, thought Oliver as he listened intently.

'Two of my officers were in a patrol car on the main highway from Montreal to the United States Border when they stopped a vehicle that kept swerving to the left hand side of the road and assumed the driver was drunk. It turned out that the driver was from Jamaica and found it difficult to remember he had to drive on the right side of the road in Canada. My officers were about to give him a verbal caution and send him on his way, when the driver was asked why he was in Canada. When he naively replied he was seeking employment, he was asked to produce his passport and his written authority to remain in Canada for the maximum period of six months.'

'As his passport had not been stamped by the immigration authority, he was arrested and taken to the nearest police post when he eventually admitted to having entered our country illegally. When he was informed he would be deported back to Jamaica, he told us it would be sentencing him to a terrible death and asked us to get in touch with you, to get confirmation that he was telling the truth.

Oliver Laneson said not only was he able to confirm that Hulio Stanza was a Jamaican citizen, and that he was wanted by the Mafia who wanted to silence him, but that there was a warrant out for his arrest for being an accomplice to the murder of a British subject on the Island of St Lucia. 'I have to admit he was an unwilling accomplice and was being held in protective custody by my officers when he escaped. I assumed wrongly that he was dead, but he did tell me while in custody he was proposing to hide in Canada or Alaska until the heat died down. I can confirm that if he is deported back to Jamaica his life would be in serious danger from the local Mafia.

Chief Superintendent Hawk thought about Laneson's response for a moment before coming to a decision. 'Superintendent, let me have that information in writing and I will place it before the court, who may allow him to stay in Canada where he will be safe providing he goes to the far north where it is less populated and they are in urgent need of experienced boatmen. I assume you will cancel the arrest warrant or the court will not grant him asylum?'

Oliver nodded his head before adding a formal 'yes I will arrange that immediately.' He made a note on his pad to advise Captain Arturo Vegas in Mexico that he had a witness that may help him bring down the leader of the massive drug ring in the Central Americas.

Ch.54

Inspector Bishop had ceased to be angry with Edwin Crosby for using the courtroom to name his deputy Sergeant Totti as a suspected drug runner. Under intense examination, the Sergeant had admitted he was being paid a monthly bonus by an unknown Mafia boss to turn a blind eye to drug distributors on the island, but refused to admit that he was distributing drugs. The Inspector had got over the initial shock of his assistant's involvement and was now hell bent on cleaning up the reputation the Island had acquired, of being a paradise for those with money wishing to 'ride the dragon'.

He demanded that ex Sergeant Totti provide names of other suppliers, or he would personally see that his ex deputy went to prison for the rest of his days. Not that the threat mattered all that much. Totti who was well aware what would happen to him once he was locked up in Dennery Penal Establishment. There were a number of hardened criminals serving long sentences, that remembered Sergeant Totti as being one of the police officers who had arranged for them to live on stodgy porridge and margarined bread, accompanied by stewed luke warm tea, day in and day out, until the smell of breakfast being prepared made them puke. He would be made most welcome.

The Inspector, a born pessimist, was of the opinion that any news was bad news. However he was proved to be wrong that morning when he was informed that two of his officers had arrested Gregori Mathis, who was found camping on a site by the Mabouya River mingling with a host of holiday hippies while hoping to escape attention.

The officers who were checking the site for drugs, were as surprised as Mathis, when they found him sitting with others around a camp fire singing hippy type songs to the accompaniment of a guitar.

Gregory Mathis was brought back to Castries in handcuffs where he huffed and puffed about innocent citizens minding their own business being harassed by the police, when all he was doing was enjoying a camping holiday with some friends. Inspector Bishop told him to shut his mouth and told him he was about to be placed in an identity parade. The change in colour on Mathis's face was noted. When the time came for him to be placed in the identity line up, he was quickly picked out by the chamber maid who had identified his photograph earlier in that month as one of the abductors at the Adelphi Hotel. Mathis was promptly charged with the murder of Rula Mooney and remanded in custody to Dennery Prison where the new Governor was warned to keep Mathis safe, or losing his job if he failed.

The Inspector determined to rid the Island of this nest of vipers, personally visited the prison to interview Mathis who the Governor had wisely placed in an individual cell in an area specially set aside for prisoners who were of the paedophile ilk, who were likely to be harmed by other prisoners who had an inborn hatred of child abusers.

Gregori Mathis was clearly a very worried prisoner when he was brought before the Inspector. His opening words before he sat down in the interview room, was 'I never shot the woman. I don't even possess a gun.'

'Sit down and shut up,' ordered the Inspector. 'If you didn't shoot the chamber maid, I want the name of the man who did. Three of you entered the hotel and abducted two innocent ladies who are now dead. I want those other two names and one way or another you are going to give them to me.'

Gregori Mathis flinched as he recognised the anger that was being disgorged from the Inspector's mouth coupled with the deep frown on the face.

'If I give you their names I am as good as dead,' he replied.

Harry Bishop gave a deep sigh. 'Without those names you are as good as dead, and you know it. Why do you think I am keeping you in an isolation cell guarded twenty four hours a day by warders? The moment after you joined the Mafia as an enforcer your days on this earth were limited. You can give me those two names now, and they can join you in adjoining cells, or continue to refuse and I will use other avenues open to me until I have them.' Without waiting for a reply he asked Mathis if he had ever heard of rendition?'

When Gregori shook his head that the word meant nothing to him, Harry Bishop explained the procedure in detail. 'We are not allowed by law to torture any prisoner in order to obtain the information we desperately need. However, if a prisoner refuses to co-operate, we fly the prisoner to another country that has no qualms about how to get the information that is required. In your case I could fly you to the American base at Guantanamo Bay in Cuba and leave it to the Yanks to obtain those names for me. They are experts at using water torture knowing prisoners talk their heads off after thirty minutes.' The Inspector allowed that to sink in to Mathis's brain for a few seconds. 'However, in your case I feel Mexico would be a better bet. They use flexible canes on your feet and back, and guarantee you will talk quicker than that used by the Yanks. That my friend.......is 'rendition'. Think about it for a few minutes and let me have your answer. The names......or rendition, what is it to be?'

The Inspector left the interview room and waited in a corridor for fifteen minutes before returning. Piling on the pressure he told Mathis that if the answer was 'no', four men in military uniform would remove him from his cell in the middle of the night. 'It will then be out of my hands,' he said, waiting for a reply.

'Stan Wazinski and Andrew Himanez' was the whispered reply from Mathis, as Inspector Bishop muttered. 'That was not so difficult was it Mathis? Now tell me who killed the maid and why?'

'Wazinski was in charge of the operation and carried a gun. He killed the maid when we discovered she was not the person we were supposed to abduct. She knew our faces and had to be killed so that she could not identify us,' he said.

'Who ordered her to be killed?' asked the Inspector.

'Wazinski called her the Warren bitch and when she told him that her name was Rula and she was employed by the hotel to keep the rooms clean he shot her in the back of the head and dumped her by the roadside.'

'Where were you ordered to take the women to?' asked the Inspector now that he had the prisoner talking freely.

'We were supposed to take her to a small bay just south of Castries where the two women were to be transferred to a cruiser, then our job was done and we would be paid.

'You only delivered one woman did the people on the cruiser ask why there was only one?'

'Yes, and Wazinski explained what had happened.'

'Did you get paid?'

'No, the captain told us we were supposed to deliver two and said he would report back to his boss who would decide whether we got paid or not.'

'Then you handed the hotel owner over to the captain'

'Yes.'

'Was she alive at that time?'

'Yes.'

'What was your reaction when you heard on the news that she had been executed.'

'I decided to hide in the hippy camp until the heat died down.'

'Do you know the name of the cruiser?'

'It was called the Southern Star.'

'What was the Captain's name?'

'I have no idea.'

'Now you are an accessory to a double murder.'

'What will happen to me?'

Inspector Bishop furrowed his brow for a moment. 'If I had my way you would be hanged. But we don't do that anymore. Instead the Judge will sentence you to thirty years without parole and you will be poisoned or hanged in your cell within two months, by mugs like you, who put their trust in the Mafia to take care of them forever.'

Gregori Mathis looked pleadingly at the Inspector. 'What happens to me now that I have provided you with the names of my mates Inspector?'

'Pray to your God if you have one, and never, never, go into the prison yard, even it is the only time you get to see the sun set.'

Inspector Bishop left the prison, but not before he had made a call from the Governor's office to police headquarters for officers' to apprehend the other two rogues.

They were arrested, one in small town of San Soucis and the other in Anse La Raye before the day was out.

Inspector Bishop was on the war path. Mafia enforcers, drug pedlars, and even the local prostitutes got the message and went to ground hoping the heat would die down once the dust had settled.

How wrong they were.

Ch.55

Edwin Crosby sent an email to Captain Arturo Vegas asking the Captain to meet him at the International Airport at Mexico City where he would be arriving on Flight K8722 at 12 noon on the following Wednesday. There are important matters relating to DFP he wished to discuss with him urgently.

Edwin recognised the importance of not naming Don Pascal in the email to ensure the Don was not pre-warned of his visit, hence the DFP instead of Don Frederico Pascal.

The reply was instant. 'You must refrain from giving me orders similar the person you named. However on this occasion I will send someone to meet you and bring you to my humble abode. Vegas.'

Edwin's plane landed at the Benito Juárez Airport outside Mexico City at 12.15pm. That was good flying time considering the stormy weather they had experienced over the Caribbean Sea giving passengers an unwelcome bumpy ride as the aircraft weathered the inclement weather.

The weather in Mexico City was not dissimilar to that experienced by passengers as they crossed the Caribbean. It was raining hard and exceptionally humid making passengers pant as they assembled in the arrivals lounge. A police officer in uniform was waiting in the lounge holding placard across his chest with CROSBY written in large capital letters to draw attention to the new arrival that he was there to act as chauffeur. When Edwin made himself known, he was ushered out of the airport into a police car and quickly driven to the Police Headquarters where he was led up to room occupied by Arturo Vegas.

Welcoming Edwin to Mexico City Arturo apologised for the appalling weather and high humidity. 'This time of the year overseas visitors tend to avoid the big cities and cling to the coastal resorts where the sea breezes off the Gulf of Mexico and the Pacific

Ocean tends to make those areas more acceptable,' he said with a smile. 'I have arranged for us to have lunch in a quiet bar a short walk from this office. We can discuss your problem over coffee without fear of interruption we can expect if I remain in the office.'

Edwin nodded his acceptance so they left the building on the short stroll to the bar that turned out to be a Tapas type bar that pleased Edwin because he was partial to the Spanish style of eating.

After a pleasant lunch they adjourned to a side table and were served coffee by an attractive waitress who quickly left them alone.

Arturo Vegas opened the conversation. 'I have already read in the local press about the murders of the two local women on St Lucia and the hostility it has caused with the local people railing against the failure of the local police to bring the murderers to justice. The press hinted that the murders were somehow linked to the Warren incident so I am guessing that is why you want an urgent meeting with me.'

Edwin nodded his head in agreement. 'As soon as the Warren trial was over and irrespective of the result, it was my intention to return to the UK and resume my legal responsibilities to my father. When the two ladies from the hotel where I was residing were abducted and subsequently murdered by the Mafia I made up my mind to resign from my father's chambers and remain in Central America in the hope that with your help I can bring the Mafia leaders to justice.'

Edwin went on to say 'I now understand the frustrations you have suffered over the years trying to bring Don Pascal to justice. In the next few days I may have sufficient evidence backed up by witnesses to at long last allow you to obtain a warrant for his arrest.'

Arturo held up his hand to stop Edwin continuing. 'Hold your horses young man. I've waited years to bring the old bugger to justice, what makes you think you can achieve what I have failed to do in just a few short days?'

Edwin explained that before leaving St Lucia he had learned that Inspector Bishop and his team had arrested all three men accused of the murders and would no doubt be putting pressure on the prisoners to disclose the names of their masters. 'He will also be trying to discover the name of boat used to carry the hotel owner away.'

'In addition, we have recordings of the man who killed Walter Warren; a recording of the Captain of the Northern Star who admits he was employed by the Mafia; while in England we have a live witness to the murder of Walter Warren who also admits to be employed by the Mafia. If the St Lucia police can discover the name of the other boat and apprehend its Captain, surely there will be enough evidence to bring Don Pascal to justice. Might I suggest you contact Inspector Bishop on St Lucia and find out how he is progressing with his investigations?'

Edwin continued. 'I gave you a list of drug suppliers and receivers that the Don wanted back. I propose you send the names on that list to the Police Commissioner on the appropriate Island and suggest they put them under arrest and question them to see if we can glean more information about the activities of Don Pascal.

Arturo shook his head from side to side. 'Your theories include lots of ifs and buts, with very few facts that I could use to obtain a warrant. What you propose is risky in the extreme, but you must remember I am no longer part of the criminal investigation branch but a Captain in charge of investigating police corruption. I would be crucified by my chief if I attempted to head an investigative team to try and bring the Don to justice. I am going to ask the chief of my previous job, the Commandante, if he is willing to head a task force to investigate all aspects of Mafia activities in the Caribbean, and Mexico in particular, to see if there is sufficient evidence to go for an arrest. The big risk is that someone will tip off the Don that a major inquiry is under way, and he will do as he did before, and scarper off to South America until the heat dies down.'

Edwin began to realise that he was not being considered for inclusion in the task force, and said so to Arturo.

Once again Arturo shook his head. 'I understand your desire to obtain revenge for the deaths of those two innocent women, but you are an English Lawyer and trying to start a fire that would soon be out of control. Leave this operation to the experts, and be satisfied that you achieved huge success to get your client acquitted against all the odds stacked against her. Don Pascal is way out of your league, and possibly out of mine. Any recommendations *I* make to the task force will be studied and taken into account. That is the best you and I can hope for.'

Edwin Crosby was not in the mood to be appeased, even though he accepted that Arturo was giving him sound advice. 'I want you to arrange for me to meet the Commandante to see if my legal expertise can be of use to the task force.'

Arturo suddenly became very cross. 'I told you earlier that 'I want' brings out the worst in me. I will have a word with the Commandante and advise him I have warned you to keep your nose out of Mexican police business. At the same time, I will put forward your request and will advise you of his response.'

Edwin apologised for his choice of words, accepted that Arturo's approach to the Commandante was a more diplomatic approach, and finished by inviting Arturo to join him for dinner that evening in his hotel.

All Edwin could now do, was await the Commandante's response to his request and hope it was successful.

Ch.56

Edwin was amazed when Arturo contacted him the next day and told him that an appointment had been made for both of them to meet the Commandante in his office at Police HQ at 4.0pm on the following day.

Promptly at 4.0pm they were shown into the police chief's office who shook their hands and invited them to sit down. 'The distribution and use of illicit drugs is on the increase,' he said as an opener. 'I welcome the suggestion from you Captain Vegas to set up a task force qualified to tackle this problem. As for you........Senor Crosby I have been brought up to date about your successful fight to save one of your English clients from a murder charge and how you stirred up a hornet's nest in the Caribbean as a result of your intensive search for the truth. I am also aware that as a consequence, you came to Mexico City and visited Don Frederico Pascal in his hacienda.....a bit like the fly walking into the spider's web. Whilst I should have been informed in advance of your intention to see Don Pascal, I have to admit that the knowledge you have gained in such a short time about drug distribution in Central America intrigues me.'

'As a result I am inviting you to join my task force, but only as an observer, and I have arranged for you Captain Vegas to be temporarily seconded to the task force that I am currently forming. It will consist of senior officers from our equivalent to your British SAS, or American SEALS; the Drug Enforcement Administration; Customs and Excise; and members of my own team of senior police officers. The first meeting will be held well away from this office to ensure there are no leaks to.......may I call them...'the enemy'.'

'I have rented an old warehouse on the Avenue Insurgentes Nostre. A police officer will be on duty outside the building to direct you to the area where we will meet. You must not discuss this arrangement with anyone under any circumstances.'

When Edwin and Arturo were outside the Police HQ they shook hands and agreed that the next few weeks were going to be very interesting.

Over dinner that evening Edwin asked Arturo how he proposed to notify the Commissioners on those Islands in the Caribbean of the names of the drug distributors on the list he possessed.

Arturo told him the letters were already prepared but now he was part of the task force he thought it prudent to agree the time of distribution with the taskforce commander to ensure all activities were co-ordinated harmoniously.

Edwin nodded his head in agreement.

As soon as the main course was finished Arturo returned to the subject of the task force. 'With such a large operation being planned, I am worried that one false move will result in the whole operation becoming a fiasco. These large scale operations have failed in the past, largely because of the enemy within. I never underestimate the long tentacles of the Mafioso. They are prevalent in every aspect of life in Mexico. Even our Commandante may be part of that organisation and this new task force being assembled is all part of a game to show the politicians that our police are diligent in tackling crime in the country. Personally I would rather place a large bomb in the Don's hacienda and when I am sure he, his two sons, and that Japanese brute are present, trigger it off and solve the drug cartel issue in one foul swoop.'

Edwin, not quite finished with the main course, dug his fork into the remains of a delicious steak and popped it into his mouth. He too was sceptical about the whole operation and tended to agree with Arturo, that a two or three man dedicated operation to penetrate the hacienda and execute the top brass of the Mafia was a more feasible plan.

Later in bed at the hotel Edwin wondered what his contribution would be in the future plans.

Ch.57

The first meeting of the task force took place in a section of a disused warehouse that had secretly been plainly refurbished as a meeting place for just such events that required a screen of secrecy.

Commandante Di Silva occupied the end chair of the table while the other chairs were occupied by a group of strangers in civilian clothes with no visible sign of personal identity.

When all were seated, Di Silver stood up and thanked them all for attending the first meeting of the newly formed task force.

'Before I commence the formal introductions is there anyone sitting round the table that is unable to speak or understand English, because that is what I propose to use during the course of these discussions. You may ask why it has to be English instead of our customary Spanish. Walls have ears, and the limited number of staff we employ are all Spanish speaking and have been checked to ensure they will not understand what we are discussing. Now I will introduce you to the other members of this task force, but not by name. Instead on this occasion I will only designate your rank or profession, and the reason why you have been invited.'

'At my immediate right is a Colonel of a highly trained élite group of military personnel. Sitting next to him is his deputy, a Major who will assume command of any troops we require to use to meet our objectives. Turning to the Colonel he said 'I appreciate you outrank me, but I have assumed the role to chair these meetings because I am in possession of facts that only a senior police officer has access to. However, if you feel that you should occupy the chair I will stand own and offer my advice where applicable.'

The Colonel replied that he had no objection at all.

Acknowledging the response with a nod the Chairman continued. 'Sitting next to the Major is a senior representative of the Customs and Excise section of our Government who is accompanied by a Commander from the Coastguard.'

'On my left is my deputy, a police sergeant who has a distinguished record and speaks several languages allowing him to converse with senior officers in other countries where there is a need to co-ordinate various activities.'

'On his left is my secretary who is making notes of this and other meetings we will be holding in the immediate future.'

'Next to her, is a Commander from the Drug Enforcement Administration whose reason for being here will become clear as we proceed.

'The last person on my left is a senior police officer from another department who has been seconded to this task force because of his intimate knowledge of a certain character who is a constant thorn in the side of many senior people holding important posts in the administration of Mexico in particular.'

'At the foot of the table is a Lawyer with considerable experience who has been invited to sit in on these meetings as an observer. At the same time I think he will be able to offer information of value once we get under way.'

'The task force will be named 'Operation Downfall' and I hope it lives up to my expectations.'

There was a pause while the Commandante waited to see if anyone had any observations to make. When none were forthcoming he continued. 'The growth of illegal narcotics in the Central and Northern Americas is on record, so you are all aware of the serious problem. Agencies all over the world have been formed to try and combat the disease with only limited success. In Mexico we have a leading figure who is the cause of our country's problem in that and other fields. It is my intention to use the expertise around this table to cut off the head in the hope it will act as a warning to all those involved in the distribution of narcotics, importation of prostitutes and formation of gambling dens. They will at last realise we are on the warpath and intend to destroy their highly lucrative illegal activities.'

'We will try to operate within the law, but occasionally in order to achieve our objectives it may be necessary to bend the rules. If any of you sitting round this table are unhappy with that situation I will accept your reasons for refusing to continue.'

No one moved.

The Chairman continued. 'While I was waiting to form this task force, certain valuable information was made available to me from our civilian observer.' he nodded towards the other end of the table. That information resulted in me making contact with officials in other countries who were happy to co-operate with our efforts. If we are to bring these despicable people to justice we need both facts and witnesses to convince a judge and jury.'

'I have spoken to a police superintendent on the Island of Jamaica who confirms he has a creditable witness safely hidden until needed. A police Inspector on another Island has three men in custody, one of whom has already indicated he will be prepared to give evidence on condition the length of his sentence is reviewed. A further creditable witness is currently being kept under a security blanket in another country far away from Mexico until required.'

'In addition we have the name of the ocean going motor cruiser that was involved with the abduction of two innocent women from the Island of St Lucia. Our Excise officers will have the task of running this cruiser and its occupants to earth but more of this at our next meeting.'

'In the meantime gentlemen I suggest you bring your individual teams up to a state of readiness as we prepare to go into battle with the enemy within a few days of this meeting. Our next meeting will be held in this room one week from now. Meeting adjourned.

Before the group departed, the Commandante provided the name of the cruiser 'Southern Star' to the Coastguard Captain, with the instructions to stop and search the boat, then detain the Captain and crew on suspicion of complicity in the murder of one Cara Phillipé a resident of the Island of St Lucia. 'I also would like you to arrange with other Coastguard Captains currently patrolling the Caribbean Sea to stop and search any cruisers or yachts with a name being used that includes the word Star.'

He told the Colonel he would supply him with a detailed layout of a hacienda on the outskirts of the city. 'I would like your team to study the layout of building closely, including the sewage arrangement and the possibility of an escape tunnel. It would help if you could arrange to overfly the area with a camera crew and check where guards are situated and the location of cars and an aircraft......most likely a helicopter. Your team may be asked to enter the hacienda so work at a plan of campaign. Arrange an early meeting with Captain Vegas.' He reminded the Colonel that Vegas was the police officer sitting at the bottom left side of the table. He has been in the hacienda and can tell you more about the armed guards protecting the place and the layout of the ground floor.'

The officer in charge of the DEA asked if the Comandante had any instructions for his team.

'Talk to our civilian observer. He has a list of known drug suppliers on various Islands. I will not attempt to tell you what to do. It is up to you to and your team to act as you wish. However, I would like to co-ordinate any operations as a joint exercise so prepare your plan of action and we will discuss it at the next meeting.

Ch.58

At the request of the DEA chief, Edwin and he met up in Edwin's hotel room where Edwin showed him a copy of the list he had purloined from a safe deposit box in the UK. I have given a copy of this list to Captain Vegas who intends to send the names of the persons listed to the Commissioner of each Island to leave it to them to deal with their local problem.

The DEA chief expressed his concern at the arrangement. 'Some of these Commissioners may be receiving backhanders from the Mafia. I suggest you ask Captain Vegas to leave it to my team to root out these criminals and I can assure you that we are all concerned in tackling the problem of illegal drug distribution in the Caribbean.

When Edwin indicated he was prepared to co-operate the DEA chief looked at the list. 'It all looks double Dutch to me,' he said, 'have you found anyone to solve the code?'

Edwin explained that it had been de-coded by friends and explained what it all meant. 'The first place on the list is the San Pedro Hotel on the Island of Jamaica. And Peter Lorenzo is the head waiter and is suspected of being the local supplier of drugs.

Puerto Rico is the next Island and the hotel is the Coral Island, where Javié Batista is the Assistant Manager.

St Lucia has the Lido Star Hotel where Rafael Bonico is the Head Chef.

Bridgetown in Barbados has a beach bar called El Dey. The owner a Nigerian called Tibo Simba was in debt to the syndicate and was about to be assassinated by the late Walter Warren. One of my compatriots went to the Island and met Simba to seek information about drug supplies. He warned Simba of his impending death and as far as I am aware he fled the Island and may be at sea somewhere in the Pacific.

Venezuela was the next on the list. Warren was meant to meet up with the owner of Wharf 7D but it never happened. I expect he is the principle supplier of drugs to the cartels and I guess he is in the pay of the Columbian Drug Lords.

MXC is not your concern so ignore it.

'No wonder your services are in great demand,' said DEA Chief John Younger. 'I recognised you were English as soon as you spoke, but how you managed to collate such a vast amount of information about the Caribbean drug ring is amazing. We have been seeking information like that for years without a great deal of success and yet you achieve that in a number of weeks. It's unbelievable.'

'What I now need my team to do as a matter of great urgency is work with the various sections of the DEA on the Islands. They need to discover the home addresses of every one of those persons you have named; discover if they have a warehouse or garage they use to store the drugs; try and find out if they have other drug dealers helping them; and most of all find out where they obtain their supplies. It's a hell of lot to ask them to achieve in just a few days. I got the impression from the Comandante that he wishes to strike every core of the drug cartel soon. Under normal circumstances it would take these sub branches of the DEA months to collate the information we now require.......' He thought about it for a moment before adding 'like yesterday.'

All Edwin could do was nod his head and wish John Younger good hunting.

But Younger had one further question before they separated. The man you named as Tibo Simba from Barbados; any idea why he went to sea?'

'It was Hobson's choice,' replied Edwin. 'If he had stayed in Barbados the Mafia would have caught up with him and made sure he paid the ultimate price for taking more than his allotted cut from the takings. Going to sea as a deck hand was a better alternative than sitting on the sea bed with a heavy chain attached to his ankles.'

'Why the hell did you let him escape? You could have arranged for him to be taken into custody.'

Edwin smiled. 'He was helped to leave the island on condition he gave us the name of his supplier from St Lucia. It turned out to be a detective sergeant who is now in custody. The sergeant will eventually tell his boss who the main supplier is to try and save himself from being sent to the local prison, where many of the inmates have a few scores to settle with Sergeant Totti'

John Younger pursed his lips and shook his head from side to side. 'You are obviously a very clever lawyer and a devious bugger to boot,' he added with a wry smile.

— — —

The Colonel called his team together as soon as he was back at the barracks. The soldiers sitting in the room represented the crème de la crème of the Mexican Army. Tough as nails, and superbly fit, after they had been trained by United States Navy Seals at their base in Coronado, California. Like the British SAS, they were always prepared for any eventuality whether at home or abroad, and had been working in conjunction with Navy Seals on a number of covert operations in Guatemala, Honduras, and even Columbia.

Now the Colonel was briefing his team for an operation at home. Plans of the hacienda had been reproduced and projected onto a large screen. 'I intend to send a small team into the area to check the surrounding land and select areas to build observation hides were we can measure the level of activity and strength of the opposition.

'I have not yet been given the name of the owner but can guess he is an important member of the Mafioso and possibly in control of all illegal operations in Mexico and the Central Americas. Something serious has happened that has triggered the fury of the Mexican police because they have put their forces on maximum alert, and involved other agencies in their decision to try and resolve this ongoing problem with some expediency.'

'Before we are ordered into action, which could be very soon, I want as much detail as possible about this mysterious hacienda, the name of the owner, who else occupies the hacienda, and whether he has any family, particularly sons who act as his deputies. I also need to know who delivers the food and other materials to the building, etc. etc? You all know the drill.'

'Sergeant Valdez, you will select your team and be responsible for the recce. Sergeant Cambrillo, you will select your team and check up on suppliers and any other homes of family members. I want to know all the facts about this troublesome hombre, even when he farts.' That brought the usual laughter from the assembled group

'I will command the main assault team and will have the guts of anyone who sends my team in blind. It is reported that there is the possibility a helicopter is stored on the estate fully fuelled, and ready to evacuate the principle if there is any threat to his security or life. If it is there, it needs to be put out of commission before it can be used. Finally a senior police officer and two three of his men in plain clothes will accompany me on the raid because of his intimate knowledge of the occupants and the layout of the building. I don't want any accidents to happen to them. They will be wearing wide orange arms bands on their right arms. Look after them like brothers, keep them out of trouble, and for God's sake don't accidently shoot any of them by mistake. That is all for the moment. Go and prepare your kit and get into place as soon as you are ready.'

Ch.59

The Coast Guard Captain became the first to score brownie points. Using his four man team of radar and ship to shore radio experts they quickly contacted most of the coastguard stations in the Caribbean and discovered that the Southern Star had been seen three hours earlier leaving Aruba in the Netherlands Antilles and gave her destination to the local harbour master as heading north to Port-au-Prince in the Dominican Republic.

With an international warrant out for the arrest of the Captain, coastguard cutters were despatched from Aruba and Jamaica who picked up the cruiser on their radar. The Dutch coastguard carried out the arrest one hundred miles off their coast and brought the cruiser back to Aruba. The coastguard reported there had been no resistance from the crew of four; automatic weapons had been discovered but here was no sign of any drugs. Police officers had already been despatched from St Lucia to affect the arrest of the crew.

At the same time, a small team of police officers had raided the Headquarters of Federated Industries Inc. in Mexico City to try and discover the location of the Southern Star and the name of its Captain. One of the staff being interviewed, and in fear of being sent to prison, confessed that there were three powerful Star cruisers left in the fleet following the capture of the Northern Star, namely the Eastern, Western and Southern Stars. An alert was put out to stop and search the other cruisers and affect an arrest if they contained arms or contraband. Arms and drugs were discovered in the cellars of the Company HQ so all senior staff were arrested and taken to Mexico City Police Headquarters for questioning.

This unexpected turn of events was not what the Commandante had envisaged and required an immediate review of his plans for the coming days. Don Pascal would have already been alerted and was no doubt already planning to depart south with the utmost expediency.

The Commandante immediately summoned his task force to a meeting and explained the reason for his concern.

The Colonel said his team were in place but he could do with a few more days to allow his men to collect more data before any attack could take place. 'In particular, I have already dropped a small team into Venezuela who have entered the warehouse on Wharf 7D and placed a number of explosive charges in strategic areas. On my signal, they will blow up the warehouse and destroy a large consignment of cocain and marijuana they discovered, together with a drug processing plant. The Venezuelan Police will be happy with the result and report that the cause was a faulty gas oven.

The Captain of the coastguard said his team were progressing well in their allotted tasks with the Southern Star already being held in Aruba.

John Younger of the DEA said his plans for co-ordinated arrests was virtually in place and all the Island's DEA Officers were awaiting his instructions to go.

Chairman Di Silva told him to go ahead otherwise some of the names on the list would disappear for a while and re-emerge when the heat had died down. 'In the meantime my officers will close down Federated Industries Inc for good that will seriously affect Don Pascal's ability to import vast quantities of drugs from Venezuela or Columbia. In addition they will standby to arrest anyone from the hacienda handed over by the army.'

Turning to the Colonel he told him not to wait for further orders and to take his team into the hacienda expressing the hope that Don Pascal could be captured and brought to trial.

– – –

That very afternoon Peter Lorenzo was arrested in his flat in Jamaica and a large quantity of illegal drugs were found stacked in one of a block of garages servicing the flats. Javié Batista the

Assistant Manager of the Coral Island Hotel in Puerto Rica was also remanded in custody by the local police.

There was a great deal of activity both at sea and on the Caribbean Islands but the skills shown by the various activities such as the Coast Guard Service, the DEA and Customs and Excise failed to alert the hierarchy in the underworld of drugs distribution.

It was now up to the élite Mexican forces to perform the coup de grâce by storming the Don's supposed impregnable castle and cut off the head of the monster that pervaded every aspect of life in the Caribbean.

Ch.60

In the Mexican Army HQ information was flowing in at an alarming rate from the various hides around the hacienda. The location of all the armed guards had been pinpointed. The outer and inner gates had been checked for strength and could be removed quickly with a series of explosive devices placed near the hinges. The hut housing the external guards had already been underpinned with an explosive device. The patio door leading into the hacienda and the kitchen door would not be able to withstand an assault but the main door would require two men to place explosives and blow it off its enormous hinges. Three cars were discovered in the main garage, two of which had already been immobilised. The third, an armoured car, had proved difficult, so a trembler explosive device had been fitted under the offside wing guaranteed to blow the heavy vehicle onto its side.

A two man team had discovered a helicopter hidden in an outbuilding and had successfully damaged the rotor blade so that it couldn't fly without repairs that would take a qualified mechanic at least two hours to correct.

It had been discovered that a fuel oil delivery vehicle was due to arrive within the next few days to top up the main tank. This was being cleaned out and converted into a troop carrier that would allow twelve armed soldiers to enter the inner courtyard unseen. In addition a meat delivery was also due and could be used as a second vehicle if required.

The only vehicle not purloined by the second team was a supermarket truck that delivered supplies to the kitchen door on a regular basis and was unsuitable for the planned operation.

The Colonel was not surprised at the thoroughness of his advance teams and sent word to Edwin Crosby and Captain Vegas to report to his headquarters within the hour. When all the assault team was ready the Colonel signalled the 'go' and the team moved into position.

As soon as some of the explosions occurred his team were passing the outer guard house that had been totally destroyed. Those guards were already in custody. The main gate was lying on its side and the two exterior guards were about thirty yards away secured by plasticuffs and guarded by two armed soldiers in camouflage dress. The rattle of automatic guns could be heard within the walls as the interior defenders decided to fight back.

The back of the fuel tanker sprung open and the troops cooped up inside, burst out into the warm barmy air and immediately commenced to return the fire. The guards at the front of the hacienda were mown down like flies by the devastating fire put down by the disciplined soldiers.

The front door of the building was slowly opening before the two men allocated to set the charges were in place. The big Japanese bodyguard appeared wielding a Beneli Mark 4 that fires .7 shells with devastating effect on whatsoever they hit. The soldiers nearest to the door, recognising the fearsome weapon, threw themselves to the ground and said a silent prayer knowing as soon as the Japanese fired at them their number was up even though they were well equipped with body armour.

A sniper looking through his telescopic lens attached to his rifle recognised the problem facing his comrades and immediately concentrated his fire power on the man in the door. Three rounds hit the big Jap simultaneously and he went down like a burst balloon, dead before he hit the floor; while the powerful gun rattled down the outside steps to the relief of the grounded troops.

The French window was the first to blow allowing the soldiers to advance into the main lounge which was empty. The hallway was also empty, but a young man wielding an AK47 firing from the top of the staircase took down two soldiers with his first and last burst before he was quickly cut down and killed by the remaining troops in the hall. Those soldiers entering the kitchen door found the staff crouched down in the corner, terrified by the noise emanating from the rest of the house. They were quickly plasticuffed and forced to lie flat on the floor where they were also covered by two armed soldiers.

The fight had lasted less than thirty minutes leaving the hacienda under the control of the army.

Arturo Vegas and Edwin Crosby wearing their orange armbands were escorted into the main house and asked to identify the Japanese bodyguard who was still lying by the main doorway. As soon as they climbed the beautiful staircase it was Arturo who identified the body with a bloodstained chest as that of Don Pascal's youngest of two sons called Ari.

'The eldest son Alfredo lives in an apartment in the Alameda Park area,' Vegas told the Colonel. 'I can obtain his address from the police computer, but as far as I am aware he is estranged from his father and has no connection with the Mafia, unlike his younger brother who is a well known hoodlum and constantly in trouble with the police.

A search of the remaining rooms showed no other presence of people. Of Don Frederico Pascal there was no sign. When the staff were questioned as to where he was, they reported he had left the building in the back of the supermarket's delivery van.

The soldiers at the road block half a kilometre down the road where questioned and reported they had stopped the van and it only contained the delivery driver. The Don had effectively disappeared into thin air. When the driver was subsequently questioned he confirmed that the Don had been in the rear of the van, but he had been forced to stop before the road block with a gun pointed at his head. He let the Don get out and left him standing at the road side.

When asked why he hadn't reported this at the road block, he said he had been threatened that he and his family would be killed if he opened his mouth.

An immediate search was made of the surrounding countryside but the Don appeared to have gone to ground. A helicopter equipped with body heat seeking equipment was called to over fly the area and that search failed to find any evidence of a human being on the open land bordering the estate.

– – –

While the intensive search was under way, the Colonel asked Edwin and Captain Vegas if they would go with six armed police officers in a van and check out Don Frederico's other son. Captain Vegas contacted the operators on the police computer at HQ and was informed that Alfredo Pascal lived in apartment 332 on the third floor of the Plaza del Sol building on the Avenue Juârez (pronounced Warez) adjoining the Alameda Park.

The police van, accompanied by a jeep containing four armed soldiers left the hacienda and returned to Mexico City where they entered the avenue adjoining the park. While the armed soldiers remained outside to prevent any unauthorised persons from entering the building, the police entered to be met by the apartments' Manager who was immediately placed in temporary protective custody while the remaining members of the team went to the third floor where a sergeant rang the bell.

The door was answered by a young woman of Mexican origin holding the hand of a young boy of about three years of age. When she saw the police officer she put her hand across her mouth obviously wondering why the police should call at her home. When she was asked if her husband was at home she nodded her head in the affirmative, so the officer pushed the door open and the remaining officers including Captain Vegas and Edwin Crosby burst into the apartment.

Alfredo Pascal was sitting watching the TV with his other son aged six and while angry at the unauthorised intrusion into his privacy, guessed that the police were involved in something concerning his father or his younger brother.

Captain Vegas explained that his father's hacienda had been raided earlier that day by an army unit accompanied by police who intended to arrest his father for a number of serious unspecified charges. 'I understand that you are estranged from your father and do not have any connection with his illegal activities. Is that so? He asked.

Alfredo handed his son over to his wife and told her to take the boys into the bedroom while he dealt with the police.

'I have not spoken to my father for the last six years since I married Anita,' he said with a deep frown on his forehead. 'In fact my father has never seen his grand children as my father has refused to come to the apartment, and I don't want them to be seen at the hacienda for obvious reasons. I am employed as a manager in a large departmental store in the city and have no connections with anyone associated with my father, or my younger brother. You can check with whosoever you like but you will find what I have said is true. Now will you kindly bugger off and leave me and my family in peace.'

Arturo sat down on the settee beside Alfredo and told him there were a number of casualties as a result of the raid. 'I have to tell you that your younger brother fired at the soldiers entering the main building and killed two young soldiers doing their duty. Other soldiers returned the fire and as a result, your brother was killed in the exchange. I'm very sorry to have to break the sad news to you, but during the battle that ensued; your father escaped and is now being sought by every officer in uniform. Airports, seaports, bus stations, and even taxi cab ranks are being checked to stop him leaving Mexico. When he is caught he will be tried in a civil court and if found guilty will serve a long prison sentence.'

Tears appeared in the eyes of Alfredo. 'I warned my younger brother many times to sever his link with my father. He was always a young hothead and had high hopes of assuming the mantle of Don Ari Pascal in the cause of time. Now it will never happen and I will be the one who has to bury him. I assume that my father would never be allowed to attend his son's funeral, would he?'

The question remained unanswered.

Aturo Vegas left the elder son to mourn, and asked the officers to leave the family home as there was no valid reason to detain Don Pascal's eldest son.

Once everyone was back in the police van Edwin turned to Arturo. 'How could two sons be so different,' he observed. 'Don Pascal's eldest son decided as soon as he was married that he had no intention of being involved in his father's shady world even though he and his family could have lived in the lap of luxury. He didn't have to live in the hacienda like his younger brother. He and his wife could have bought an upmarket property on the outskirts of Mexico City and employed a mass of servants to see to their every need. Instead he trained to be a manager in a departmental store and appears to have been able to provide adequately for his family. One can only admire his determination to be independent, but due to his father's record we have found it necessary to invade his privacy. No wonder the young man is angry at our intrusion. Now perhaps everyone will leave him alone to let him live his private life.'

Arturo who had listened intently shook his head. 'That will never happen. It is often quoted that 'blood is thicker than water' and I'm sorry to say Alfredo Pascal will never be allowed to live in peace.'

Edwin failed to see the logic in Arturo's observation. 'What will you do now that Don Pascal appears to have escaped capture?'

Arturo grimaced. 'I'll be ordered to return to my substantive post and spend my days chasing bent police officers. While the salary is acceptable, personally I hate the job. I was trained to catch criminals and I suppose that is what I do now. However, it is much more rewarding putting rogues like Don Pascal and his ilk behind bars than seeing a bent police officer sent to prison. The poor sods face a life of hell never knowing when a screw will cut them up; throw acid in their face; or die in a managed brawl.'

He grasped Edwin by the hand. How about you my friend' what do you intend to do now that the trial is over?'

'Back to the UK and see what opportunities are available?'

Epilogue

Throughout the world, large Banks, Corporate Businesses, International Drug Manufacturers, Arms Manufacturers, Technical Industries, Loan Companies, Housing Agencies, and Left Wing Political Parties etc., have a cadre of people at the top who will use any method whether legal or illegal to achieve their goals. The use of muscle is not unknown to achieve their objectives, so why should the Mafia be any different?

The acceptance of the Mafia in countries like Russia, Italy, Corsica, Sardinia, Mexico, and the Unites States of America are largely tolerated because they are difficult to remove or contain.

That there are smaller conclaves in the area of the Caribbean comes as no surprise. Nor is the acceptance that local politicians, bent police officers, and even the judiciary are paid to look the other way, or assist in spurious activities such as narcotics, prostitution, and gambling.

Such is the way of life that was alien to young lawyers like Edwin Crosby, who have to learn the hard way that the rules laid down by society in general have little effect when dealing with the unscrupulous.

His experiences in the semi tropical zone of Central America were completely out of kilter with the challenges he faced daily in Liverpool.

On return to his father's chambers, Edwin hoped that with the situation in Mexico not resolved to his entire satisfaction, the instruction and sound advice given by his father not to get involved with a client no longer applied. He made several attempts to make contact with Julia Warren, inviting her to dinner so they could make the initial move towards forming a long term relationship.

Unfortunately for Edwin this was not to be. Julia regarded Edwin first and foremost as her rather expensive lawyer with little prospect of ever being in the same financial league as her late husband. Some would regard her as a gold digger, but Julia, young and exceedingly beautiful, had already experienced the rich trappings of life and was already in a relationship with an 'unhappily' married Stock Broker from Cheshire County, whose mansion and way of life was even more affluent than that of her recent marital experience. Poor Edwin was forced to accept that he had to seek elsewhere if he wanted a stable relationship with someone of the opposite sex in the future. It was to be a number of years before Miss Right walked into *his* Parlour.

When his father suddenly had a stroke that left him paralysed down one side of his body he could no longer head the chambers. His partner Welland, bought out his father's share and became head of the business with his son appointed as joint partner. Edwin heartbroken, moved to another legal firm in Liverpool, dealing with shipping and dockland development. The financial rewards were similar but his previous experience of dealing with people problems no longer applied.

Emille became terribly unsettled in the UK and eventually decided to return to Jamaica sincerely hoping that all would be forgotten or at least forgiven. Two enforcers called at his flat late one night and the following morning he was found with his head in the gas oven and his body full of alcohol and drugs.

Ex Detective Sergeant Totti is still serving a long sentence in Dennery Prison and has a number of scars on his face following numerous attacks from police hating prisoners to remind him of his past,

Franklin Jenson decided to move to the United States of America to further his law experience and soon afterwards became the Public Prosecutor for the State of Maddison County.

Private Detective Roberto Sanchez was discovered dead in his car in the hills above Castries with a length of hose connected to the exhaust pipe. The coroner recorded a verdict of suicide but his family were convinced he had crossed swords with the Mafia one time to many.

Ex Captain Hulio Stanzer of the Northern Star was granted residential status in Canada and joined the Hudson Bay Company as first mate on one of their cargo boats.

Tibo Simba ex owner of the beach bar on Barbados is still with the same shipping line ploughing across the Pacific Ocean, but with one of the large passenger liners where he is head barman and loves his job.

Detective Harry Bishop is still Detective Harry Bishop and with a black mark on his personnel record will remain that way until he reaches the age of retirement.

Alfredo Pascal who carried the blood line of his family found it difficult to avoid family ties. After a period of mourning the loss of his brother he loved so dearly, he changed. Bitterly angry at the way his brother had been slaughtered instead of arrested and sent to prison, he accepted the role of Mafia Don and moved into the hacienda and became as ruthless as his father before him. Many people asked the question as to who had authorised his appointment as supreme head of the Mafia in Mexico. A telephone call from his father in Peru to the Mafia committee who served the old Don was the answer, but it was never broadcast for obvious reasons.

The mystery of how Frederico Pascal disappeared was known only to his late bodyguard. They were both aware that the police would expect the Don to have more than one escape route from his hacienda. Possessing a helicopter, the other alternative was likely to be a tunnel, and that is what the police would search for if they decided to mount an attack on the hacienda. Pascal with all his animal cunning decided to provide a temporary hideout. He purchased fifty acres of land on the other side of the highway adjoining his vast estate. He employed four ex miners from Guatemala and had them tunnel under the highway with the permission of the local authority, on the grounds he needed access to the other land for his tractors and workpeople. The four men built the tunnel and at the same time provided a smaller secondary excavation running parallel to the main tunnel that was fitted out to become a small secret shelter. It contained folding camp beds, food store, chairs and lighting where two or three persons could hide out for a few days until the heat died down. When the men were finished, Don Pascal paid them handsomely and sent them back to Guatemala richer than they had been in the past with the knowledge that his secret enclave would ultimately be disclosed had he used local miners.

The delivery vehicle he used in his escape dropped him a short distance from the hide, where he stayed for a week until he was satisfied the road block would be removed by the police. It was easy for him to call a taxi on his mobile phone and ask to be picked up at the roadside using the excuse that his car had broken down and been towed to the nearest garage for repairs. He was dropped by the taxi driver on the outskirts of Mexico City where he purchased a second hand car and crossed the border into Guatemala. From there, he flew to Peru where he had considerable assets to sustain his previous luxurious way of life. He told his son he would not be returning to Mexico as life in prison was not something he wished to endure.

In Mexico City Arturo Vegas waited patiently for the day when he could place the cuffs on Frederico Pascal and watch the bull dozers demolish the hacienda until it became a pile of rubble. Arturo would never discover that is old enemy died in Peru the following year, assassinated by the local Mafia when he tried to muscle in on their territory.

Neptune continues to be Lord of the sea. His command for thunder and lightning; storms and hurricanes; and the crashing of waves on sea shores is always obeyed; to remind mankind that they must abide by his rules or accept the consequences.

- finito -

Robert was born in 1926 in the picturesque village of Whitburn on the North East Coast of England. He joined the mining industry in 1940 prior to serving four years in the Royal Air Force, mainly in South East Asia towards the end of the 1939/1945 war.

Leaving the industry in 1968 he moved with his family to Staffordshire to take up an appointment with a world renowned manufacturer of classic pottery - Josiah Wedgwood. He became a Management Executive of the Earthenware Division of the Company before retiring in 1989

He has enjoyed sailing, golf, walking in the Lake District, gardening, spending time with his family and grandchildren, and in recent years writing novels, an autobiography, and building in wood, complex scaled models of sailing ships.

Apart from his memoirs, 'Journey into Manhood' he has written the following novels that have also been converted into ebooks for Kindle type readers.

Girls in Grey
*The Second Girl in Grey
Friends in Grey
Private Trimble
The Italian Mission
The Silver Cane
Zero Principles
Journey in Fear
Java Bond
Storms Clouds over Malaya

*available from Amazon, or lulu.com

Other novels and the autobiography
are available from the lulu.com website.
ebooks available from Barnes and Noble.

What comes next?.......... Time is not on Roberts's side.